# Murder on the Île Sordou

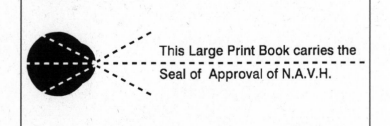

This Large Print Book carries the
Seal of Approval of N.A.V.H.

A VERLAQUE AND BONNET PROVENÇAL
MYSTERY

# MURDER ON
# THE ÎLE SORDOU

## M.L. LONGWORTH

**THORNDIKE PRESS**
*A part of Gale, Cengage Learning*

GALE
CENGAGE Learning·

Farmington Hills, Mich • San Francisco • New York • Waterville, Maine
Meriden, Conn • Mason, Ohio • Chicago

GALE
CENGAGE Learning®

LIBRARY OF CONGRESS CATALOGING-IN-PUBLICATION DATA

Longworth, M. L. (Mary Lou), 1963–
  Murder on the Île Sordou : a Verlaque and Bonnet Provençal mystery / by M. L. Longworth. — Large print edition.
    pages ; cm. — (Thorndike Press large print mystery)
    ISBN 978-1-4104-7576-3 (hardcover) — ISBN 1-4104-7576-X (hardcover)
    1. Murder—Investigation—Fiction. 2. Large type books. I. Title.
PR9199.4.L596M89 2015
813'.6—dc23                                                    2014042151

Published in 2015 by arrangement with Penguin Books, a member of Penguin Group (USA) LLC, a Penguin Random House Company

Printed in Mexico
1 2 3 4 5 6 7 19 18 17 16 15

*Dedicated to my cousins*

# AUTHOR'S NOTE

There are many islands off the coast of Marseille. Some are closed to the public, but Frioul and the Île d'If can be visited by boat from Marseille's old port. Sordou, however, has been invented by the author.

# CHAPTER ONE:
## LACYDON

From here he could see La Canebière rolling straight down into the old port, splitting the downtown into two equal parts, as though someone had drawn a line in the sand with a stick. It made sense that the main street would dump into water, for it had once been La Lacydon, a river. Eric Monnier tried to balance his hip against the handrails of the boat in order to relight what was left of his cigar. He noticed that the farther out from Marseille they got, the more the mountains behind the city seemed bigger, as if they were pushing — thrusting — the city into the sea. Funny, he thought, when you're in the city you don't notice the white chalky limestone hills. You only hear the beeping car horns, the cry of seagulls, and see the dust, and smell the sea, and dirt. He knew that Marseille made no attempt to fancy itself up for tourists, and each time he returned to the place where he was born it took him a few days to learn to love it again.

*Lacydon* had been his first and only book of poetry, written in the early 1960s when he was twenty-two and published on a shoestring by a friend in Arles. It was an ode to Marseille, and its history, its bright light, and its fast-talking inhabitants. He had sold a dozen or so copies at weekend flea markets and then had given out the rest to friends and family. He still had a cardboard box under his bed with the proofs — typed by the older sister of a friend — and five remaining copies of the slim, elegant tome.

With the nonsuccess of his poetry Monnier took a job at a high school in Aix-en-Provence teaching French literature, just until, he initially hoped, his poetry took off. An elderly great-aunt on his father's side died and gave the apartment in Aix's Quartier Mazarin to her great-nephew. He still lived there, surrounded by wealth: his neighbors being a count and countess (below) and a Parisian architect (above). And here he was, one month newly retired from that same job and same high school, never having put his poems into book form again. His new poems were now written out, in longhand, in black bound books that he bought at Michel's on the Cours Mirabeau.

He knew that the staff at Michel's called him "Le Poète" as soon as he left the shop, and he didn't mind.

Monnier's eyes watered as he looked at Marseille. He had always loved the port, its golden stone medieval forts protecting the harbor, and the fortress-like church, Saint-Victor, lovelier in its simplicity than the elaborate nineteenth-century Notre Dame de la Garde. He turned to his right and saw the bunkers, built by Germans during World War II, on the hill below the Pharo Palace. As kids they had played around the bunkers, until getting chased away by a Pharo guard. As the boat went farther out on the sea more of Marseille came into view: the private swimming club just beyond the bunkers, where now membership took years and multiple recommendations, and beyond that the three-star Passédat restaurant.

He turned his back to Marseille now; not because he was displeased with the city, but to break the wind. On the third try his cigar relit — barely visible hints of red shone at the tips — and he puffed madly to get it going again. With his back to the city he saw that they were close to Les Îles du Frioul, a group of islands that included the abandoned prison on the Île d'If, immortalized by Alexandre Dumas in *The Count of Monte*

*Cristo.* Two of the larger islands of the Frioul archipelago were joined by a causeway, with a large natural port that faced Marseille. They too had limestone cliffs and craggy hills, dotted with bright-green shrubs, all of it shimmering in the late July sun against the blue-green sea. When he was young an uncle (his mother, daughter of Italian immigrants, had been one of twelve children; his father, an only child) had had a cabin on Frioul, and Eric would spend weeks on end swimming and fishing with his cousins, and when alone, writing.

Farther out to sea the waves got bigger and the boat hit one and fell down with a thud. The poet heard a cry and what sounded like "Whoopee!" from a middle-aged couple who had boarded the boat just ahead of him. It was the wife who had yelped. She had her back to the city, arms spread out firmly gripping the boat's railing, as her husband comically jutted around trying to stabilize himself so that he could take a picture. He wore white tennis shoes that seemed too big for his feet, and one of those hats that had a bill to keep out the sun but a hole on top. They never made sense to Monnier. He had no idea what the caps were called, but on the basis of that — and the wife's "Whoopee!" — he guessed the couple to be American. The woman saw Monnier looking at them and she smiled and waved, yelling, "Rough sea!" Monnier waved back with his panama hat in his hand, having understood that she had said something about the waves.

He tried not to stare, but the poet was mesmerized by the American couple's glee, and their shared enthusiasm. He had had love affairs but never married; the woman whom he would have married had died more than fifty years ago, and he hadn't enjoyed dating after that. He used his poetry as an excuse to be a recluse; people believed him, as the making of poetry was too abstract for his few friends to understand.

A week on the island was a treat to himself for forty years of teaching ungrateful seventeen-year-olds (with some exceptions) the beauty of Flaubert. As a retired civil servant he would be earning his full salary — small at 2,000 euros a month — but it was more than enough for someone who lived rent-free, had no children, and never traveled. As he smoked his cigar he saw himself reflected in the boat's window: he imagined that he looked like any retired teacher who loved to eat and drink (this was something he spent money on); his half-moon-shaped reading glasses permanently hanging around his neck; his paunch; his white Guayabera shirts that a friend bought on visits to Cuba (this one stained, he noticed, with last night's beef daube); his red bulbous nose; a scruffy white beard; and his flyaway white hair, thinning, but not bald.

The Americans were still giddy at the waves, and he was thankful that the language barrier would be an excuse not to have to socialize with them once they got to the island. Not very social at the best of times, Monnier wanted silence on the island; time to reflect, and to write. And then he heard French.

A new couple had emerged on his side of the boat; they must have been on the starboard side and boarded after him and the Americans. They were younger by five years than the Americans, and younger than him by . . . twenty years perhaps. At least she was. He nodded as they walked by, their arms linked, and they smiled and nodded back. The woman was tall and slender, but not skinny, with a head full of curly auburn hair that flew about in the wind, just as Élodie's had. She had a long thin nose, high cheekbones, and a thin mouth, and lots of freckles. Her partner was equally striking, but did not have her classic good looks. He

14

was her height, if not a tiny bit shorter, and wide at the shoulders, with a paunch that Monnier could just make out. His nose had been broken . . . an accident? a sporting injury? and his hair was thick and black and streaked with gray. His eyes were much darker than hers, but they were as intelligent. He had a large, wide mouth, and a hearty laugh.

Monnier's cigar went out again and he turned back to look toward Marseille. The city's details were now difficult to make out, except for Notre Dame de la Garde sitting atop a hill east of the city, much like Paris's Sacré Coeur — a beacon — in this church's case, for sailors. The boat had made its way around the Frioul islands and was now heading out farther to sea, southwest, to an island seven hundred meters wide and two kilometers long that was their destination.

"Is that a Cuban you're smoking?" a deep voice said beside him. It was Broken Nose, the one with the beautiful freckled companion.

"What else?" Monnier answered. He may be just a humble civil servant, but he would only smoke Cubans. "An Upmann. But it's out now, and I'm holding on to it still because I don't want to throw it overboard."

"I have an Upmann in my pocket," the

man answered, patting what looked to be, to Monnier's inexperienced eye, an expensive linen jacket. "A Magnum forty-six. But I'm saving it for when we get to the island. My companion thought it silly that I smoke a cigar while on a boat, out at sea. I think she thinks the idea of a cigar and fresh air is incongruous."

Monnier laughed. "Tell that to the Cubans." He held out his hand. *What the hell,* he thought. *They speak French and we'll be together on a small island.* "Eric Monnier," he said.

"Antoine Verlaque," Broken Nose said, shaking his hand. He looked at Monnier and smiled again. "Here for some R & R?"

"I hope so," Monnier said. "Just retired from forty years of teaching. And you?"

"Vacation."

"Have you brought more cigars with you?" Monnier asked. "I'm not sure the hotel will sell them."

Verlaque nodded and smiled. He was charmed by the teacher's naivety; hotels such as the one they were heading to always had a humidor. He had brought his own cigars, but knew he would be able to fall back on the hotel's stock if he fell short. "They're filling up about half of my suitcase," Verlaque answered. "*She* doesn't

16

"know." At that point they both looked across the boat to Verlaque's companion, who was taking photographs of the sea.

"She's beautiful," Monnier said, surprising himself that he would be so forthright.

"Yes, and she carries it so well. Some women are ruined by their beauty, but not Marine."

Monnier thought that this man Antoine was used to getting compliments on the beauty of his girlfriend, or wife; at least, he hadn't been at all surprised by a stranger's comment. "Marine," Monnier repeated. "Appropriate name for someone who takes pictures of waves."

Verlaque nodded. "It is, but I think she's taking photos of waves because she's actually frightened of them."

Monnier did a half smile. "I knew someone like your Marine once. Wonderful girl . . ."

The boat hit a wave, and both men grabbed on to the edge. "I've never been beyond Frioul before," Verlaque said. "It's magnificent to be out on the sea like this, with Marseille off in the distance."

"We'll be going out eight kilometers," Monnier answered. "Sordou was the first island that Mediterranean mariners came to; hence the importance of its lighthouse.

The other islands in the Riou archipelago are uninhabited . . ."

"Yes, I know . . ."

"Protected by the coast guard and used only by scientists and divers and seagulls . . ."

Verlaque waited for Monnier to take a pause, as he was obviously in teacher mode, but didn't get a chance to speak. "Neolithic peoples came to Sordou looking for shell-fish," Monnier went on.

"Mmm," Verlaque said. "We'll no doubt get some good fish on the island. I've heard great things about this young chef . . ."

"Of course there are plenty of rabbits, and some rare birds like the protected Puffin cendré . . ."

"*Of course,* with its bright-yellow beak and ashy-colored feathers . . ."

"But the puffins hide out in the island's rocky crevices, so it's unlikely that we'll see one."

The boat slowed down and Marseille was but a golden haze in the distance.

"Well, here we are!" Monnier said, shielding the sun from his eyes with his hat.

Now that the boat had pulled up to the island's dock, the passengers could feel the July heat. The American woman reminded her husband, Bill, as they excitely ran inside the boat to get their suitcases, to be careful of his back.

"Ah . . . Sordou," Monnier said, looking at the island.

"Have you been here before?" Verlaque asked. "As I understand it, Sordou has been abandoned for decades."

"Oh, I've been here before, *mon ami,* I've been here before."

# CHAPTER TWO:
# THE WELCOME

"Watch your step," the captain said to the passengers as they got off his boat — *Le Sunrise* — and hopped on to Sordou's main pier. The captain was anxious to get back to Marseille, as the sea was getting rough, and by the time he got back his friends would be well into their second pastis at the Bar de la Marine.

A handsome, rugged-looking man in his thirties was there to greet the guests and help them with their bags. Hugo Sammut was glad to have the job; he worked during the winters in the Alps as a ski instructor but had needed to earn some cash this summer season. He was hired on as gardener and boatman — he had his blue boat badge in sailing and could take the guests out in the hotel's small motorboat if they desired. It was no surprise to him that he would also get asked to do odd jobs such as greeting the guests at the pier; at their first staff meeting in early May he had been shocked that the staff consisted of only six people, plus the hotel's owner and his wife.

*"Tenez, madame,"* Sammut said as he offered his forearm to a middle-aged woman getting off the boat.

"Oh, don't mind if I do!" she answered in English, giggling and taking his tanned muscled arm.

"Shirley!" her husband called out from behind. "You'll want to watch out with these Frenchies!"

She patted Sammut's arm as thanks once she had both feet on solid ground and reached for her husband's suitcase as he almost lost his balance getting off the boat. "Bad back," she loudly said to Sammut, pointing to her husband and then motioning to her lower back with her hand. "And Parkinson's too," she added. Eric Monnier cringed; the woman's openness about her husband's various ailments embarrassed him.

"In that case, madame, please allow me to take your suitcases up to the hotel for you," Sammut said in perfect but accented English. He was extremely popular in the mountains with the Anglo-Saxon — women, in particular — skiers.

"Oh my, thank you . . ."

"Hugo," he answered.

"Hugo, *dear.* I'm Shirley Hobbs, and this is my husband, Bill."

"Glad to meet you, son," Bill Hobbs said, shaking Sammut's hand. Monnier looked on in amazement at the American couple's friendliness and noted that the man's hand trembled as he shook hands. Monnier had never been to "the States" as some of his ex-colleagues had annoyingly referred to it.

"Hugo, are you sure you can handle both of those bags?" Bill Hobbs asked. "I'm afraid I can't be of much help."

"Yes, sir. It won't be a problem," Sammut answered, and to his relief saw Serge Canzano, the hotel's bartender, walking quickly down toward the dock.

"I'll help you with your bags, sir," Canzano said to Monnier as Sammut gave his colleague a *where have you been?* look. Canzano didn't have the chance to tell Sammut that he had been busy making a second mojito for one of the guests when the boat had pulled in. He had finished making the drink and called Marie-Thérèse — who had been busy in the laundry room — to tend bar until he returned.

"And then I'll be back for your bags," Sammut said to Antoine Verlaque and Marine Bonnet.

"Oh, no no," they protested in unison. "That won't be necessary," Verlaque said. "We can manage."

"I'll take your bags," a throaty female voice sounded. The group turned around to see a petite, short-haired woman in her late twenties as she bounded down the pier and took Marine's suitcase from her. "Welcome to Locanda Sordou," she said. "I'm Niki Darcette, the hotel manager."

Marine looked at Niki Darcette's thin tanned arms and legs and estimated that she was a size 0. Darcette wore a sheer white cotton blouse with short sleeves and a red miniskirt with high-heeled sandals.

"Mme and M. Le Bon, the hotel owners, will be meeting you in the hotel lobby," Darcette continued. "A few of the guests have already arrived, two more are coming on a later boat this evening, and then we'll be uninterrupted for a blissful week."

It sounded to Marine like Darcette had rehearsed the greeting; the addition of "blissful" was a little too much. But she liked her low, raspy voice, even if it was probably due to too much smoking.

"M. Verlaque," Darcette said, walking beside Verlaque. "I hope you had a pleasant boat ride."

"Very pleasant, thank you," Antoine said,

turning around and smiling at Marine.

Marine was relieved that Mlle Darcette hadn't said "judge"; she had insisted that Antoine's profession — he was Aix-en-Provence's examining magistrate — remain hidden that week. This was to be a no-work holiday; neither of them would be giving out free legal advice. She had finished her term from teaching law in late May but since then had been busy researching and writing.

"Wow. Wow wow wow," Shirley Hobbs said, adding a whistle, when she looked around her.

"Shirley, that's four 'wows,' " Bill Hobbs told his wife. Steep white cliffs surrounded the island's harbor; the cliffs were dotted with green shrubs, and in some places small hearty umbrella pines grew out of rock. The cliffs dropped sharply off into the blue-green sea, like the *calanques* the Hobbses had seen in Cassis on their previous vacation to this part of Provence. It had been that pleasure-boat ride five years ago — three *calanques* for 15 euros Bill remembered — that had persuaded them to book this luxurious week on Sordou. "It's just like a place in those decoration magazines you're always reading, isn't it, Shirley?" Bill asked, taking his wife's arm.

"*Design* magazines, not *decoration,* Bill," his wife replied.

The guests gazed up at the hotel; it was a light-pink adobe building sitting on a slight rise, overlooking the sea. It curved along a hill and rose up in blocks, working to fit into the hilly landscape instead of imposing itself on it. A series of curved balconies and terraces lined the hotel's front, some grand with sweeping views, and others small and intimate. This side of the island faced south; the view was, except for the white cliffs at either side, of the sea. The guests seemed to all turn around at once to look at the view once they were on the top step leading to the hotel's front door.

"Sea, and only sea, all the way to Africa," Hugo Sammut told the guests. He had been on the island for two months and was still mesmerized by the view.

"*Messieurs-dames,*" a voice called out. Maxime Le Bon was standing in the arched doorway of the hotel, holding open the double glass doors. "*Bienvenus,*" he continued. "Welcome," he said to the Hobbses, guessing, because of Bill Hobbs's visor, who they were. Le Bon wore what was required in the July heat — linen pants and a short-sleeved white shirt. He was trim, and tanned (like the rest of the staff), and he seemed,

25

thought Marine Bonnet, to be genuinely excited by the arrival of his guests. "My wife, Catherine — we all call her Cat-Cat — is inside. Please . . ."

Le Bon and Sammut held the giant glass doors open, and the guests passed into the hotel's lobby.

"No more wows, Shirley," Bill Hobbs said as he looked around the spacious cathedral-ceilinged lobby. The walls were painted a warm cream, and the accents — window frames and light fixtures — were black. To the right of the front door was an arched alcove — Marine thought it might have been a chapel at one time — where there was a curved wooden reception desk. An elegant middle-aged woman quickly came out from behind the desk and welcomed the guests.

*"Bonjour,"* she said, smiling. "I'm Catherine Le Bon. Please call me Cat-Cat. Your suitcases will be taken to your rooms while Mlle Darcette and I check you in. While we're doing that, you're all invited to pass through the lobby into the bar . . . the Jacky Bar we call it, in honor of one of Sordou's bartenders from the 1950s . . . and have a complimentary glass of champagne."

Eric Monnier saluted Mme Le Bon and made straight for the bar, saying, "I'll check in last. You folks go first," as he walked out of the lobby.

"Well, we are very tired," Shirley Hobbs said after Niki Darcette had translated Cat-Cat's welcome. "I'd love to see our room and put my feet up."

"Of course, Mme Hobbs," Maxime Le Bon replied. He gestured toward the reception desk. "Please . . ."

Verlaque looked at Marine and said, "I'll check us in if you want to go to the bar."

"I don't mind waiting with you," Marine answered.

"Don't you want to find Sylvie?" Verlaque asked. He secretly wanted to check in without Marine knowing that he was going to try to upgrade their room.

"You're right," Marine said. "And the bar is a good place to start."

*Putain de merde!*" a teenage male said as he passed between Marine and Verlaque, causing them both to step back.

"Excuse us!" Marine said, visibly annoyed.

The boy turned around and quickly said, "Sorry," before throwing open the front doors and running out of the hotel.

"Brice!" a woman called, walking quickly into the lobby.

"He went that way," Verlaque said, pointing outside.

*"Merci, monsieur,"* the woman said. "Teenagers!" the woman said to Verlaque, flashing him a smile, as she walked out of the hotel.

"M. Verlaque," Maxime Le Bon said. "We're ready to check you in."

"See you in a bit," Marine said. "You know where to find me."

If the hotel's lobby was elegant Tuscan in decoration, the bar was riotous Capri, circa 1962. Marine stood in the doorway with her hands on her hips and looked around the bar, smiling. Hugo Sammut approached her with a glass of champagne. "Thank you," Marine said. "This is a beautiful bar."

Sammut looked around as if he hadn't noticed the bar before, and shrugged before walking off.

"Hey!" Sylvie Grassi called from the end of the curved, white bar accented with large black polka dots. "Finally!"

Marine quickly walked over to her best friend, gave her the *bise,* and hugged her. "I'm so glad we're here!"

Sylvie held up her mojito and clinked glasses with Marine's champagne flute. "To summer vacation," she said.

"Chin-chin," Marine replied, sipping her bone-dry champagne.

"Sit down 'cause you're gonna fall over when I tell you who's here," Sylvie said, slightly slurring her words.

Marine laughed. "Is that your first mojito?"

Sylvie shook her head back and forth. "My second, and then I'm going to take an afternoon nap. I haven't had a nap since Charlotte was born."

"How is she?" Marine asked of her ten-year-old goddaughter.

"We spoke yesterday, just before I got here. . . . There's no cell phone reception here, by the way," Sylvie said. "She'd been on a two-hour walk through Alpine meadows with my parents, and later they were going to buy cream at Charlotte's favorite farm."

Marine sighed. "That's idyllic."

"Mmmm, and so are these mojitos, and this hotel! Isn't this bar too much?"

Marine looked around at the aqua-blue and green curved sofas that lined the walls, bright-yellow armchairs, glass-topped bronze tables, and white wooden venetian blinds that held the sun at bay. Ceiling fans slowly turned above their heads, giving the bar a tropical feel. She saw Eric Monnier, whom Verlaque had told her was a retired teacher, sitting alone at a round marble table under a massive black-and-white framed photograph of a Cuban farmer. He was writing in a notebook and had seemed to already have finished his champagne as there was now a glass of what looked like whiskey beside him.

"Marine," Sylvie said.

"Oh, sorry," Marine said. "What?"

"I have to tell you who is here, as a guest."

"Right. Who, then?"

"Please show some enthusiasm!"

Marine laughed and sipped some champagne. "Sorry, judging from your voice it must be a movie star, and you know I don't know much about cinema. I can't remember the last time I went to the movies. Stars to me just seem like moderately talented people who won the beauty lottery at birth — and who have little up here . . ." she said, pointing to her head.

"Those are Hollywood stars. This person you would *not* have recently seen in a movie, *chérie.*"

"Their career is over?" Marine asked.

Sylvie frowned. "He does commercials now. I heard he was trouble on the film sets. You still haven't guessed who . . ."

"Hey, you two," Verlaque said, leaning down to give Sylvie the *bise.* "Don't get up," he said.

30

"I can't," Sylvie answered.

Verlaque laughed loudly and Marine beamed, pleased that her two favorite people might actually get along this week.

"I was just telling Marine that we have a French film star among us on Sordou," Sylvie said, loudly finishing her mojito.

Verlaque raised an eyebrow. "Really?"

"And, there's fireworks between him and his wife — whose face has been lifted about a million times — and her surly teenage son."

"We saw them in the lobby!" Marine said, more interested in the boy's angst than the movie star's wife.

"M. Verlaque, you'll be needing some nice cool champagne," Niki Darcette said as she handed Verlaque a *coupe*.

Sylvie Grassi looked at Marine and Marine whispered, "I swear she's flirting with him!"

"Pardon?" Verlaque said.

Marine made sure that Niki was out of earshot and repeated what she had said to Sylvie.

Verlaque laughed. "That's crazy."

"No, it's Sordou," Sylvie said. Verlaque and Marine looked at Sylvie, who herself was a young-looking forty-year-old who kept her petite frame trim, much like,

Verlaque thought to himself, Mlle Darcette. "The guys on staff here are all making eyes at me. I think it's partly due to the beauty of this island, the warm sun on your skin, and how great the saltwater makes you feel once you've been swimming."

Marine laughed. "And the fact that they can't get off the island unless a boat shows up probably helps too," she said.

Sylvie frowned but then whispered excitedly, "Don't look now, but just behind you . . ."

Marine and Verlaque instinctively turned around to look.

Sylvie groaned and hid her face in her empty mojito glass.

"Alain Denis!" Verlaque whispered.

"He's the only film star that I think my mother can name," Marine said in a low voice. "She loved him in that sixties movie he did in Venice . . ."

*Acqua alta,*" Sylvie supplied.

"My mother loved him too," Verlaque said, making no bones about the fact that he was openly staring at the actor, who was at the far end of the bar ordering a drink. "*The Red Night* was her favorite, if I remember correctly."

"Mine was *The Longest Road Home,* without a doubt," Sylvie said. "That great scene, shot in black-and-white, where the screen is split in two by a wooden post, and he's on the left of it, alone, but you can hear her voice, off screen, and she's crying . . ."

"Ah yes, Isabella Piccolini," Verlaque quickly said, smiling. "Now, she was my *father*'s favorite screen star."

Marine tried to be discreet as she looked at the actor; he did look a bit like his younger self: he still kept his fine straight hair slightly long, but it was now mostly gray. His long aquiline nose and full, almost girlish lips were still very striking, as were his high cheekbones. But his skin was wrinkle-free, which Marine thought was odd for someone who must be in his late sixties, like her parents. "What happened to his career, anyway?" she asked.

Sylvie leaned forward. "It began with film-set problems between Denis and Isabella Piccolini," she said, whispering and playing with her empty mojito glass, toying with the idea of having a third. Sylvie read *Paris Match* whenever she could; she was too proud to buy it, so picked up used copies when she saw them at the dentist's or doctor's office, or at her sister's. "Not only was he lazy — he had problems remembering his lines." Sylvie then touched the side of her nose and made a snorting noise. "But he used to sexually harass the female co-stars, including Piccolini, who was a happily married nice Italian girl with four children, Daniella, Dario, Davide . . . um, I can't remember the last one . . ."

"Go on," Verlaque said.

"He began making too many demands during filming, asking for more and more money, much of which was going straight to his coke dealer."

"What do you think he's doing here?" Marine asked.

"On vacation," Sylvie answered.

"I think Marine means here, on Sordou, and not in Saint-Tropez or Ibiza," Verlaque suggested.

"Good question," Sylvie said. "Maybe he wanted to be out of the limelight?"

"I thought movie stars craved that," Marine said.

Sylvie leaned back on her bar stool and gave Alain Denis a sideways glance. "He certainly looks like the type who would be happy with cameras flashing in his face," she said. "Especially since he's been reduced to making dog-food commercials. But who knows?"

Marine and Antoine looked at Sylvie, surprised that she would end their discussion of Alain Denis on a pseudo-philosophical note.

"Should I have another mojito or a nap?" Sylvie asked.

"A nap," Marine and Antoine said in unison.

# CHAPTER THREE:
## ABOUT THE CHEF

Circles had been one of the decorative themes of the original Jacky Bar, and during the last two years of painstaking renovations Émile Villey had convinced the Le Bons to keep that iconoclastic 1960s shape. There were circles on the side of the long, curving, white bar, made from wood and painted black; discreet circles on the woolen and silk area rugs; and round bronze mirrors and picture frames adorned the walls. Villey believed that circles were relaxing; just the thing needed in a seaside hotel. But they also served as his window onto the bar, and its adjoining restaurant, as four of the bronze spheres had been turned into two-way mirrors, allowing the chef to observe his clients, and staff, from the kitchen.

Émile Villey, a young chef at twenty-five years of age, was lucky, and he knew it. Running his own restaurant, even though it was small, was a dream job. Maxime and Cat-

Cat Le Bon treated him as an equal — even consulting him during the kitchen and restaurant renovations — and gave Émile full control of the menu and the kitchen. He had fallen in love with the island the first time he saw it — he had been born and raised in landlocked Berry, in the middle of France, and had done his training, which began at the age of fifteen, in similar land-locked restaurants from Picardie to Paris. During his interview, while on a rare week-end off from his job at Le Meurice in Paris, Émile had cooked for the Le Bons, using plants he had foraged on Sordou's rocky cliffs — rosemary, thyme, lavender, and wild arugula — and he had hired the island's only full-time inhabitant, Prosper Buffa (paying him too much), to catch some fish to grill. The meal had been simple, but fresh, and the Le Bons had been wildly enthusiastic. They told Villey he would be welcome to arrive early that spring, to get the kitchen ready, and experiment with menus on the staff, until the first guests would arrive in July. Émile Villey and Maxime Le Bon had finished the evening of his interview drinking twenty-year-old Armagnac and dreaming of Michelin stars.

It was only after Villey had signed a three-year contract with the Le Bons that news was passed down to him via the extensive and rapid French chefs' network: the Le Bons had been so enthusiastic because Villey had been the only applicant. After a few more visits to the island, Villey figured out why he had been the only one to apply for the job: given the remoteness of the island it would be almost impossible to produce a varied menu. There would be no exotic ingredients; even the basics would have to be delivered by boat from Marseille. And Marseille was still rough-and-tumble Marseille; it would never be, even with investments like the ones the Le Bons had made, Saint-Tropez, Capri, or even Aix-en-Provence. Apprehensive, the young chef had been ready to break his contract, disappearing into some restaurant in New York, or Italy, until he went back to the island in August for yet another meeting with the Le Bons, who were virtually camping out, overseeing the hotel's renovations. After their brainstorming session, Villey went swimming along the cliffs and, floating weightlessly on his back, looked at the blue sky above. There was silence all around him, except for the splashing noise he made with his hands, and the far-off noise of the *cigales* who hung out in Sordou's few trees. Putting his goggles on — a gift from his parents, who themselves had only once been to the sea — he swam along the underwater cliffs and marveled at the sea life, each tiny colorful fish swimming in the same direction as he did, each one living in a group, but alone at the same time.

As Villey heaved himself up onto a flat rock and dried off in the sun, he reminded himself of his apprenticeship years: the rude awakenings at 6 a.m. in freezing-cold Berry, when it was still dark out and frost covered the ground and every other surface; working solidly in a large restaurant kitchen, long after midnight, six days a week, until his hands ached and were covered in cuts and sores. Saturday night was the apprentices' only solace, which they shared with the nursing students at the opposite end of town, drinking beers and playing foosball. He soon became a *saucier,* then rose to the post as sous-chef for a manic-depressive two-starred chef near Lille who thought it funny to play practical jokes on his kitchen staff in the middle of a busy Sunday lunch. And then came his coup: a position as the fish chef at Le Meurice in Paris, where working conditions, despite the glamorous hotel and three-starred restaurant, were no better than his first *apprentisage* at the Auberge des Oiseaux in Berry. At night he would fall into his small bed in a studio in the twentieth *arrondissement,* exhausted. And the studio, where his neighbors didn't seem to work and listened to rap all day and night, cost him 850 euros a month; half of his salary.

Sordou would be *his* challenge, Émile decided as he toweled off that hot August day. Were there not other great restaurants in remote places? Iceland, for example? Or some South Seas islands? He almost ran back to the hotel, and sat down and drew up a plan, which included a kitchen garden and pots for herbs. If he planted in early spring of the opening season, then he could have Provençal summer vegetables to plan the menu around. If Villey would tend to the garden, the Le Bons promised they would set aside a plot of land. The architect even planned a six-foot-high stone wall that would protect *le potager* from the sea's winds.

Villey continued to make notes on the train back to Paris that evening; he would buy fruit in season and preserve it, as his grandmother had done. He'd make liqueurs from thyme and lavender. Fish would feature highly on the menu; he'd arrange with local fishermen to stop by the island on their way back to Marseille: Prosper wasn't reliable enough and made it clear that he hated the Le Bons' presence on what he claimed was *his* island. Émile knew he'd have to get up at some godforsaken hour to meet the fishermen, but at least he wouldn't be breaking the snow off of the inner windowpane as he had done in Le Berry. Buying meat would be difficult, but he'd arrange to have Provençal lamb delivered, or send Hugo Sammut out to pick it up. Pasta would be his saving grace; he loved making it, and everyone liked eating it. Le Bon also agreed to invest in an Italian meat-carving machine that cost the same price as a small Citroën or Renault, but it was the most beautiful machine Villey had ever seen; brilliant red, its chrome glistening. Its mechanics were as precise as a telescope's, and with a gentle turning of its wheel, a leg of Bellota or Pata Negra ham from Andalusia could be carved down to one-tenth of a millimeter. Extra legs could be hung from the rafters in the kitchen, Villey thought, or even in the bar.

He looked out one of the *hublots* at the clients, drinking their celebratory glass of champagne, and he liked the look of them. This would be a good group to start off on; for the Le Bons had reported that they were a bit of everything: a rich film star, Parisians, an American couple, and some middle-class Aixois. Villey was especially intrigued by the mojito-drinking artist, or he thought she was an artist, with her punky clothes and multicolored bracelets up and down her thin but muscular arms. He liked her laugh and could hear her laughing with her friends — a man and a woman — who had just arrived. The movie star was there too, looking sullen, pretending to be busy with his iPhone even though there was no reception, and there was an unkempt elderly man sitting at a corner table busily writing in a notebook. A diary? Villey watched him carefully and decided that the stained Cuban shirt and shaggy beard might be a ruse and that he could be a restaurant critic. Or hotel critic. But so soon? He'd have Serge and Marie-Thérèse keep an eye on him.

Émile Villey had decided to be a professional cook when he was twelve. He had helped his mother and aunt cook and serve for a party — his grandparents' fiftieth wedding anniversary — and had rejoiced at the sounds of the happy diners while he worked away in the kitchen with a lazy, older cousin. Had he known just how difficult his years of training would be, he might have chosen a different field, but what were the choices for a nonbookish boy in the middle of

France, whose father was a farmer? He had two older brothers who would split the family farm. The lazy cousin was now the worst electrician in France, and Émile was here, on a sun-soaked Mediterranean island, where the rich came to de-stress.

And this morning had been a blessing; after his daily swim he had walked around the south side of the island and up over a rocky hill, through a small pine forest, where he came across a small, wild orchard. Someone years ago — when the hotel had been at its climax, no doubt — had planted fruit trees. The trees were in terrible shape; as a farmer's son he knew that. But two of them were still laden with apricots, although it was late in the season, and Émile took one off the tree and, splitting it apart, ate its warm, juicy, sweet fruit. He put as many in his backpack as he could and rushed back to tell Maxime Le Bon the good news. There was also a huge, umbrella-shaped fig tree, covered in hard little figs. They would be ripe in late summer. He had been making both apricot and fig tarts since he was an apprentice, using a deceptively simple shortbread crust that he laced with almond extract, an elixir unknown in France that an English sous-chef had once introduced him to. He carried the tiny glass bottles, as he did his knives, from kitchen to kitchen, and had friends who were going to London pick some up for him, along with sharp cheddar and oat cakes.

This week had also brought another gift, that of Isnard Guyon, a friendly fisherman from Pointe Rouge in Marseille, who had not only been bringing Émile excellent fish throughout the spring, but had recently offered to bring the chef meat and other products — at a small commission, naturally — via a cousin who was a butcher, known for his fresh lamb from the hills of Provence and the dairy products he ordered from a farm in the Alps. Guyon had delivered the first batch the previous morning, as promised, pulling up to Sordou's dock at 5 a.m. Villey tasted some of the cream as soon as he got back to the kitchen; it was richer and thicker than any cream he had ever tasted.

Émile Villey turned away from watching the guests, put his thick, curly blond hair in a ponytail, adjusted his apron, and washed his hands. It was time to get to work on the evening's menu: the guests could choose between cold zucchini soup with a dollop of Alpine crème fraîche, or a stacked vegetable terrine made with layers of phyllo dough and anchored down with a sprig of rosemary; for the main dish Isnard's freshly caught sea bream braised in olive oil with cherry tomatoes, black olives, and artichokes, or lamb chops cooked over an open fire served with a wet polenta; and apricot tart for dessert, with the vanilla ice cream he had made before he went to bed. Villey had picked lavender and used it to make cookies, which he planned on serving with a delicate sweet wine from Beaumes-de-Venise in the Luberon.

He didn't mind not having kitchen help; the Le Bons had spared no cost in buying him the best appliances, and he had been taught to clean as he cooked. He almost preferred it that way, enjoying the silence and calm. If pressed, Serge had promised — or rather, Maxime had promised — Serge's services in tidying up or helping chop vegetables. Marie-Thérèse had offered to help in the kitchen, and so far her enthusiasm outweighed her inexperience. Tonight would be their first dinner with clients, and Émile knew that how well it went off could predict the rest of the summer's success, and even the future of Sordou.

# Chapter Four:
## Dinner for Ten

Marine sat on their room's private terrace, her bare feet resting on the wrought iron balcony. She wore a short, pink fitted cotton dress, and a large floppy beige sun hat trimmed in light blue. A cool wind was beginning to blow, and the sun would soon set, but she relished these few moments — outside, away from her computer and research. She looked out at the sparkling sea and wriggled her toes, which had just been subject to a poor pedicure. She inspected the spots where she had missed, and the red nail polish had leaked out onto her toes. She told herself that no one would notice, and if they did, they surely must be bored.

"Did you put sunscreen on your legs?" Antoine Verlaque asked as he came out on the terrace to join her.

Marine looked at her legs and then up at her boyfriend. "Not yet, but I will tomorrow, I promise," she answered. "It's just been so long since these white, freckled legs have seen any sun." She turned her legs from right to left and frowned.

Verlaque reached down and tapped on the brim of her hat. "I love your white, freckled legs," he said. "They match all the polka dots in the bar downstairs."

"Thanks," Marine said, rolling her eyes.

"Aren't you hungry?"

Marine laughed. "No, but *you* are, I take it. Aren't there any snacks in the minibar?"

"There was a small bag of peanuts, but I already ate them."

"Thanks for sharing!" Marine said.

"It really was minuscule," Verlaque replied. "About this big," he added, putting his thumb and pointer finger about an inch apart.

Marine looked at her watch, made of white gold and encrusted with very discreet diamonds. It had been a birthday present from Verlaque, and she dreaded to even think of how much it cost, probably as much as a down payment on a smallish apartment in Aix.

"Let's go down to the dining room," Verlaque said, rubbing his hands together. "It's almost eight-thirty."

"All right, don't rush me," Marine said as she slowly got up from the very comfortable deck chair she had been sitting on and took one last look at the sea.

"Come on, slowpoke," Verlaque said, already heading for the door. "Let's get a good table."

"Wait a minute, Antoine," Marine said, catching up to him and gently grabbing his shoulder. "I don't want to be rushed, or stressed, this week. There are other guests here, and so what if they get the dining table with the best view. Okay? Look at the view out of this bedroom window."

"I'm just hungry."

"I believe that you're hungry," Marine said, laughing. "But I also know that as an examining magistrate, and an independently wealthy one at that, that you're used to getting your own way. But there are other wealthy, even famous, people here, and they too are used to getting what they want. So let's let them have their . . . way."

Verlaque took Marine in his arms and kissed her. He then drew away and said, "Do I have the right to send the wineglasses back if I don't like them?"

Marine laughed and looked up at the ceiling, knowing that Antoine would be restless the entire dinner if the wineglasses were too small or their rims too thick. "Yes!"

He took her once again in his arms and

kissed her, lifting up the back of her dress and running his hand up her leg toward her buttocks.

"Antoine," Marine said, reaching behind and taking his hand in hers. "We already made love, twice, after we got here. Remember?"

"Yes," Verlaque replied, kissing her. "That's the problem. I remember."

"Besides —"

A knock at the door interrupted their embrace.

"Who could that be?" Verlaque asked.

"Sylvie," Marine whispered.

"Why?" Verlaque asked, adopting Marine's hushed tones. "Can't we just meet her downstairs?"

Marine shook her head back and forth. "No, she doesn't like going into dining room, or even to parties, alone. Shhh . . ."

"That's ridiculous," Verlaque whispered when the caller knocked again, this time harder.

"It's just a phobia she has," Marine whispered, moving toward the door. "She sees herself as a loser if she enters a place alone."

Verlaque tapped the side of his head, putting his hand down just in time as Marine had opened the door and Sylvie rushed into their room. "Didn't you hear me knock?"

she asked. "Nice dress, Marine." She looked over at Verlaque, who earlier had changed into a short-sleeved blue linen shirt and clean khakis, his bare feet in a new pair of Tod's. "And you, Antoine, look very . . ."

"Elegant?" Verlaque asked.

"Preppy," Sylvie replied. "But it suits you."

Verlaque pressed his lips together, knowing that "preppy" for a contemporary photographer — who this evening wore a short gold-lamé dress and high-heeled strappy sandals — was an insult, but he had promised Marine he would try to get along with her best friend. He looked over at Marine, who was smiling, and she winked at him.

"What did you two do all afternoon?" Sylvie asked, walking around their large room and inspecting it.

"We had sex twice, then a nap," Marine said flatly.

Verlaque laughed.

Sylvie took a step back and looked at her friend, wide-eyed. "Are you under some kind of Sordou spell?"

"Perhaps," replied Marine.

"Well, I had a nap too," Sylvie replied, still looking sideways at Marine. "And then went for a swim in the pool where both the young godlike chef and rugged boatman were ogling me, and then saw a huge fight between Alain Denis and Botox wifey, whose name, I found out, is Emmanuelle."

Verlaque yawned. "Who's hungry?"

The dining room's décor was more subdued than the Jacky Bar's, but every bit as interesting, and also Capri-inspired. Cat-Cat Le Bon and Émile Villey had spent weeks poring over the Internet and design magazines, choosing what they agreed were the most comfortable chairs, elegant linens, and tasteful table settings. The chandeliers were made from colored Murano glass; everything else was a shade of ivory or cream, save for the bunches of pale-pink peonies on the sideboards.

Niki Darcette, who had changed into a short black evening dress, was there to greet the guests, and she escorted the trio to a round table set for three, which did have a view of the sea, as did most of the other tables, given there were only ten people eating that evening. "I'm sorry that it's too cold to eat outside on your first night here," Darcette said. "We weren't expecting the wind to pick up like it did."

"That's Provence for you," Sylvie answered. Despite living and working in Aix-en-Provence for over twenty years, she still hated the Provençal wind.

The dining room was big but didn't feel too cold, partly thanks to the low carved ceiling and the expansive windows. The architect had renovated a second, smaller dining room, which was now closed off by sliding wooden doors but could be opened to join the main room when the hotel reached — the Le Bons hoped by next summer — its maximum capacity.

Verlaque, Marine, and Sylvie politely nodded at the other diners, who nodded back. Eric Monnier was just tucking his napkin into the top of his shirt and Verlaque shook his hand and wished him well. As they passed the Hobbses' table Verlaque said bon appétit to the couple, who were already halfway though their main dishes.

*"Merci,"* Shirley Hobbs said, visibly thrilled to be able to understand the man's greeting.

"Darn fine lamb chops," Bill Hobbs said, pointing to the meat with his fork, his hand gently shaking.

Verlaque stopped and said, in English, "Is that so? I'll order them, then."

"Oh my God," Sylvie whispered to Marine as they sat down. "Next we'll be playing musical chairs with the other guests."

Marine smiled. "Antoine loves to talk about food, and especially use his English."

"What's the sauce surrounding the polenta?" Verlaque asked Hobbs.

"It's just the meat juice, pure and simple," Bill Hobbs answered.

Verlaque rubbed his stomach. "Sounds perfect. Enjoy the rest of your meal."

"Thank you," the Hobbses said in unison.

As he walked away Verlaque heard Shirley Hobbs whisper, "The French are *so* nice, not at all like Susan and Ian Bertwhistle said."

Verlaque smiled, glad to have proven the Bertwhistles wrong. And what did he have to be snooty, or sour, about? Why not be nice, and kind, to strangers, even if it had horrified Sylvie Grassi? He liked his job as the examining magistrate in sleepy and affluent Aix-en-Provence; he was very in love with Marine Bonnet, who was the most intelligent, cultured, and warmhearted law professor he was sure to ever meet; he enjoyed, and respected — apart from Prosecutor Yves Roussel — his colleagues at the Palais de Justice; and he was, as the heir to a flour fortune, financially more than well-off. What was missing? he asked himself as he sat down, still smiling.

"Why don't you go and chat with the rest of the diners?" Sylvie asked.

"I would," Verlaque answered, shaking

open the pale-blue linen napkin and setting it on his lap. "But I'm too hungry —"

Verlaque's sentence was cut short by what sounded like a gunshot, quickly followed by two more. Sylvie held her hand to her chest and said, "What in the world?"

"Hunters?" Marine asked. "It's off season . . ."

Maxime Le Bon rushed into the dining room, motioning to the diners with his palms pushing the air. "Please, do not be alarmed," he said.

"Those were gunshots," Bill Hobbs said.

"Dear guests," Max Le Bon continued. "As I said, please do not be alarmed. As you saw from the boat as you arrived at Sordou, the island is home to one of France's tallest lighthouses . . ."

The guests nodded, perplexed.

"And in that lighthouse lives our very own eccentric islander — every island needs one, ha-ha — Prosper Buffa."

Verlaque leaned over and quickly translated for the Hobbses.

"M. Buffa, having never lived on the mainland, hunts and fishes for his food," Le Bon went on. "That was Prosper now, obviously hunting rabbits. I'm dreadfully sorry, and I'll ask him to stay on his side of the island from now on, and to restrict his hunting to the early morning."

"That's so dangerous," Bill Hobbs said, looking at his fellow diners for approval.

*"Mais oui, certainement! Très dangereux!"* the Parisian woman called out.

"Oh, Bill," Shirley Hobbs said. "Don't be such a square. We're in France, and people still hunt here." She smiled kindly at Verlaque and Marine and Sylvie. Sylvie waved.

"Zank you for ze understanding," Max Le Bon said in heavily accented English. "Bon appétit!"

"Good, here comes the waitress," Verlaque said.

*"Bonsoir,"* Marie-Thérèse Guichard said, still nervous on her first official day as waitress. She had practiced over the whole month of June on the rest of the staff, but hadn't taken it seriously as she had grown to know, and feel comfortable with, her coworkers. At twenty-two she was the youngest person on staff and had heard about the job through her uncle, who had overseen the masonry work during the renovations. "There's a simple menu this evening," she began. "In fact, a simple menu all this week."

Verlaque and Sylvie laughed, and Marine kicked both of them under the table.

Marie-Thérèse coughed and went on.

"Um, tonight's specials are . . . cold zucchini soup served with crème-fraîche from the Alps . . . I mean the cream, not the zucchini . . . and stacked, roasted vegetables layered with the chef's own phyllo dough." She looked seriously from Marine to Sylvie and went on, too shy to look at the chubby man, whom she could see was sitting forward staring intently at her, his elbows on the table and his chin resting on his fists. "Um, for entrées . . . freshly caught sea bream . . . Isnard caught it . . . he's our fisherman . . . he's really nice . . ."

Verlaque laughed and Sylvie and Marine held their napkins up to their mouths, Marine's eyes filling with tears.

". . . braised, um, in olive oil with cherry tomatoes, black olives, and artichokes, or wood-fired lamb chops served with polenta." Marie-Thérèse sighed and shifted her weight, daring to glance at the male diner, who was know sitting back, his thick arms crossed, still smiling.

"I'll have the soup," Marine said.

"So will I," Sylvie added.

"Stacked vegetables for me," Verlaque said.

Marie-Thérèse nodded. "Okay. And to follow?"

"The sea bream," Marine said.

"Lamb chops," Sylvie said.

"Another lamb here," Verlaque said, raising his hand.

"Thank you," Marie-Thérèse said, turning quickly on her heel to go. "Oh, here's the wine menu!" she added, handing Verlaque a thick white book.

"Impressive!" Verlaque said. "Small food menu, and big wine menu, just the way it should be."

Marie-Thérèse nodded, but looked baffled. "I'll be right back!" she said.

"Take your time," Marine said, smiling. "My friend will be a while looking at your wine list."

"We'll need a red and a white," Sylvie said. "Marine ordered the fish."

"Oh, I like red with fish —"

"Yes, definitely two bottles," Verlaque cut in, putting his reading glasses on to read the menu. He read the list, whistling softly as he turned the pages. "White from Cassis?"

"No," both women said in unison.

"Too close to home?" Verlaque asked. "Okay then, a Nuragus di Cagliari from Sardinia. And a red from . . . Sicily?"

"Perfect," Sylvie said, having no idea what a Nuragus was. But if Antoine liked it, it would be good. She looked around the room. "Alain Denis and his wife are here without the teenager."

"Poor boy," Marine said. "Does he have to eat alone, in his room?"

"It would appear so," Sylvie said. "They were arguing about him this afternoon."

"That must be the new couple, who arrived here on the later boat," Marine said as she saw Sylvie looking across the room at an elegantly dressed couple in their late thirties or early forties who sat in silence.

"Parisians," Sylvie said. "Obviously."

Verlaque ignored the women as he continued to read the wine menu, which for him was as interesting as a novel. He turned to the last page to see what kind of Armagnacs and whiskies they offered.

"I hope this place isn't going to feel like a retreat," Sylvie said. "With half of the guests not getting along, and the rest of us watching each other."

"You're the one who's watching," Verlaque said, looking at Sylvie over his reading glasses.

"I can't help it," Sylvie said. "And there's that man, eating by himself."

"He's a French literature teacher, from Aix," Marine said. "I'd say he looks happy enough. Perhaps another night we'll ask him to join us."

"See what I mean?" Sylvie said. "This *does* feel like some camp. Next you'll suggest that we each change seats every dinner, so we all get to know each other."

Marine laughed. "That would be fun . . ."

"Clément!" Verlaque called out.

Marine and Sylvie stared at each other.

"Clément Viale!" he continued. Verlaque got up and set his napkin on the table. "Clément Viale is over there. We went to law school together." Verlaque excused himself and began to walk across the dining room.

Viale saw his old friend and cried, "Dough Boy!"

Verlaque and Viale embraced, and Viale led Verlaque over to his table, where he was introduced to Clément's wife of twelve years, and mother of his three children, Delphine. Marine saw Verlaque turn and point to her, and she was about to get up when Verlaque came back.

"We're meeting them after dinner, for a drink in the bar," Verlaque said, sitting down.

"Dough Boy?" Sylvie asked, winking at Marine.

"I was thinner then, believe it or not," Verlaque said. "But the name came from my family's flour business."

*"Bien sûr,"* Sylvie replied. "Here comes the

waitress," she said. "No laughing this time!"

Verlaque ordered the wines, and Marie-Thérèse took the wine list from him, almost dropped it, and left.

"How's dessert?" Verlaque said to the Hobbses, leaning back in his chair.

"Wonderful!" Bill Hobbs yelled.

"The cookies have lavender in them," Shirley Hobbs added. She held one up.

"Excellent!" Verlaque said, turning back to Marine and Sylvie.

"They're very enthusiastic," Marine said.

"Yes, not at all affected," Verlaque agreed. "My poor friend Clément isn't having as much fun as our Americans." He glanced around the room. "Nor is the movie star-slash-dog-food-salesman."

"See, you're just as curious as us," Sylvie said.

"As *you,*" Verlaque replied. "Marine could care less."

Marine sighed. She hated when Antoine put her on a pedestal, or when he assumed what she was thinking. The maddening thing was, he was usually right.

Marie-Thérèse came back, holding a bottle of white wine in her hand. She bit her lip and tried to remember her lesson with Émile and Serge; she could have killed Serge right now. She had looked for him at his post in the bar, as he usually opened the wines, but he was nowhere to be seen. She had rushed into the kitchen and Émile had calmed her down, and told her to open the wine herself. They had practiced it numerous times. "Pour a little, then taste," Émile repeated twice.

She tilted the bottle gently toward *him* — Chubby Man, she'd already named him in her head — and showed him the label. Both Émile and Serge had warned her that it could be the woman who chose the wine, but Marie-Thérèse knew that in this case it was definitely the man deciding. He looked at the label, and nodded, smiling up at her, and she took the bottle by its neck and cut off the lead wrapper. She slipped the piece of foil in her apron and then slowly twisted the screw into the cork, pleased that it was going in straight, and easily. Pulling up on the corkscrew, the cork came slowly out, letting off a tiny "pop" sound, and Marie-Thérèse almost cried tears of relief.

She poised the bottle over the monsieur's wineglass, from a set of glasses that Marie-Thérèse had been warned were handblown in Austria and were the world's best. Serge had joked that they were also so fragile they could break if you looked at them the wrong way. She knew he hated them, and she did too. Shaking, she began to pour a little white wine into Chubby Man's glass, and just then she looked up and saw her boss, M. Le Bon, come into the dining room. She was sure that Émile was watching her too, through those little round windows that looked like mirrors. And then her head went all fuzzy. Her face was hot, and red, as she strained to remember the next step. And then she had it; Émile's kind voice in her head, saying, "We pour a small bit in the glass, and then we taste." Marie-Thérèse silently repeated the phrase as she finished pouring. And, before Antoine Verlaque had time to reach out for his glass, Marie-Thérèse had grabbed it and lifted it to her mouth and tasted the Cagliari. "It's good!" she said, putting his empty glass down with a confident thump.

# Chapter Five:
# Stranger Than Fiction

Maxime Le Bon froze in his tracks. Émile Villey, taking advantage of a small pause between cooking lamb chops and sea bream, had indeed been looking out the *hublot* onto the dining room. He held his head in his hands and went back to the stove. Taking a juice glass off of a shelf, he poured it half full with a good cognac he used for cooking and downed it in one sip.

Antoine Verlaque was, for one of the first times in his life, speechless. He looked up at the waitress and saw, in her big brown eyes, his own at twenty-two. She looked terrified. Hadn't he been just as nervous and bewildered by adult life as she was now? The Verlaque family wealth and prestige only partly softened all the apprehension he felt at that age.

And then he laughed and put his hands together and began to clap. Marine and Sylvie quickly followed suit, Sylvie adding some fist pumps, and Eric Monnier, who had witnessed the whole thing (as he couldn't take his eyes off of Marine Bonnet), clapped and yelled, "Bravo!" Bill Hobbs began to film the scene with his new iPhone and couldn't wait to show it to Ian Bertwhistle.

Maxime Le Bon looked around the room and saw his diners happy, and laughing. Even Clément and Delphine Viale seemed to be having a good time.

Marie-Thérèse had at once realized what she had done wrong. She had practiced sipping wine with Serge and knew what a good wine should smell, and taste, like. And she knew that it was Chubby Man who was meant to have tested the wine, not her. But now he was clapping, as was Maxime Le Bon.

Serge Canzano, having heard the commotion, came running into the dining room, and Le Bon motioned for him to take another wineglass to Verlaque's table. Canzano set down an empty Riedel glass, and Marie-Thérèse slowly poured some wine into it. She smiled at Verlaque, who swirled the wine around and then sniffed at it, and tasted it. "You're right," he said. "It is good. Very good indeed." He didn't want to teach her that you only need sniff the wine, to see

if it was corked, and then say, "It's fine."
She'd learn that, probably first thing tomorrow morning.

"Bravo!" Monnier yelled once again.

Marie-Thérèse then poured wine into Marine's glass, who said, "Thank you," and into Sylvie's, who said, "Chin-chin!" and took a big gulp.

"I'll be back . . . *momentarily* . . . with your first course," Marie-Thérèse said. She felt, all of a sudden, a surge of power and confidence. She had a feeling that the job would be easy from now on, and she would grow to like it more and more with each passing day. She turned around and walked through the dining room, beaming. It was the first time in her life that, although she had made a mistake, she had made people laugh, and be happy. It made her joyous. She walked by the famous actor's table (she had never seen any of his films, but thought he was funny in the dog-food commercials), and Alain Denis raised one eyebrow at her and frowned in a way that she knew was not kind. Émile Villey, back at his lookout post, also saw the actor's callous stare and rushed to be at the kitchen door when Marie-Thérèse walked in.

"That was quite a scene back there," Clément Viale said, swirling his whiskey in a cut-crystal tumbler.

"She'll be able to tell her grandchildren the story," Marine said.

Viale smiled. "At any rate, that was nice of you to applaud her, Dough Boy. A younger Verlaque would not have taken that so well, if I'm remembering correctly."

Verlaque rubbed his stomach, not seeming to care about his nickname. He crossed his legs and sipped a bit of the eighteen-year-old Lagavulin. "Stranger than fiction," he said. "If you were to put that scene in a novel, no one would believe it. It made my day."

"What was *Clément* like at that age?" Delphine Viale asked, leaning forward and resting her chin on her incredibly thin and bejeweled hands.

Verlaque laughed, sensing the tension between the couple. "Like the waitress," he said. The group looked on, perplexed. "Full of bewilderment for what lies ahead in life, and naïve too," he continued. "Not yet aware of all the crap."

"Oh, I don't know," Clément replied, straightening his back. "I think I knew quite well what I was doing back then."

"Really?" Verlaque asked. "You were one hundred percent sure that law school was for you? And that you'd enjoy being a law-yer?"

"I think so . . ."

"And you were sure you'd marry, and have children? And you were confident in the fact that the earth was a safe place to be; that there'd never be anything like global warming, or tidal waves, or maniacs driving airplanes into the World Trade Center?" Verlaque began to remember the things that had frustrated him about Viale all those years ago: his smugness, the smugness that came from their elite backgrounds and schools.

"Nobody could have known those things," Viale suggested.

"But I think that's what Antoine means about naivety in the young," Marine said. "We don't know yet, and don't even want to know, that evil exists. We all saw it in that young waitress this evening."

"At that age I was just into getting drunk and laid," Sylvie Grassi said. Verlaque laughed and the Viales looked on, Clément with a strained grin and Delphine with a look of disgust.

"Fancy Alain Denis being one of the guests this week," Delphine Viale said in an awkward attempt to change the conversation.

"He was the only person not laughing this evening at dinner," Marine said.

"Really?" Verlaque asked.

Marine nodded. "I think it's because that waitress stole the show."

"You're right," Sylvie said. "An aging actor, once having worked with the most famous Italian and French directors of his day, now selling eyeglasses and dog food. He shows up to a small exclusive resort and expects people to be fawning over him, and then at dinner no one gives him the time of day and the gaff of a young waitress steals our hearts."

"Oh, I don't know," Clément said, turning to his wife. "Delphine asked for his autograph this afternoon, didn't you *chérie*?"

"It was for Mother," Mme Viale replied, pursing her lips and glaring at her husband.

"Oh, my mother loved him too," Marine said, smiling, in an attempt to lighten the strained atmosphere between the Viales.

"Poor guy; we should stop speaking of Denis in the past tense," Sylvie said, finishing her whiskey. "Well, I'm off to bed; the boatman has promised to take me . . . um . . . rowing . . . tomorrow." Verlaque and Clément Viale laughed, and Delphine glared at her husband. Sylvie stood up and pulled down her dress, which had risen up while she had been sitting.

"I'll come too," Marine said. "It's been a long day."

"Well, I'm not going to be the only woman here, listening to Antoine and Clément relive their glory days," Delphine Viale said. She got up, taking with her a small Fendi clutch bag that Sylvie had been eyeing with interest.

"Sleep tight, ladies," Viale said, saluting them with his right hand.

The men watched the women leave the bar and the minute they were out of the room Clément called over to Serge Canzano, ordering two more whiskies. Viale then sighed, leaning back in the armchair and closing his eyes for a few seconds.

"Going through a bad patch?" Verlaque asked.

"Only for about the last ten years," Viale said. "No, six years. Things started going downhill after the birth of our third child."

"I'm sorry."

"You've never married, have you?" Viale asked.

"No."

Serge Canzano set two more whiskies down on the table and cleared away the empty glasses. When Canzano was out of earshot, Viale went on. "I'm having financial problems too. That's the one thing I never thought I'd have. So I guess you were right before; when I was a student I didn't think unhappiness, or failure, was possible. Cheers," he said, holding up his glass.

Verlaque lifted his glass and had a small sip; he didn't feel like drinking anymore but wanted to keep Viale company.

"Do you have a course of action?" Verlaque asked. "I mean, is there any way to straighten out your financial problems?

Viale made a sweeping gesture around the room.

"Here?"

"I'm an investor in Sordou," Viale said. "It's the last of my family money. The rest I lost; who was to know that Alcatel-Lucent would take a dive in the stock market?"

Verlaque said, "It's a good idea, Clément. This is a beautiful place, from what I've seen so far. You'll make back your investment." Verlaque took another sip of whiskey; he knew all too well how risky the hotel and restaurant business was. And this one was set on a remote island. "It must be a coup having Alain Denis here. Has someone called *Paris Match* and arranged for some paparazzi to come?"

"Niki Darcette is supposed to be working

on that, and Denis himself promised to call some journalist contacts, but so far, nothing. He's a prick, actually." Viale finished his whiskey with one final big gulp and set his glass down.

Verlaque smiled; anyone who at sixty-something tried to look as he did at twenty-something was sure to be a prick. "Speak of the devil," Verlaque whispered. Viale turned around to see not Alain Denis but Emmanuelle, his wife, enter the room, wearing what looked like a long white silk housecoat but was actually a dress, split up the front to her midthigh.

"I'm glad to see there are still some men awake in this hotel," she said to no one in particular as she walked to the bar and ordered a glass of champagne.

Verlaque couldn't take his eyes off of her; not because she was beautiful, but because she was so odd looking. Emmanuelle Denis was of average height and had long blond hair piled in an elaborate bun on top of her head. She was outrageously thin but had very large breasts, a look that always seemed imbalanced to him. She was tanned, and well groomed, right down to the French manicured toenails. He smiled to himself, having overheard Marine trying to paint her own toenails, every second word a *"merde!"*

Mme Denis had obviously paid a lot of money, and taken much effort, to look the way she did, and yet she looked like a half human. He glanced across at Clément, who was also staring at her, but with a look, it seemed to Antoine, of admiration.

Emmanuelle Denis was used to receiving the attention of men and slunk off her bar stool, expertly maneuvering between the bar's small tables in her evening gown and high heels, and carrying a full glass of champagne. "Do you mind if I join you?" she asked.

"Not at all," Verlaque said, rising. "But I was just headed off to bed."

Clément Viale also got up and pulled out an armchair, the same one Delphine Viale had been sitting in, and motioned for Emmanuelle to sit down. "I'll have another whiskey, please," he called over to Canzano. Serge Canzano grabbed the Lagavulin and gave the Parisian a double hit; maybe it would knock him out and Serge could close the bar at least before 2 a.m.

"What a shame," Mme Denis said to Verlaque. "Are you sure you can't stay?" She liked his look and guessed that he was a powerful man. A surgeon, or politician . . .

"Quite sure," Verlaque said. "Good night, madame. Good night, Clément. See you tomorrow."

Verlaque walked through the quiet, marble-floored hallways, up a flight of stairs to their room. He quietly opened the door and walked through the room, looking at the sleeping figure of Marine, lit up by the moon. She lay still, on her back, with her hands clasped on her chest. She rarely moved in her sleep, unlike his thrashing. Was Clément right in suggesting that Verlaque, as a young man, had been short-tempered? Verlaque knew that over the years he had softened; 30 percent due to aging, and 70 percent due to the calming effects of the woman sleeping in the bed opposite him now.

He opened the doors to the terrace and stepped out; the wind had stopped and he could see the hotel's garden, lit up by well-placed spotlights, and beyond that, the still black sea. What had he wanted when he was in his early twenties? Probably a bit of Sylvie's getting laid; he had also wanted, and received, love and affection from his grandparents; he wanted to get good marks; and had loved running fast, alone with the ball, during his rugby games. He must have had fantasies of being a famous courtroom lawyer, but these memories were fuzzier. He breathed in the night air, which smelled of pine trees and the sea.

Did he dream of marriage, and children? No, probably not. Half of French marriages ended in divorce; the Viales were a perfect advertisement for staying single. But there were successful marriages too. His commissioner, Bruno Paulik, was happily married to a winemaker, and at this moment they were watching their first crop of grapes ripen in the July sun; their funny, chatty little daughter, Léa, most likely dancing and singing among the vines. If he had children, he wanted girls. What in the world would he do with a boy?

# CHAPTER SIX:
# ABOUT THE MANAGER

The village of Néoules was in the middle of Provence, a region that some enterprising local mayors had coined La Provence Verte to try to entice tourists. It was south of the A8 — a highway that stretched from the Riviera all the way to, as the signs proclaimed, Barcelona. There were few reasons to go to Néoules, unless you knew someone there: no sea or mountains; the roads were windy; and there were no cultural sites or Michelin-starred restaurants. The economy was thinly spread: chickpeas were the local specialty crop; there was a sprinkling of winemakers making good to mediocre wines; a bottled-water company was one of the bigger employers with a staff of fifty-five; an enterprising Dutch woman made soaps and cosmetics out of donkey's milk; and the rest of the inhabitants appeared to be either retired or unemployed. And it had never been green — *verte* — to Nicola; for her it would always be orange, the color of rust.

Rusting farm equipment was her parents' idea of garden decorating. They had been unemployed as long as Nicola could remember; when she was very young her father had worked part-time fixing motors, but he grew so unreliable that farmers began taking their work to a mechanic in neighboring Rocbaron. But M. Darcette loved the motors, and instead of taking broken, useless motors to the dump, he arranged them around their half-finished terrace, as if they were art objects. Her mother found a broken cherub fountain behind an abandoned hotel in Garéoult and had made her husband put it in the middle of the terrace, surrounded by the rusty engines. He had given up trying to rig water up to it — they couldn't afford a pump — so every now and then, when Mme Darcette was feeling energetic, she filled the basin with old dishwater.

Nicola and her older sister Aude went through the first half of their childhood thinking the Darcettes' way of life was normal. They didn't think it odd that their parents went almost everywhere, even into the village, wearing their slippers — with cigarettes hanging from their mouths — as the other villagers weren't much better dressed. But Nicola knew that at least some of the other men in the village met at the *bar des sports* and laughed a bit. Not her father; he and Mme Darcette kept to themselves, nourished by a constant supply of bulk wine they got from the *cave co-operative*. Mme Darcette had inherited two acres of vineyard outside of Néoules, and she rented the grapes out to a local farmer, who took them, along with his own harvest, every September to the co-op. The farmer offered to pay them in cash or wine; the Darcettes chose wine.

The Darcettes had, surprisingly, enough money to live on. The girls needed next to nothing; school was free, and the state paid for their books and most of their clothes. Mme Darcette made endless pasta (with no sauce) and cucumber salads (with white vinegar and salt). As soon as Aude was ten, she began doing the cooking, sometimes adding ketchup, which she stole from the school cafeteria, into the pasta. The girls ate better at school than at home and soon learned to take extra servings when they were offered by the canteen ladies and gladly finished the tossed-aside food on their friends' plates.

Nicola realized that her family was abnormal when she was ten, and Aude was in her first year of high school, being bused to Brignoles. A Parisian family moved to Néoules; the father commuted to his job as a lawyer in Toulon, and the mother stayed at home with the three children and restored their two-hundred-year-old farmhouse. M. and Mme Masurel bought the house on a whim; they loved Provence and had long wanted to get out of their cramped eight-hundred-square-foot apartment in Paris. They moved in the summer, when Néoules was looking its best, and enrolled their three young children in the village school. Claire Masurel, their oldest, and Nicola Darcette became fast friends; Claire, being a secure, loved child, didn't know that the other students left the Darcettes alone. Nicola was bright, and athletic, and, thanks to an energetic first-year gym teacher, the girls were encouraged to play soccer and run track together.

Nicola would always remember her first visit, after school, to the Masurels' house. She had seen other old houses, but never one like this. The garden certainly didn't look like hers, nor did it look like "rich peoples' " gardens, as her references were the manicured gardens of Americans, as seen on 1970s reruns poorly dubbed into French. Mme Masurel had left the olive trees in front of the house, and the Masurels had planted the cypress trees that lined the driveway. A wrought iron table and four chairs sat under an umbrella pine. Ivy grew up the sides of the stone walls, but even Nicola could see that it was neat, and clipped.

But it was the smell inside the house that Nicola remembered most acutely, more than the furnishings, for at that age she didn't really know what was beautiful, or tasteful; she just knew that it all looked good, and comfortable. The house smelled like cooking — Mme Masurel liked to bake — mixed with Mme Masurel's perfume. It took Nicola years to find that smell again, and she found it when robbing a department store in Nice. It was Yves Saint Laurent's Rive Gauche.

Nicola experienced many firsts *chez les Masurel.* Her first lasagna, her first bubble bath, and her first games and puzzles. She had never seen an activity book before, and Mme Masurel began buying them for her, slipping the books into her backpack. Nicola and Claire would walk through Néoules together, hand in hand. They'd make up stories about the people and choose their favorite houses. Nicola would have pink roses growing up beside her front door; Claire, jasmine. They began, along with some of the other, brighter, students, to put on elaborate spectacles for the end-of-the-year party. M. Masurel filmed them; the Darcettes never came. Both girls were voracious readers, lying on Claire's frilly bedspread, locking the door on Claire's two younger siblings, whom they referred to as Pest No. 1 and Pest No. 2.

It all came crashing down on Nicola a week in May when she turned thirteen. Claire came into school one spring day looking gloomy and had a hard time meeting Nicola's stare. At recess they sat together with their backs against the chain-link fence and Claire gave her the news: they were selling their house and moving back to Paris. Living in Néoules was too hard on Claire's mother: she hadn't met any friends; the villagers shied away from her. And M. Masurel had been offered a much better job in Paris; he'd be a partner in a law firm, which meant that they would be able to buy a big apartment in a fancy neighborhood. A German couple had seen their farmhouse from the road and had offered them a lot of money for it.

Nicola was stunned. The rest of the day she couldn't concentrate. She couldn't believe that she would lose Claire, and that there would be strangers living, and only on vacations, in the Masurels' beautiful house. The Masurels moved that August, and Nicola knew that she would never see Claire again. There was no way that she could ever invite Claire to her house. She now knew that her family was awful. Aude, at nineteen, had escaped; she was already married, with a toddler, but Nicola hated her husband. Aude was going to have another baby at Christmas.

Nicola saw her future: either end up like Aude or get out of Néoules. But it would be five years before she would even graduate from high school. She found solace, as one would expect, in new friends. They met every day after school in the bus shelter (it had a bench, a roof to protect it from the sun, and three walls to protect it from the wind). Boys would pull up to the shelter on their mopeds, resting their feet on the shelter's low front wall, while the girls sat side by side on the bench, facing the boys. By the time she was fifteen Nicola had become one of the ringleaders; she was brighter than the rest of them and had more reasons than the others to stay away from her house as much as possible. Teachers at the school, remembering her enthusiasm for reading and theatre, tried to get Nicola to participate in the annual concerts and plays, as she had done with Claire, but she refused. Her new friends would have seen this as childish, and she desperately needed her new friends, thick as they were.

Before moving, Mme Masurel and her husband had discussed the possibility of inviting Nicola for vacations to Paris. But they had both seen, from afar, Nicola's house, and her parents, and didn't know how they would ever arrange such a voyage with the Darcettes. M. Masurel was torn: he saw that his wife had grown very attached to the sprightly young Nicola — whom they lovingly called Niki — and he worried that she would be too sad if she saw Niki again, knowing what they were sending her back to in Néoules. He even asked a colleague, who specialized in family law, about the possibility of adopting Niki. But, as he had half-presumed, that would be impossible unless there were claims of abuse or life-threatening neglect. So once they were installed in their fifteen-hundred-square-foot apartment in the seventh *arrondissement,* he purposely threw away his condoms, and Mme Masurel became happily pregnant for the fourth time.

# CHAPTER SEVEN: LUNCH POEMS

Antoine Verlaque could barely remember the last time he had had such a pleasant "lie in," as his English grandmother would call it. His father, industrious and hardworking, had not permitted the boys — Antoine and Sébastien — to just do *nothing* or especially to sleep in. His mother — emotionally absent — had no opinion whatsoever. M. Verlaque saw idleness as laziness, but Emmeline and Charles, the grandparents, gave the boys time to do nothing. "It's a luxury," Emmeline would tell them. "You have the time. Let your wonderful minds wander." Emmeline had one rule for this time, though: they had to be outside. It was one of the reasons that Verlaque so enjoyed a cigar: it was a quiet one or two hours of tasting, thinking, looking, and it was often outside. It was time to ponder over a current case, but more often than not he thought of words (his own, or those of poets) or faces (Marine's, Emmeline's). It was never wasted time.

Each room had a Nespresso machine, and Marine made them each a coffee and they sipped, and read, in bed. As was usual with Marine she soon had a half dozen books, and various sheets of paper, surrounding her, and a pen poised behind her right ear. Verlaque peered over his reading glasses at her, setting down the hotel's complimentary copy of the *International Herald Tribune.*

"How are Jean-Paul and Simone?" he asked. It had been over a year since Marine had embarked upon the ambitious project to write about the love life of philosophers Jean-Paul Sartre and Simone de Beauvoir. Verlaque was encouraging her to take a year's sabbatical, but that proved more difficult than either of them thought in her state-funded university in Aix.

"Wonderfully complicated," she replied. "And yet so simple too, at least in terms of their own relationship, and work habits."

"They didn't work in bed," he said, smiling.

Marine laughed. "Lots went on in their beds, but not work. They wrote diligently every morning, stopped for lunch, then worked until eight p.m. or so. Every day. In many ways they were a perfect couple."

"Except they didn't have children," Verlaque said, finishing his coffee. Marine stared at Verlaque, but before she could reply, he asked, "Where did they go for lunch? Café de Flore?"

"Of course," Marine said. "You know, I've never been there."

"You're kidding!" Verlaque said, taking off his glasses.

"No. I've always been turned off by the six-euro espresso."

"My father still goes there regularly."

"Why don't we go with him?" Marine suggested. "The next time we're both in Paris." The truth was, she had only been to Paris once with Antoine, and that was for an art opening of Sylvie's photographs. They had stayed one night in a mediocre modern hotel near the Louvre and caught the morning train back to Aix. Antoine had not introduced Marine to his parents, nor had he walked her by his old haunts, which she knew were close to the Seine. It was forbidden territory.

"I think," he answered slowly, "that that's a very good idea." He put his glasses back on and opened the newspaper, signaling that the conversation was finished.

By late morning Marine and Sylvie were

sitting by the pool, and Verlaque, having swum several laps, left them to their gossiping and walked up to the hotel to get changed.

"Antoine's being nice to me these days," Sylvie said to Marine, while she applied SPF-0 suntan oil to her already tanned legs.

"There's something . . ." Marine began, "changed about him. This morning he actually agreed to my suggestion that we meet with his father in Paris."

"That's front-page news," Sylvie said.

"And another thing," Marine said, putting down Sartre's *Being and Nothingness.* "He's been speaking about children . . ."

Sylvie began humming the wedding march.

"Stop it," Marine said. "It's all been very indirect, boys versus girls, that sort of thing. I think he's terrified of having a son."

"I get that," Sylvie said. "When I see the boys at Charlotte's school, I think of them as extraterrestrials. Did Antoine really talk of children?"

"Yes, but like I said, only when it has to do with other people," Marine said. She thought for a moment and then added, "But that day we arrived here, Antoine did say how much happier he'd be with a daughter. Because of Brice, Alain Denis's son, storming out of the hotel."

"Stepson," Sylvie said.

Marine looked at her friend, puzzled.

"I read it in *Paris Match*," Sylvie said. "Oh, look. Here he comes now."

The teenager strode onto the terrace, a book and towel under his arm. Marine thought that in his swimsuit he looked even thinner, and more fragile. He threw his affairs on a chaise longue not far from Sylvie and muttered, "I hate him," and then dove into the pool.

"Wow," Sylvie said. "That was pretty frank."

"It might not have been about Alain Denis," Marine whispered. "What's he reading?" she asked, craning to see the book.

Sylvie, who was closer, got part way off of her lounger to see the book's cover. *"Death in Venice,"* she said, sitting back down. "Must be on next year's reading list."

"I'm not so sure," Marine replied. She had been a great reader at that age, as had Antoine. She knew that Sylvie's reading consisted mostly of photography journals and fashion magazines. But she didn't fault Sylvie for that: how dull life would be if one's friends did exactly the same thing as you.

They watched in silence as the boy swam

lengths. They smiled as he did a few somer-saults and then floated on his back, looking up at the cloudless sky, framed by the dark-green needles of the umbrella pine trees that circled the south side of the pool. Marine found it curious that, even though there were available chairs on the opposite side of the terrace, Brice had chosen one near them. Perhaps he had thrown his towel on the closest chair and was going to leave as soon as he got out of the pool. She was about to ask Sylvie something about Char-lotte — her beloved goddaughter — when the boy got out of the water, shook himself off like a dog, and sat down.

"Fun book?" Sylvie asked, pointing to the Thomas Mann novel.

"I wouldn't say fun," Brice answered, not showing his surprise that this woman, who must be more than twenty years older than himself, would refer to Thomas Mann as "fun." "Disturbing. And dense, but highly readable too."

"Oh. Well, if it's too treacherous," Sylvie went on, as if she hadn't heard his answer, "there's a great film version with Dirk Bo-garde in the lead."

"I've seen it," Brice said. "Now, *Bogarde* was an actor."

Marine and Sylvie exchanged quick looks.

As if Brice too regretted his comment, he quietly added, "Thanks for the recommendation though." He slipped on his earplugs, and like Antoine with his newspaper, Marine saw that their short discussion was over.

But Marine kept the image of Brice, floating on his back, in her head. What was he thinking when floating, looking at the sky? What *do* we think of when we're teenagers? Food? The opposite — or same, given your preferences — sex? Music? She thought of herself at sixteen, seventeen: a studious and polite girl. But it had also been the summer when she had been so conscious of a new silence that enveloped her parents — a doctor and a theologian in Aix — and Marine, an only child, had been unable to speak to anyone about it.

Antoine Verlaque walked into the Jacky Bar to the sounds of Billie Holiday. He was hungry and felt good after his long swim. He saw Eric Monnier sitting at his usual table, under the large framed photograph of the Cuban tobacco farmer. Monnier, seeing the judge, held a finger in the air. "Ze Lady," he said in heavily accented English. Intrigued, for Verlaque had always preferred the scratchy and sad voice of Billie Holiday over the too-perfect one of Ella Fitzgerald, he saluted and walked over to the teacher.

" 'Ain't Nobody's Business If I Do,' " Verlaque said, sitting down.

"Written by Bessie Smith, I believe," Monnier said.

Determined to outdo the teacher, Verlaque added, "Yes, and the lyrics a smack in the face to all the journalists who were so obsessed with Billie's private life."

But Monnier had one up on the judge. "Look at this book of poetry," he said. "I swear to God, when the song came on, I was reading this exact poem: 'The Day Lady Died.' " He passed the slim volume — *Lunch Poems* — to Verlaque, who turned around and asked Serge Canzano for a whiskey.

Verlaque turned back and looked at the cover. "Frank O'Hara?"

"One of my colleagues at the high school — an English teacher — recommended him," Monnier said. "Never a professional poet, this O'Hara. Worked at the Museum of Modern Art in New York in the fifties and sixties."

"A curator?"

"Not even," Monnier said. "He took the tickets. Front desk. At lunch he'd walk around New York and then come back and hit the typewriter. Hence the title of this collection. Or that's what the jacket says about him, anyway. Lunch was his favorite meal."

"Much better than breakfast," Verlaque said.

"I hate breakfast," Monnier admitted. "Always thought it something to get quickly over with."

Verlaque laughed. "No alcohol."

"Exactly. Lunch: I've gotten through the dismal morning and am feeling like working. Really working. I treat myself to a nice restaurant lunch and am surrounded by chatting people — workers, students, tourists. The food is salty, not sweet like at breakfast, and I can have a glass of wine to get the creative juices flowing and that perfectly complements my meal. And it's still bright out, and the world looks happy."

Verlaque picked up the book, feeling Monnier's loneliness. He said, trying to be light, "Not much boozing goes on anymore at my work lunches." Dinner was Verlaque's favorite meal, but he kept that to himself: the evening meal he shared with Marine. He began reading the poem, set on a Friday in July in 1959, as Canzano quietly slipped a Lagavulin in front of him. He finished reading and took a slow concentrated sip of the single malt.

"What did you think of the poem?" Monnier asked.

"I'm speechless," Verlaque said. "It's beautiful," he went on, "and I've never heard of this O'Hara."

Monnier nodded, smugly smiling. "Could you help me translate a few lines?" he asked, leaning forward and taking the book. "Especially at the end."

"Sure."

"John door?" Monnier asked, pointing to the sentence.

"Ah. The door to the toilets," Verlaque said. "It sounds like the 5 SPOT he writes of is a New York bar."

"Whispered?"

*"Chuchoter,"* Verlaque answered.

"There's almost no punctuation," Monnier said. "I'll have to loosen my poems up a bit. Breathing?"

*"Respirer."*

Verlaque had another sip and asked Monnier for the book. He read aloud:

". . . and a NEW YORK POST with
her face on it
and I am sweating a lot by now and
    thinking of
leaning on the john door in the 5 SPOT

while she whispered a song along the
   keyboard
to Mal Waldron and everyone and I
   stopped breathing"

"It gives me goose bumps," Monnier said.
"Very wise that he doesn't end the sentence
with a period."

"Yes," Verlaque said. "Like there's still so
much to say about her."

"Or he really did stop breathing . . ."

Their reflections were cut short by Alain
and Emmanuelle Denis, who entered the
bar, loudly arguing. Eric Monnier folded
his arms across his chest and quietly barked.

"He's *your* son," Alain Denis said, flop-
ping down in a vintage rattan chair. He
motioned to Serge Canzano with his pointer
finger twirling in the air, and a few seconds
later the cork gently popped out of a bottle
of expensive champagne.

"That's right," Emmanuelle Denis replied,
still standing. "Brice — he has a name — is
*my* son, and I'll decide where he'll go to
school."

"It seems like you're making a decision,
all right," Denis said. "Between the kid and
me." He turned around and yelled to Canzano, "Having trouble finding a glass, or
what?"

"Alain, you're such an ass," Mme Denis said.

"A famous ass," Alain Denis replied, grabbing his glass of champagne from Canzano. "You seemed to like that fact when we first met."

Monnier coughed, barely disguising another bark, and Verlaque tried to hide his laughing face in the glass of whiskey.

# CHAPTER EIGHT:
# LITTLE SQUID, SHIRLEY

Cat-Cat Le Bon could see the Mediterranean from her office window. She turned away from the view and opened the third drawer in her desk, pulling out a stack of black-and-white photos of Locanda Sordou from the 1960s. Someone had taken color slides too — luckily — and using those, along with vintage magazine articles from *Life* and *Paris Match,* she and Max were able to design the new hotel. Bright greens and pale blues, with touches of pink and orange, had been the original color scheme, and they stayed faithful to that. Those happy colors would be a perfect match for the white stone and marble floors and the cream-colored walls. The Le Bons had gone over budget, of course. The architect, when he saw Cat-Cat's file of clippings, fabric swatches, and tile samples, warned her that she would. But Cat-Cat hardly listened, because here, at Sordou, it belonged to them. They had saved and worked hard — always for other people — in order to someday run their own hotel. Their goal had been to own a hotel by the time they were fifty; Max was fifty-one and Cat-Cat had just turned fifty in March.

The next drawer down was full of design ideas that she had been collecting for over ten years. She had recorded furnishing and room arrangements that worked, and those that didn't, in every restaurant and hotel she had ever worked in, and put them in the envelope. The envelope had grown to two binders. She and Max had sourced the best linen drapes in Tuscany; colorful cement tiles in Morocco — a fraction of the cost than those bought in Parisian tile stores — and they prided themselves on purchasing crafts from living French designers: tall, fragile porcelain vases; small marble end tables; thrown-glass goblets made by a designer in Brittany. Even the light fixtures were handmade, in forged metal by an artisan in the Luberon, with silk shades made by an obsessed seamstress in Montmartre.

Cat-Cat knew that guests would like to see the photographs of the hotel in the sixties, and especially try to identify the many stars, singers, presidents, and millionaires who came in those days. She wasn't sure herself why she didn't get the photographs framed and hung as Niki had suggested; but she knew, down deeply, that she was superstitious: she hid the photos away in a drawer because she was afraid they would bring them bad luck, as if the photographs could taunt the Le Bons, saying, "Look at what a tremendously successful hotel I was back then. See if you can do as well."

As if the photos could speak, she turned them over and slipped them back into their envelope and looked at the computer. The bank manager in Marseille who worked on their loan had worried about them having a luxury hotel on such a remote island. The screen flickered, reminding Cat-Cat of his concern. "It was different in the 1960s," he had said. "Guests didn't need Internet, or cell phones, and neither did the hotel. One phone line was enough." He took a sip of coffee and then added the words that she and Max had dreaded, "And even then, the hotel didn't last."

But Max had an old friend from Bordeaux who convinced the Le Bons, and the bank manager, that they could get by with an old-style modem to run the hotel's computer. And Cat-Cat did research on successful hotels around the world that *didn't* have cell phone reception or Internet for their clients and were doing quite well. "It's the twenty-first century," Max had argued at the bank. "Wealthy people want to get *away* from their families and businesses and the press." Cat-Cat looked at the screen and tried to block out the bank manager's high-pitched voice, still protesting down to the last minute, but finally giving in and signing their loan papers.

*"Coucou, Mme Le Bon,"* Marie-Thérèse said, sliding into the office with a tray balanced on her hip. "I brought you an afternoon tea."

"How lovely," Cat-Cat said, turning toward the girl. "Thank you." She sighed.

Marie-Thérèse saw the computer lit up on the reservations page. She bit her lip and then said, "Don't worry, madame."

Cat-Cat tried to smile. "I wish I could."

"Today is Sunday . . ."

"And?"

"We'll fill up. Couples will have spoken over the weekend about trips they want to take," Marie-Thérèse explained. "And so tonight, or tomorrow, when they get into the office, they'll book here. At Sordou. You'll see."

"Have you always been such an optimist?"

"Yes, I think so," Marie-Thérèse replied,

shrugging. "I've never really thought about it before."

"I used to be too."

"You still are. This hotel will work, I'm sure of it."

"How so?"

"Because you love it so much."

Cat-Cat's eyes filled with tears.

Marie-Thérèse went on, "And because you love it, and work so hard, it will work. *Voilà!*"

"Another dinner alone," Eric Monnier wrote in his Moleskine. He crossed it out and wrote "Dining Alone," and began a poem. As he always did when writing a poem, he wrote down key words in the margin: words that filled his head, words that described what he was looking at or feeling. He began with colors, and at Sordou they were always the same: "white," "blue," "green." *He* then tried to remember what other clients or guests had said to him that day, as he enjoyed putting other people's words in his poems. But it was only their second day on the island, and he had stuck to himself. Surely someone had said something to him? Oh yes, the bartender. Monnier chuckled and wrote down "The usual?" The waitress must have spoken to him at lunch; and he had passed the hotel's owner, Mme Le Bon, standing on the terrace looking out to sea. He had commented on the fine weather. "Cooler than in Aix," he had said. And what had she replied? He couldn't remember, so wrote down an image instead: "the worried owner and the cheerful waitress."

Monnier took a sip of white wine and looked around the room. He wrote down what the waitress said at the Amercian's table, *"Petits supions au Vin Blanc."*

"Pardon?" the wife had asked.

"Little squid, Shirley," her husband answered.

"Very good translation," the cigar smoker named Antoine said, leaning over his table to congratulate the American gentleman, who shrugged and laughed, amazed that he knew the translation. Eric liked the words better in English, and quickly wrote them down before he forgot them. "Little squid, Shirley." He went back up to the top of the page and put a line through "Dining Alone" and replaced it with "Little squid, Shirley." He sat back, smiling, and pushed his book aside when the waitress came with his first course.

"Good evening," she said, carefully setting down a bowl. "Chef Émile's *amuse-*

*bouche . . .*"

"*Petits supions,*" he said.

"Exactly!"

"Thank you," Monnier said, tucking the napkin up under his chin. "And to follow?"

"Puttanesca," Marie-Thérèse answered, smiling.

"Ah, the whore's pasta!" Monnier said, breaking some bread to have with his squid.

"Pardon me?"

"Go ask Chef Émile what 'puttanesca' means," he said, pointing with his bread toward the kitchen.

Marie-Thérèse turned away and quickly walked to the kitchen door.

The squid were tiny and had been fried quickly in garlic followed by a white wine reduction. They were fresh, and delicious, and Monnier realized that he had eaten them too quickly, for when he looked around he saw the other diners still eating. He pulled out his book and realized that it would be difficult to find words to rhyme with Shirley. Someone laughed and he looked up; it was Marine, Antoine's girlfriend, and he wrote down her name.

He noticed that Alain Denis wasn't dining, nor was his family. They were probably eating in their room, or suite, more likely. The poor boy, Monnier mumbled to himself. Should be out swimming with his buddies, not stuck in a small hotel with his unhappy parents. The Parisians were at the table next to him, talking of their own children; one was at camp and the two smaller ones were with their grandparents, he gathered. Monnier imagined that's what married couples do: speak of their children. He tried to block out their conversation; he didn't like eavesdropping, especially if it wasn't interesting. But then the wife said Sordou more than once, and *investment,* and her husband whispered for her to be quiet.

Monnier became restless when the Viales began to talk once again of their children, and, self-conscious of having eaten his squid too quickly, got up and walked to the Jacky Bar to grab the wine menu. He'd need a nice strong red to go with the puttanesca; Serge — they too were on a first-name basis — would have a good recommendation.

"What would a whore from Naples drink with her tomato-based pasta?" Monnier asked as he leaned on the bar.

Serge laughed, and Monnier smiled. "A southern-Italian red," Serge replied. "But let's go farther afield than Sicily."

"Yes, let's."

"You'll need a fresh fruity red to match

the tomatoes and red peppers and anchovies."

"I can handle that."

"Calabria," Serge said. "Chef Émile and I have picked out a special wine to go with the pasta —"

"Oh, I love Calabria," a female voice sounded. Monnier swung around and saw Marine standing beside him.

"I've come for the wine menu," she said.

"I'm sorry," Serge said. "There should have been one out there."

"It's no problem," Marine continued. "Have you been to Calabria?" she asked Monnier.

Trying to be nonchalant, as he always did in the presence of beautiful, kind women, he leaned an elbow on the bar and shrugged. "I'm sad to report that no, I've never been south of Rome."

"I'm Marine," she said, extending her hand. "Antoine told me you had a nice talk today about poetry."

"Eric Monnier," he replied.

"I'm pleased to meet you." She turned to the bartender and said, "So you're recommending a wine from Calabria? We were hoping you'd have one."

"We're a small island with a big wine cellar," Serge said. Happy to share his knowledge, he showed them one of the bottles. "The ancient Greeks — the Oenotrians — made wine in Calabria as early as the seventh century B.C."

"Oenotrians?" Marine asked. "As in oenology?"

"Well done," Monnier said. "It means people from the land of vines."

Serge tried to smile, having lost his place center stage. He continued, "Their Greco di Bianco might be the oldest wine in the world. But we've selected a red for the pasta, made from three different Calabrian varieties and aged in chestnut barrels."

"Not oak?" Marine asked. "How interesting."

"It's fresh and young and fruity," Serge continued, "with notes of tobacco and black licorice."

"Tobacco sounds good," Monnier said.

"So does licorice," Marine followed. She looked at the poet, as Antoine called him, and asked, "Would you like to eat with us, M. Monnier?"

Monnier hesitated. "Thank you, but no," he said. "Too much work," he continued, patting the fountain pen in his pocket. "But perhaps another evening."

"That would be very nice," Marine answered.

# Chapter Nine: About the Boatman

Hugo Sammut had not begun walking until he was almost two years old, but when he did, he had, as his mother bragged, "Run for it, and hasn't stopped since." He was a naturally gifted athlete, coordinated, and wasn't nearsighted like his siblings. He was good at both soccer and rugby but he excelled at sailing and alpine skiing, two sports dear to the French middle and upper classes. His parents, now retired, had been high school teachers and had spent their numerous school vacations with their three children either skiing (in winter, in the cheaper Alpine ski resorts like Saint-Martin de Belleville, or Les Houches) or boating, in summer, at Mme Sammut's parents' vacation apartment in Arcachon on the Atlantic coast near Bordeaux.

As the third child, and an unexpected one, he had been pampered. His older sister and brother had been good at sports, but better at academics, and were now a family doctor and accountant, respectively. Hugo's love was the outdoors, and sports, but a grave dyslexia — which even in the mid-1980s still wasn't diagnosed as a treatable learning disability in France — had made studies for him unbearable.

Difficulties with reading and writing, and attention deficit disorder, finally diagnosed along with dyslexia when he was fifteen, meant that Sammut was put in remedial studies, and he graduated at nineteen with a 10/20 on the technical baccalaureate, on his second attempt. His classmates went into trades: plumbing, masonry, and electricity for the boys and hairdressing for the girls. But his athletic skills and cheery disposition — cheerier now that he was finally finished with school — gave him employment as a skiing instructor in the winter and as a boating teacher in the summer. His good looks helped too: his olive skin and dark curly hair often meant that he was mistaken for an Italian or Spaniard; odd, when both his parents, and his brother and sister, were blond.

M. and Mme Sammut were thrilled that their son found employment, even if it was seasonal. In between jobs Hugo would be in Nancy, helping to garden or do fix-it jobs around their large suburban house. Hugo was easy to be with and loved his mother's cooking, and was an ideal uncle to his nieces and nephews, who, with their parents, all lived in Nancy. But Hugo had a temper, brought on, his mother now knew, by his ADD. When he had been young, she and her husband and Hugo's siblings had learned how to treat his rare — but powerful and frightening — outbursts by making sure that he couldn't hurt himself or anyone else and leave him to his screaming. When he first came home, elated, with the news that he had found employment as a ski instructor, Mme Sammut's first worry was his temper. But Hugo seemed to control his anger while on the slopes; it was if the constant exercise and fresh air wiped away his tantrums.

After his fifth year as an instructor in Les Houches he abruptly switched ski stations; he told his parents that the pay was better in Chamonix. Had they read the local Savoie newspapers they would have learned that their son's dismissal was due to a fight with another ski instructor who wasn't calling the emergency services fast enough for Sammut's liking. Sammut had been skiing on his afternoon off when he came across an injured skier whose red ski vest he saw

through the bushes. The skier had been skiing off-slope and had suffered a heart attack, and was alone. Sammut called for
help, his colleague on the other end not paying close enough attention to Sammut at
first, until he realized the extent of the
emergency. An emergency crew arrived nine
minutes later, by snowmobile, but the skier
had been dead for five minutes. Sammut
watched the crew lift the lifeless middle-
aged man on the stretcher, and he skied
down, following them. He found his colleague in the bar, entertaining fellow ski
instructors with stories, and Sammut walked
over and punched him in the face, knocking
him out.

At thirty-four years of age Sammut considered himself young and was in no hurry
to settle down with a wife and children,
maybe not ever. He would have continued
his winters in the Alps and summers in Arcachon had it not been for the successive
announcements from his two siblings that
they were moving, with their families, to the
south of France. His sister had been offered
a job in Nice's biggest hospital, and his
brother, the same week, had been hired as
the financial director of a helicopter company based in Marseille. M. and Mme Sammut, seeing their children and grandchildren

disappear for the sun and blue skies of Provence, sold their house — it was too big for them now — and bought a two-bedroom apartment in the seaside village of Cassis. Hugo, after seeing the Sordou job advertised in a boating magazine, soon followed.

Sammut wasn't convinced, as his family seemed to be, that the south of France was worth all of the talk. He loved the crashing waves of the Atlantic, and the tides, and the miles of sandy and underpopulated beaches. He had easily made friends in Arcachon: with fellow sailing instructors — who had nicknamed Sammut "Hugo-of-the-Dunes" for his talent in seducing vacationing women in nearby Pyla's great 110-meter-high hills of sand — and he had made good friends with local *commerçants* and an oyster farmer across the bay in Cap Ferret. But he knew that he would miss his family too much, and so he traded all that for the rocky, crowded beaches of the Mediterranean. He would still have the winter skiing, at least.

And so it surprised no one more than Hugo-of-the-Dunes himself when he fell in love with rocky Sordou. He knew that Jacques Cousteau, his childhood hero, had explored these waters, but Sammut had had no idea just how close Cousteau had been.

For five years, beginning in 1952, Cousteau and his team on the *Calypso* explored the underwater around the Île Grand Congloué, finally discovering a Greek shipwreck from the third century B.C. forty meters under. Over seven thousand pieces of tableware alone were brought up to the ship's decks and taken to two museums in Marseille, along with thousands of wine and oil amphorae. Sammut had little interest in these and had never been to the museums to look at them. It was more the heroics of the exploration that he loved: that Cousteau and his wife Simone had put their life savings into the *Calypso,* along with help from rich Americans and the Guinness family; that Cousteau and engineer Émile Gagnan had built the first self-contained underwater breathing apparatus in 1943, out of a sheer love of being underwater; and that Cousteau, as a young man, was meant to be a pilot, but a car accident ended his aviation career and he became fascinated by the sea when swimming, wearing only goggles, near Toulon. "What if Cousteau had become a pilot?" the young Hugo used to ask his parents. "Well then, he would have become fascinated by birds, and clouds," his mother replied.

Hugo was in the water whenever he got

the chance; he kept his goggles draped over his bedpost, and he swam close to the rocks — without flippers or a mask — just as the young Cousteau had done in nearby Toulon. From there, under the water, he could observe the aquatic life — the variety and busyness of the fish and shellfish made their little skeleton crew at the Locanda Sordou seem ridiculous.

The battered Cousteau poster that had been taped above his bed in Nancy was long gone, but Sammut knew the quotation on it by heart: "From birth, man carries the weight of gravity on his shoulders. He is bolted to earth. But man has only to sink beneath the surface and he is free." And Hugo Sammut felt free, indeed, on water, and flying over snow. Never a great lover of people, except his own immediate family, and a detester of cities, he knew from the first time he saw it that he could be happy on Sordou.

# CHAPTER TEN:
# THE RISING SEA

Marine Bonnet and Antoine Verlaque stepped out onto the dining room's terrace, its small red marble tables set with fine white china for breakfast. The only sound was made by Hugo Sammut; wearing neatly pressed shorts and a tightly fitting polo shirt, Sammut was clipping the fragrant hedge that separated the terrace from the gardens that gently slopped down the hill.

"This view is just as spectacular as the view from our room," Marine said, slipping her hand around Verlaque's waist.

Verlaque nodded and looked out over the island's small, protected bay toward the limestone cliffs in the west that fell abruptly into the sea. "I'm glad we came," he finally said, kissing her.

"Lovebirds!" Sylvie called from under an enormous white sun hat.

"Hey," Marine said, walking over to Sylvie's table and giving her the *bise.* "How's the coffee?"

"Divine," Sylvie said, lowering her oversize vintage sunglasses for special effect. "It's illy, not French, thank God."

"Great news," Verlaque said, sitting down and pouring two glasses of orange juice for himself and Marine from a cut-glass pitcher.

"French coffee is good, you two," Marine said. She always felt that she had to defend their country, as Verlaque was a quarter English, and proud to be, and Sylvie was just a reactionary.

Marie-Thérèse had seen Pretty Woman — the name she gave Marine the moment she first saw her — and Chubby Man walk onto the terrace, and she came out to greet them.

"How are you this morning?" Verlaque bellowed.

"F-fine," she answered, adjusting her white apron. "Chef Émile has baked scones this morning. Would you like some?"

"Scones?" Verlaque asked. "Fantastic. And two cappuccinos, please."

"Yes, that sounds great," Marine added.

"I'll have another scone, pretty please," Sylvie said. "And another cappuccino."

Marie-Thérèse nodded and almost ran off.

"It's charming how she refers to the chef as Chef Émile," Marine said. "They're almost the same age, I would guess." She looked out over the blue-green, almost transparent water. "Incredible to think that there are underwater caves all around these islands," she said. "With prehistoric paintings and carvings."

"Weren't those a hoax?" Sylvie asked.

"Oh no," Marine answered. "They've been dated as the real thing."

"But how did those little prehistoric dudes get into those underwater caves, with their paints and all?" Sylvie asked.

"First they went to the art store and bought the paints, then to the hardware store for the flashlights," Verlaque said.

"By land," Marine answered, smiling. "The sea was farther away then. Those caves, tens of thousands of years ago, were at the water's edge. Today you have to swim in to get to them, with scuba gear."

Sylvie sighed and looked out at the sea. "The sea keeps rising, doesn't it?

"Yes. With global warming the glaciers are melting," Marine said.

Sylvie moaned. "What a depressing thought."

"Time to buy a beach house in Skagen," Verlaque said, looking over his *Le Monde* at the women.

"I'm in," Sylvie said. "I love the Danish. That *is* in Denmark, right?"

"On the northern tip," Verlaque said, sitting up as Marie-Thérèse came back with their breakfast.

Marine continued to look out at the cliffs and the sea. It was indeed depressing to think that one day it would be too hot to sit out in the south of France, even at 9 a.m.

"What's amazing to me is that we have the *calanques* and islands right here, just a few miles from one of the world's biggest cesspools," Verlaque said, smearing his scone, which had just appeared, with too much butter.

"Are you in one of your anti-Marseille moods?" Marine asked.

"I've never liked it," Verlaque replied. "Just the restaurants are better than ours in Aix, that's all."

Marine winked at Sylvie and asked, "Has everyone else already eaten breakfast?" she asked.

"The Yanks were on the way out when I came," Sylvie said. "Dressed for the golf course. The poet was here but left just before you came. Other than that, no one. Oh, here comes Alain Denis . . ."

The actor, dressed in a pink linen shirt and white linen shorts, walked out onto the terrace and gazed through his Ray-Ban aviator sunglasses for a table. He made no attempt to say good morning to the only other people on the terrace and chose a table far away from them.

Verlaque saw Marie-Thérèse waiting in the wings, playing with her apron strings. He saw her take a deep breath and walk across the terrace's red terra-cotta surface and bend down to ask Denis what he would like for breakfast.

"Of course I'm alone, what does it look like?" the actor cried loud enough for everyone to hear. Marine, Sylvie, and Antoine Verlaque tried not to wince.

Marie-Thérèse straightened up. "I'm sorry," she said. "I thought that Mme Denis might be arriving any minute."

"Obviously not," Denis said, sighing. "I'll just start with an espresso, no food yet," he added in a lower voice, as if he regretted his prior outburst. "No, I'll have a bowl of fresh fruit with that."

Marie-Thérèse said a loud and firm "Coming right up!" and left. Verlaque had to look into his newspaper for fear of laughing. The young waitress was having a go at the aging actor, but like all self-possessed people, he had no idea.

When Marine, Sylvie, and Antoine were finishing up breakfast Mme Denis appeared, wearing a beach sarong and high-heeled sandals. "I can't believe it," she said to her husband.

"This is excellent," Sylvie whispered, taking off her sunglasses to see well.

"You're sitting there, calmly having breakfast, when my son is missing!" Emmanuelle Denis yelled.

Denis looked up at his wife, slowly setting aside his *Paris Match.* "Brice has gone swimming, or walking, or . . . I don't know. . . . He's gone off just to worry you. He'll be back when he's hungry." He picked up the magazine again and Mme Denis swung around and saw Marine, Sylvie, and Antoine — who had been pretending to read the newspaper — all staring at her.

Verlaque got up and said, "Maybe one of the staff have seen him," he said quietly but firmly. "This is a wonderful place for a teenage boy to explore," he added.

"I'm sorry to disturb your breakfast," Mme Denis said, reaching out her hand. Verlaque was so surprised at the offer of an introduction that his foot got caught on the table's wrought iron leg and Sylvie snorted out a laugh. He hadn't told Marine of Emmanuelle Denis's late-night appearance in the bar the previous night.

"Antoine Verlaque," he said, shaking her hand. "And this is Marine Bonnet, and . . .

our friend, Sylvie Grassi."

"Emmanuelle Denis," she replied, and nodded in the direction of Marine and Sylvie. "It's Brice, my son," she continued. "I can't find him, and it looks like he didn't sleep in his bed last night."

"Perhaps he made it?" Verlaque asked. But before Mme Denis answered, Verlaque said, "Oh, he's a teenage boy . . ."

Mme Denis forced a smile. "Exactly."

"This is a small island, and it's summer, but I can't imagine someone sleeping outside," Verlaque said.

"He's done this kind of thing before," Mme Denis replied. She looked at her husband and he rolled his eyes. "As you say, this is an island, but Brice doesn't know it. It's not the same as Paris."

Marine looked at Mme Denis and remembered the boy's absence at dinner last night. But his mother had been there, without him, and was now decked out for a bathing suit photo shoot, not frolicking in the waves with her son, or playing games with him, or whatever Marine supposed mothers should be doing on vacation with their children, even teenage ones.

Mme Denis went on, "Brice wouldn't eat with us last night. . . . He was too upset."

"I really don't think you should go telling

strangers our family history," Alain Denis hissed, now standing beside his wife.

"*What* family?" she answered back.

"Come have something to eat," Denis said, taking her arm.

"I'm not hungry," she replied, shaking off his hold.

"Emmanuelle, don't be a daft cow," he said.

"Leave her," Verlaque said. "She's obviously upset."

"Mind your own business, asshole," Denis said, grabbing his wife's arm once again.

"I said I'm not hungry," she cried. "I'm going out, to look for my son!" She pulled herself away from Denis but he lunged toward her, pulling on her arm.

Verlaque was about to reach out to help Mme Denis when Hugo Sammut's body appeared out of nowhere, as if he had flown over the hedge. With one fast gesture he grabbed Alain Denis's arms, forcing them behind his back with his hands in a locked position. Hugo threw Denis against the wall of the hotel, while Denis shouted protestations of having Hugo fired, and suing the hotel.

"Hugo!" Max Le Bon shouted, now standing at the edge of the terrace, having heard the commotion. "Release M. Denis this instant!"

The actor's face was reddened, and his sunglasses had fallen and broken in the scrimmage. Verlaque quickly bent down and picked them up, hiding them under a napkin.

"What kind of staff do you have here?" Denis cried, tucking his shirt back into the waist of his shorts. "That man will be fired, I assume!" Denis walked over to his table and picked up his iPhone and left the terrace.

"Come, Hugo," Max Le Bon said. "I'm terribly sorry for this," he then said to the patrons.

"He did nothing wrong," Sylvie said. "He was defending —"

"Thank you, mademoiselle," Le Bon said, gently taking Hugo by the elbow and leading him away.

"I hope he doesn't get fired on my behalf," Mme Denis said, slowly sitting down.

"Hugo went too far," Verlaque said. "Right or wrong, your husband is a guest."

Maxime and Cat-Cat Le Bon had toyed with the idea of not putting in a swimming pool when they renovated Locanda Sordou. They thought the whole idea of it idiotic, with the sea surrounding them; budget was a concern too, and toward the end of the renovations they had started using up their money and had little left for a pool the size and quality a hotel like Sordou would need. In the end an investor — a colleague of Clément Viale's — stepped in with 50,000 euros, which enabled them to add a pool, pool house, and bar, and buy the necessary lounge furniture from B&B Italia.

The Le Bons had both grown up privileged, and their first swims had been at family vacation homes on the sea, in Deauville. And so one of the first things they had installed, before the renovations had even begun, was a small ladder that led from the flat rocks in the beach's harbor down into the sea about five feet below. The flat rocks provided perfect, natural areas to recline, and the ladder made it feel like the Mediterranean was one big swimming pool, which, compared to the Atlantic, it was.

Marine had climbed down the ladder and swam close in, where she could see down to the seafloor. But Antoine swam far out, and when she was tired she climbed out and stood on the rocks watching him, with her hand shielding her eyes from the sun. She didn't like the idea of his swimming alone, but she was too afraid of the sea, and its black depth, to venture out with him.

They had been out there all morning, alternating between reading, talking, and swimming when it got too hot. She waved to the Americans, who were sitting on the next cliff over, Mr. Hobbs fishing and Mrs. Hobbs sketching. She bent down and pulled her watch out of her beach bag; it was almost 1 p.m., and time to head back in for lunch. She waved out to Verlaque and he began swimming toward her.

"If I got you some goggles," he said as he swam up to the cliff's edge, "I think you'd enjoy swimming in the sea more." He swam over to the ladder and pulled himself out. Marine was always amazed that despite her boyfriend's love of good food and wine, and his ample girth, he rarely seemed out of breath after swimming, or running. "When you do a lot of sports when you're young, it stays with you," he had explained. Marine's sports had been walking to the library when she was a young girl, and then walking around Paris's sixth *arrondissement* where she had studied law.

"Perhaps," Marine called out, as she sat on the rock's edge and dipped her feet into the cold sea.

"Time for lunch?" Verlaque asked once he was out and was toweling off his hair.

"Yes," Marine replied. "And I predict that Sylvie will be a no-show, and that boy, Brice, will be there, and starving."

"I think you're right," Verlaque said. "It would be hard to have a son, wouldn't it?"

Marine looked over at Verlaque, surprised. "You mean instead of a daughter, or just a child in general?"

"No, I think as opposed to a daughter."

"Oh, I don't think I was easy to get along with at fifteen."

"Easier than I was, or any other boy," Verlaque said, picking up his newspapers, which he had held down with a rock. "I'd be terrified to have a son, actually. My parents did such a botched job on Sébastien and me."

"But that's just it," Marine said. "It wasn't your fault, being a boy. It was your parents' botched job, as you call it, at raising you, and your brother."

Verlaque laughed. "Now there's a piece of work, eh? My brother, Parisian real estate mogul who dines every night alone."

"You don't know that for sure."

"Yes, I do," Verlaque said. "Reports from acquaintances tell me that Séb has pissed off so many colleagues in Paris that he's usually alone these days."

Marine said nothing; what could she say?

She'd only met Sébastien Verlaque twice and hadn't enjoyed either meeting.

The Hobbses, having seen Marine and Antoine packing up, realized that they had lost track of time. They had caught up to the Frenchies on the path that led back to the hotel. "Hungry!" Shirley Hobbs called, rubbing her stomach.

"I hope lunch is as good as last night's dinner," Verlaque said in English.

"Wasn't that a treat?" Shirley Hobbs said.

"I'm hoping to make my own contribution," Bill Hobbs said, lifting his blue bucket up. The four of them stopped and looked at the dozen or so small reddish fish. "What are they?" Hobbs asked.

"They're little rock-clinging fish called *rougets,*" Verlaque answered. "They're one of the ingredients of a bouillabaisse in Marseille."

"Oh, we ate that last time we were in Provence," Shirley Hobbs said. "I'm surprised you'd forget their name, Bill."

Hobbs shrugged his shoulders. "I'm going to show them to the chef," he said. "Have to earn my keep."

Marine smiled and she pointed to Shirley Hobbs's sketchbook.

"Would you like to see?" Mrs. Hobbs asked. She stopped and opened her sketchbook to the first page. It was a watercolor of the sea and Sordou's westerly cliffs.

"You've made the water sparkle," Marine said, amazed at the painting's effervescent quality. Verlaque translated for Shirley Hobbs, who smiled.

"I've been taking art classes since retirement," Mrs. Hobbs said.

"She really keeps at it," Bill Hobbs said, beaming. Marine understood the gist of what he said and smiled.

They walked into the hotel, through the lobby, then through the dining room, out onto the same terrace where they had had breakfast, but it was now shaded by parasols and by white awnings that were suspended from the hotel's walls. Verlaque gave Marine a quick look as if to ask, "Do we join them for lunch?" and Marine nodded in the affirmative. Verlaque posed the question aloud and the Hobbses said that they would be delighted. Bill Hobbs went into the dining room and knocked at the kitchen door, wanting to give his offering to Émile Villey. Verlaque, Marine, and Shirley Hobbs were shown to their seats by Niki Darcette.

"How did you find out about Sordou?" Verlaque asked after helping Mrs. Hobbs into her chair.

"It was Bill's idea," she replied.

"Where are you from?" Marine asked in slow, careful English.

"Bellingham."

"Where's Bellingham?" Verlaque asked.

"Washington," Mrs. Hobbs answered. "Washington State, not the capital."

*"Washington, mais pas D.C.,"* Verlaque said to Marine.

*"J'ai tout compris,"* Marine said.

"Marine speaks beautiful Italian," Verlaque said. "She's shy about her English, but she just understood our conversation."

"Please tell Marine that she looks like a movie star," Shirley Hobbs said. "But a proper one, not a made-up one."

As if on cue, Emmanuelle Denis walked into the room, now wearing tennis shorts and sneakers, which emphasized just how skinny her legs were. She saw Marine and Verlaque and walked over to their table, raising her hands in the air. "Still no sign of him!" she cried.

Marine, Shirley Hobbs, and Verlaque saw the panic in the woman's eyes. Verlaque quickly got up and put his hand on her shoulder. "He's lost track of time," he said.

Emmanuelle Denis wiped her eyes dry with a much-used tissue. "But he could have fallen . . ."

Verlaque pulled out a chair and motioned

for Mme Denis to sit down. She said, "He fights with Alain . . . my husband, and his stepfather, and this April Brice walked out on us. The mother of a friend called us the next day, telling us he was at their place. He stayed the week. . . . It was the longest we've ever been apart."

Marine looked at Mme Denis with more sympathy than she would have imagined herself capable of. It surprised her that a woman who looked like such a bimbo would be so attached to her son. She wasn't putting it on, either. Her eyes were red and her hands trembling.

"I have two boys," Shirley Hobbs said in English, reaching across to Emmanuelle Denis and taking her hand. She had understood that the woman's son was missing, and she was pleased that after so many vacations in France, she was finally able to understand the language; she vowed to take a French class once they got back to Bellingham. "They caused us grief in their teenage years, each one in his own way. But they grow up, and if you love them as much as you obviously love your son, they get on with things and end up doing fine. You'll see."

Verlaque was about to translate when Mme Denis caressed the American's hand

and said in flawless English, "Thank you, madame. I know that you're right, but it seems as if I'm still learning this . . . parenting. I've made so many mistakes."

"Who hasn't?" Shirley Hobbs said, smiling.

"What happened last night?" Verlaque asked. He realized as soon as he said it that it sounded as if he was challenging Mme Denis, but she seemed to take no notice of it.

Mme Denis replied, "They fought again, and I brought Brice up some food from the kitchen. Alain wants Brice to go to a boarding school next year, since his grades slipped this semester."

To Verlaque, Marine, and Shirley Hobbs, the choice was easy: get rid of Alain Denis. But they remained silent.

"I brought the food up just before we ate, around eight p.m.," she said. "And this morning saw his unmade bed."

"Well, Brice can't go far on Sordou," Verlaque finally said. "We'll look for him if he doesn't show up by three p.m., okay?"

Marine nodded in affirmation. "Please eat lunch with us," Marine said. "You'll feel better with some food."

"Thank you," Mme Denis replied. "I think I'll have a glass of rosé too. I normally don't drink at lunch."

"I'll order us a bottle of Bandol," Verlaque said.

Bills Hobbs came back and seemed nonplussed that there was a guest at their table. He pulled out a chair from a neighboring table and introduced himself to Mme Denis. His wife leaned over and quickly explained about Brice.

"Well, I saw the boy last night," Bill Hobbs said in English.

"Where?" everyone asked in unison.

"I was here, on the terrace, after dinner. Shirley had gone to bed, and I was . . . having a little after-dinner whiskey," he replied. "It was late . . . about eleven p.m. He had shorts on and headed out behind the hotel, away from the harbor."

"Bill," Shirley exclaimed. "Why didn't you say something?"

"Well, I'm telling you all now, aren't I? Besides, the boy wasn't carrying anything, so I thought he was mad about something and was just going for a walk, to let off some steam."

"Steam?" Marine asked.

*"Vapeur,"* Verlaque said.

"Our Jason used to do that," Bill reminded his wife.

"You're right," Shirley said, turning to

129

Emmanuelle Denis. "Our oldest son, Jason, had a hot temper, and whenever he was angry with us he'd go for a walk down to the harbor. So you see, I'm sure there's nothing to worry about."

# CHAPTER ELEVEN: HOUSEKEEPING

"If he ogles me one more time . . ." Niki Darcette whispered to Cat-Cat Le Bon as they were checking their bookings for August. She drew her hand across her throat and made a sawing gesture.

"I told Max there's a problem with Alain Denis and women," Cat-Cat said, taking off her reading glasses and turning toward Niki. "I remember it from the press long ago. And after what happened this morning at breakfast, we'll all have to be careful around Denis. But you have to understand, he's . . ."

"A big shot," Niki replied. "Or was."

Cat-Cat nodded. *"Was, indeed,"* she whispered. "Nevertheless, I've asked Serge to keep an eye out for you when Alain Denis is around, and you both need to watch out for Marie-Thérèse. She's so young."

Niki pursed her lips, remembering her own young self, stuck in Néoules. "Okay, you're right. I can stick up for myself around guys like that — don't worry, I'll be professional — but Marie-Thérèse is so innocent."

Mme Le Bon smiled. "She is, isn't she? It's so refreshing." She thought of her spoiled nieces and nephews in Paris, and their demands for the latest Apple this and that, the right kinds of shoes, and handbags, and sunglasses.

"I would prefer Hugo looking out for us," Niki said. "Serge isn't too . . ."

Cat-Cat held up her hand. "No Hugo discussion right now," she said. "We're all fond of Hugo, but we had to fire him."

"He was defending her."

"I know, I know," Cat-Cat said. "But we have to show our guests, and staff, that we won't accept violent behavior."

*Unless it's a movie star being violent,* Niki thought. "When is Hugo going?"

"In the next few days," Cat-Cat replied. "We've told him to lay low and stick to his cabin; we need him here until a replacement can be found. But Max is furious; now Hugo's gone out somewhere with the boat."

"Really?" Niki asked, feigning surprise. She knew that Hugo, when upset, went to the sea. And she guessed that he was probably with Mlle Grassi, the artist. It didn't bother her; she wasn't the slightest bit attracted to him.

Both women turned their attention toward the computer screen, lost in their thoughts: Niki worried about Marie-Thérèse, wondering if such a young girl could be happy working on an island. She vowed that at break later this afternoon she'd try talking to Marie-Thérèse; more than just a chitchat. Cat-Cat Le Bon looked at the screen, thankful that the slow modem brought the hotel Internet; and she was thinking, as she did almost daily now, that she regretted not having children. If she had, when she and Max were first married, they would now be Marie-Thérèse's age.

Maxime and Catherine Le Bon knew enough about hotels before opening their own to guess that one of the biggest occupations at Sordou would be the laundry. This is where Yolaine Poux, the head housekeeper, found herself now, thankful that her bosses had wisely thought to make the laundry area large enough to comfortably work in, and with windows on two sides to allow a cross draft. The Le Bons, worried about their budget, and the heat that electric dryers would let off, had rebuilt an existing high-walled courtyard where the housekeeper could hang the sheets, towels, and tablecloths up to dry, out of view of the hotel's guests. The island's sun and wind dried the sheets, sometimes in under an hour, and they needed minimal ironing afterward. Mme Poux hummed as she ironed the crisp white pillowcases, spraying them with lavender water.

It was almost a luxurious area to work in, every bit as luxurious as the hotel itself, and it was by far the best job Mme Poux had ever had. The terra-cotta floors and stone walls reminded her of a posh redone farmhouse, the kind that she knew Parisians and foreigners bought in the Luberon and around Saint-Rémy. There were long, wide wooden tables in the middle of the room on which she could spread out her folding and sorting, and an armchair in the corner for when she needed a break. From the chair, where she would have an espresso made by Serge every day at 4 p.m, she could stare, not out to sea, as the laundry room was in the back of the hotel, but out onto the *garrigue* that led to Sordou's interior. She loved the view; for years she had worked in the laundry rooms of the Hôpital Nord in Marseille, where the small, high windows gave onto the employee parking lot.

Marie-Thérèse came into the room, carrying a linen bag, dumping its contents onto the floor in front of one of the industrial-size washing machines. Mme Poux treated these machines like some young men treat their cars; she washed them every second day, cleaning their round windows and buffing the stainless steel handles and window surrounds. She set down the iron and walked over to where Marie-Thérèse was standing, gazing at the washing machine.

"He sure uses a lot of these tea towels," Mme Poux said, lifting them up and setting them into an empty machine. "But he's a good chef, I'll give him that."

"Mmm . . ."

"Cat got your tongue?"

"It's that boy, the sad one . . ."

Mme Poux said, "He missed lunch, right? He'll be back for dinner, you can bet on it."

"The judge — oops, I'm not supposed to know that — and his girlfriend went out looking for him," Marie-Thérèse said, bending down to help Yolaine load the washing machine. She liked to help Mme Poux, whom she thought to be about one hundred years old.

"Is that so?"

"Yep. They made it sound like they were just going on a walk, but I know they're trying to help Mme Denis. She's really upset."

"*Ca, alors,*" Mme Poux replied, pouring

soap carefully into the machine and turning it on. "That woman doesn't look like she would care one bit about her son, but I've only seen her once, in the hallway." Mme Poux, who dressed in traditional aprons and flat comfortable shoes, didn't like the high heels and leopard prints.

Marie-Thérèse shrugged. "She does care. She was crying, and yelling at her husband after lunch yesterday. They're not even sharing a room; she sleeps in Brice's room, in the extra twin bed; did you notice? She said —"

Mme Poux put her hand up. "I don't want to hear. You shouldn't be listening to them."

"I couldn't help it . . . ."

"Still, I don't want to hear about other people's problems, especially rich people's problems. I worked in a hospital, where people were sick and dying, but every day I thanked my lucky stars that I wasn't a nurse or doctor, having to deal with all that mess."

Marie-Thérèse didn't reply that she'd rather *that* mess — helping people get better — than the hospital mess Mme Poux must have found daily on the sheets and towels: blood, shit, piss, vomit, and who knows what else. She knew that the other employees didn't like Mme Poux very much; it wasn't like she was mean or anything; she just kept to herself, and was a maniac about her laundry room. But, then, Émile was fanatical about the kitchen; he climbed up on the stove every night and cleaned the hood, and Serge was constantly wiping down the bar and checking glasses for spots, so why did they make fun of Mme Poux? If it was because her name, Poux, was the same name for lice, then they were stupid and immature.

"Want me to get you your coffee?" Marie-Thérèse asked.

Mme Poux pulled her watch out of her apron pocket. "It's a quarter to four. That would be awfully nice of you."

"It's no problem; then I'll take my break."

"Yes, you should," Mme Poux said. "You get a long break; don't forget that you need to rest as you work at dinner this evening." Mme Poux then made a hissing sound with her mouth. "They really need more employees."

"They have to watch their money the first year," Marie-Thérèse replied.

"Oh, so you're an expert, eh?"

Marie-Thérèse put her pointer finger up to her eye and tapped three times. "I keep watch, and listen too."

"*Ah oui!* You listen a little too much,

missy," Mme Poux said, laughing despite herself.

Marie-Thérèse swung around, grinning. It pleased her to make Yolaine smile. She'd get the coffee and then see if Émile had any cookies left that she could put on the saucer. It was just a little bit extra effort, and if it made people feel better — whether they were staff or guests — then it was a good thing in her books.

Mme Poux finished ironing a pillowcase — it was her last of the day — and carefully folded it and set it in a wicker basket. She walked across the room and sat in her armchair and looked out at the bright-blue sky. She reached into her pocket and took out her watch, flipping it over and rubbing its smooth back, tracing the inscription with her fingers: *Yolaine, ma chérie.* She remembered clearly the day that Rémy had given her the watch; a clear summer's day, much like this one. He had saved for months, and bought it at Levy's on the Rue Paradis. She still had the velvet box. And it was a day like today that he had died, at forty-two years of age.

"Oh, you're alone," a voice said from the doorway. "I thought Marie-Thérèse was here."

"She was," Mme Poux replied. She didn't

care for Niki Darcette; there was something about her that was just a little *malhonnête.* Yolaine Poux didn't like the way Mlle Darcette waltzed around the hotel in short skirts and tight blouses, thinking that she was on the same social standing as the Le Bons, or even crazier, as the hotel's guests. If Niki wanted to speak to Marie-Thérèse she could just go and find her.

"Ummm, sorry to bother you," Niki said, smiling and not hiding the sarcasm.

Mme Poux said nothing, but turned her head back toward the window, signaling that their conversation was over.

*"Oh mon dieu,"* Niki muttered as she walked away. "What did I ever do to Mrs. Lice?"

Yolaine Poux put the watch back in her apron pocket and began humming Charles Aznavour's *"Elle."* It had been Rémy's favorite song. She looked outside the window but then quickly leaned back; she didn't want to make it seem like she was snooping on the clients. For Alain Denis was not far from the window, a small white piece of paper in his hands, and it seemed to Mme Poux that he was laughing.

# Chapter Twelve:
## Pirates

"Neolithic peoples came to the islands look-ing for shellfish," Hugo Sammut said as he dropped the *Calypso*'s anchor.

Sylvie stared at his tanned, flat stomach and hoped he couldn't see her eyes through her giant sunglasses. "Oh yeah?" she asked, moving toward him and rubbing his muscu-lar forearm.

Sammut dipped his baseball hat into the sea and drew up some water, carefully drop-ping it on to Sylvie. He took his hand and gently rubbed the water on her stomach, then her arms and shoulders. Sylvie moved her face toward his and he kissed her, slowly and carefully.

"Tell me more," she whispered, leaning against his chest.

"In the middle of the island are the ruins of a twelfth-century watch tower," Sammut said, stroking Sylvie's hair.

"What would they watch out for?"

"Barbarians," Sammut hissed, tickling Sylvie. "Barbarian pirates from North Africa. They would attack ships in the Med and take prisoners — white Europeans — that they'd sell in the slave trade."

Sylvie sat up. "That's sinister."

Sammut nodded. "They took over a million prisoners, over the centuries, until they were finally stopped in the early nineteenth century by the French invasion of Algeria. Anyway, the watchtower here would send warning signals to Marseille, where they had a similar lookout post up in the hills behind the city."

"Except it wasn't a city yet," Sylvie interjected.

"Of course, silly," Sammut said. He kissed Sylvie again and drew her close to him, circling the outline of her breast with his finger. "When I was a kid I read an English book translated into French called *The Lustful Turk;* I found it at our local library in Nancy when I was about twelve or thirteen and would read it under the blankets at home."

"Under the blankets, eh?" Sylvie asked, stroking his chest. "What was it about, dare I ask?"

"Pirates," Sammut explained. "A ship that was sailing from England to . . . India, I

think . . . gets attacked here, in the Mediterranean, by Barbarian pirates. There's a
young Englishwoman on board, a virgin,
naturally . . ."

"Naturally . . ."

"And she's taken into custody and delivered to a harem in Morocco or some such
place. Anyway, she's taught lots of things
about sex by Ali, her rich captor."

"And she grows to like these . . . sexual
acts?"

"Mmmm," Sammut whispered. "She becomes *obsessed.*"

Sylvie closed her eyes and let Hugo's
tongue explore her mouth, then neck, then
breasts. Her senses were alive to their sur-
roundings: the gently rocking boat, the
sound of the water licking the boat's sides,
the bird song, and the sawing noise of the
*cigales,* audible even from their anchored
spot a few dozen yards from shore.

"Let's swim a bit," Sammut suddenly said,
readjusting Sylvie's tiny bikini top.

"Sure thing," Sylvie replied. She would
have preferred to go on kissing her handsome boatman, but it was getting hot.

Sammut dove off of the boat and Sylvie
watched him swim, his strong arms gracefully slicing the emerald-blue water. She
climbed down the boat's aluminum ladder

and fell backward into the sea, her arms and legs stretched outward as if she were a starfish. She floated in the water for a minute, squinting up at the blue sky, until Sammut came up behind her and slipped his hand inside her bikini bottom. She rolled over toward him and, treading water with no apparent effort, he held her in his arms, his left hand now exploring her. Their faces were covered in saltwater and they kissed passionately, Hugo Sammut now thrusting his fingers inside of her with more urgency. Sylvie began to shake and then crumpled in his arms.

"That was fast," Sammut said, smiling. He kissed her again and poured some water onto her head with his hand.

"Um, it's been a while," Sylvie replied, now treading water beside him.

"If we swim to shore, I know of a secret place we could go to, to . . ."

"To do this properly?" Sylvie asked, wrapping her arms around Sammut's shoulders and kissing him. "Show me the way."

They were both strong swimmers and quickly got to the shore, Sammut holding out his hand to Sylvie as they walked up onto the pebbly beach. Sylvie looked down at her bare feet and said, "I hope it's not far."

Sammut pointed to a cropping of large rocks to their left, stretching out into the sea.

"Oh, I see it," Sylvie said. "The flat rock in the middle?"

Sammut nodded and took her hand. They climbed up onto the rocks, jumping from rock to rock until they came to Hugo's flat rock, hidden from the sea by a bigger, steeper, and taller rock.

"It's incredibly smooth," Sylvie said as she lay down.

Hugo Sammut slipped off his swimming trunks and set them under Sylvie's bum. He then quickly took off her bikini bottom, and Sylvie threw off her wet top. "Tell me more about the book," she whispered, taking Sammut's erect penis in her hand.

"The Englishwoman has a friend who comes on another ship, looking for her," Sammut said, licking Sylvie's breasts. "And her boat is also captured by pirates, and guess where she ends up . . ."

"At Ali's harem?"

"Yep, and she too becomes insatiable in her appetite for . . ."

"Carnal pleasures," Sylvie said, wrapping her legs around Sammut's lower back. "Oh, please give me some carnal pleasures," she cried.

■ ■ ■ ■

"Did you hear that?" Marine asked.

"All I can hear are the bloody *cigales,*" Verlaque said. "I would have thought that they'd be minimal here, given there are hardly any trees."

Marine waved her hand through the tiny pale-pink blossoms of a short willowy bush. "There are pine trees growing out of the cliffs, and these tamarisk trees, but that's enough for the *cigales,*" she said.

"Is that what those trees are called?" Verlaque asked. "You see them at the sides of the highway sometimes."

"Yes, they're hardy little things," Marine said. "They love the sun and can withstand strong winds, so they love the seaside too. My parents have one in the backyard."

"Would you have one? A tamarisk? In your ideal garden?"

Marine smiled. "I suppose I would. They're always the first trees to flower, in late spring."

Verlaque sat down on a rock. "I'm beat and too hot. How are you?"

"Same," Marine said, sitting down beside him. "We should turn back, or go and jump in the sea. With this breeze you don't feel the sun so much, but we should be careful. Did you wear your bathing trunks under your shorts?"

"I did indeed," Verlaque said, pulling at his shorts to reveal the waist band of his blue-and-green trunks.

"Hermès?"

"Of course," Verlaque replied.

"I never thought I'd love a man who wears Hermès bathing trunks."

"My mother bought them for me," Verlaque said, straightening his back. "And Séb got the same ones, but in orange and yellow."

"Oh my God, matching presents for brothers in their forties."

"The good thing about this island being so small is that you can't get lost," Verlaque said, getting up. "You can see the lighthouse from almost any spot on the island, I would guess."

"You don't think that Brice is out there, lost, do you?" Marine asked.

"No, I think he's back at the hotel by now, complaining about the nonexistent Internet connection."

"Well, I'm sorry that we didn't see him."

"Let's go," Verlaque said, taking Marine's hand. "A swim would feel great right now, and we can't do that in Aix."

They walked over a small rise that was covered in rocks mixed with bright-yellow miniature daisies. Small, chatty birds flew around them, in and out of the low *garrigue* plants and shrubs. "Look, there's the *Calypso* anchored in that small bay," Marine said.

"Oops," Verlaque said, laughing out loud. "Looks like Sylvie and Hugo were out identifying the flora and fauna of the island."

Sylvie waved at her friends as she quickly adjusted the thin straps of her bathing suit. Hugo looked like he was dancing a jig, hopping on one foot as he put on his bathing trunks.

"Ahoy, mates!" Verlaque cried.

"Oh, Antoine!" Marine said, laughing.

"Let's get a ride back with them."

"Great idea," Marine said. "Hugo doesn't look too upset for someone who probably just lost his job."

"I agree," Verlaque said. "But perhaps he wanted to go anyway? People in hospitality are changing jobs all the time."

They walked quickly down the rocky hill, careful not to slip, toward the cove and flat rocks. Different flowers appeared, these ones violet, growing in thick small bunches out of crevices in the rocks. Marine bent down to get a better look when she saw a bit of dark-blue fabric draped over a wild rosemary bush. She stood up and walked over to it.

"What's that?" Verlaque called out.

She picked it up and held it in her hands, turning it around. She then held it in the air.

*"Mon dieu,"* Verlaque said.

"Brice's New York Yankees cap," Marine said, quickly looking around her. "Brice!" she called out. "Brice!"

Verlaque said, "He could be hurt and can't talk." He waved to Sylvie and Hugo and gave them a "time out" signal while he and Marine checked behind bushes and rocks for more traces of the boy.

"Nothing," Marine said when they rejoined each other.

By the time they got down to the flat rocks that jutted out into the sea, Sylvie and Hugo were adequately attired.

"Thanks for waiting. Can we get a ride back with you?" Verlaque asked.

"No problemo," Sammut replied. "We can swim to the boat, or I can pull it up close to the rocks; you can follow that path that hugs the cliff and jump on from that low white rock."

"We'll swim," Marine said.

Hugo said, "Fine, but let's get going. The sea is getting rough."

"Really?" Sylvie asked, looking at the calm water.

"Yep," Hugo replied. "Believe me."

"We found this," Marine said, passing Brice's hat to Hugo.

"Brice," Hugo and Sylvie said in unison.

Sylvie shielded her eyes from the sun and looked up at the cliffs for signs of humans; while she and Hugo had been making love she had had the funny feeling that they were being watched.

"He's probably back at the hotel by now," Verlaque said as he put the cap on his head.

"Nice," Sylvie said.

"I don't want to get it wet," Verlaque explained.

Marine looked at her boyfriend, with his bathing trunks covered in tropical plants, and now a New York Yankees ball cap that seemed a little too small for his large head and thick hair. Sylvie and Hugo were laughing but Marine, however odd Antoine looked, couldn't joke about it. For some inexplicable reason her stomach was taut. As she started swimming she tried to forget what kind of creatures were silently moving under her body. A bird flew overhead and made a piercing cry. She was the first to arrive at the boat; her fear had made her swim the fastest. She pulled herself up by the boat's small rickety ladder and sat on the hot plastic bench, looking back at Sordou. As beautiful as the island was, she saw that its barren scrubland and jagged white cliffs could be sinister. There were few trees to provide shade, and it would be so easy to fall while walking along the limestone cliffs. Why had Brice gone out? She never would have ventured off on her own; she couldn't even imagine Antoine doing it, late at night. But young men were fearless; centuries of wars and eighteen-year-olds signing up for battle proved that. They couldn't imagine any harm ever coming to them.

# CHAPTER THIRTEEN: ABOUT THE BARTENDER

Serge Canzano loved Bloody Marys. For him, it was the all-purpose drink. Great for curing a hangover, but equally fine as an aperitif, in the true meaning of the word: a drink that gives one an appetite. The tomato juice he made fresh, every day. If the hotel's clients didn't order a Bloody Mary then Serge would drink the tomato juice at the end of his shift.

He knew the history of the drink — most drinks, and wine too — by heart and would gladly relay that information to anyone who cared to listen. With this first group at Sordou, he had already determined who those interested parties would be: the judge and the schoolteacher, both from Aix. Perhaps also the judge's girlfriend, who might be interested in the drink from a purely historical standpoint.

During one of his too-short breaks, and during a rare time at Sordou when there were three bars of Interent connection, he had googled Marine Bonnet: history of law professor at Aix's esteemed law school, graduated from law school in Paris second in her class, just after Renaud de Montille, and Serge did not need the Internet to tell him that Montille was now minister of the interior. Marine Bonnet also seemed to write, or coauthor, historical papers on law. He skimmed over these titles, lost on the jargon that he could not understand. But it sounded good: "All that Glitters: Sumptuary Laws in Sixteenth-Century France," "Beyond Paris: French Law in Provence During the Middle Ages," and "Shedding New Light on Andrea Alciato's *Emblems.*" He smiled to himself, glad that some of these pampered civil servants were actually working over their long summer break. For the *patrimoine* of France had always been important to Serge Canzano. And he sometimes thought of bartending this way: protecting and teaching *la patrimoine de la France,* his beloved country's cultural heritage.

Canzano looked up from his post behind the marble-topped bar, where he had been daydreaming of Mlle Bonnet, to see Alain Denis take his usual seat, in a vintage wicker armchair in the farthest corner of the bar.

Serge got out a champagne glass, ready for what would be the actor's usual predinner drink: an overpriced glass of champagne. Hey, if the Le Bons could make money on that, all the more power to them. Denis glanced over in Canzano's direction as if to say, "I'll have the usual" and Canzano nodded as if to say, "Coming right up." He stifled a yawn.

Much to his delight the retired schoolteacher came in and took a seat at the bar, directly across from Canzano. "Good afternoon, Serge," Eric Monnier said. "Quiet around here in the afternoons."

Canzano watched as the sixtysomething, slightly overweight ex-teacher struggled to make himself comfortable on the narrow bar stool. "What will it be, M. Monnier?" he asked.

"I'll leave that up to you," Monnier replied, taking out of his pocket a Montecristo limited-edition cigar and rolling it around in his hands. "What do you suggest on this warm and breezy beautiful day on Sordou?"

"A Bloody Mary," Canzano answered. "The tomato juice is fresh, using our tomatoes. Unless you want a rum with your cigar."

"No, a Bloody Mary sounds good. I

haven't had one in years. Gotta love a drink named after an English queen, even if she did only reign for five years, and even if she was in fact less bloody than her sister Elizabeth."

"Coming right up," Canzano answered, smiling. He poured Alain Denis a glass of chilled champagne and delivered it to the actor, who couldn't be bothered looking up or saying thank you.

Canzano returned to the bar and got out his favorite French-made vodka and shaker and began preparing the drink.

"I hope you add Tabasco to that," Monnier said.

"Of course," Canzano replied, seizing the opportunity to show off his skills. "Tabasco became one of the all-important Bloody Mary ingredients in 1952, in America."

Monnier leaned forward. "Is that so? Does the drink date from the fifties?"

Canzano smiled as he got a sprig of celery out of the fridge, thrilled to have an eager student. "No, 1917."

"Really? Right in the middle of the Great War?"

"Yup. A hotel in Indiana ran out of orange juice during breakfast service. The chef, a Frenchman I believe, replaced the oranges with fresh-squeezed tomatoes, with sugar and a special sauce he had concocted."

"So who was the genius who added the vodka?"

"An actor, George Jessel. In 1927. He also added lemon and Worcestershire sauce. He made the drink in Florida for a bunch of his friends, and it became an instant hit."

"I'll say."

"I think the horseradish and celery salt around the rim came later, and they're equally important ingredients, as is the lime juice." Canzano finished making his concoction and shook the cocktail shaker in his hands.

"Ah, what a lovely sound," Monnier said.

The barman put the finishing touches — the sprig of celery and a twist of lime — into the bright-red drink and passed it carefully over the bar to Eric Monnier. "I'm not sure it's the best match with a cigar."

"It doesn't matter," Monnier answered. "I can have the cigar later."

Canzano got to cleaning his shaker and cutting board. He was a bartender of the old school: he didn't chat with clients unless they wanted to. And he never gave anything away about himself, no matter how gritty the information and divulging got on the other side of the bar. He had bartended for over thirty years in various hotels and bars around Marseille's old port, from sleazy holes-in-the-wall that barely fit ten people to the elegant Sofitel high-rise, its rooftop restaurant boasting some of the best views of the city and the sea. It was at the Sofitel that Canzano realized that Marseille was best seen from up above, with the double-paned picture windows firmly closed.

Over the years on the job he had seen one shooting (drug related), one stabbing (drug related as well), and a dozen or so fistfights — between couples, between best friends, between opposing soccer fans. He had listened to clients as they told him of their failing marriages, their affairs, their jobs, their children, their parents, and the most common topics of all: politics, and how much they either loved or despised Marseille. There were good times too and that was probably one of the reasons why he kept at it. Behind the bar he was competent, and left to himself. He didn't have a boss hovering over him. And he had made friends with some clients and coworkers. They weren't all a complete mess. He had helped celebrate job promotions, anniversaries, first dates, soccer victories, and general Friday-night glee. He had poured beer, pastis, martinis (mostly for foreigners or the more well-traveled enlightened French), cheap rosé wines that the bosses bought in bulk, and had opened bottles of red wine from Bordeaux and Burgundy that cost his month's salary.

But the more promotions Canzano had earned the further away from the client he became. At his last job at the Sofitel his job consisted of managing the bar and assisting the sommelier, a kid fresh out of the wine school in Orange who could barely work a corkscrew. Canzano missed the chitchat at the bar, and the people watching, that he had done years back. Once, when he had run the bar at a tiny place on the Cours Julien, every night for six straight years one man had come into the bar on his way home from work. He was nicely dressed: polished shoes, pressed pants, and expensive jacket. Every night he ordered a pastis, and every night he'd pull out his wallet — just before his last sip — and ask how much the drink was. And every night Serge had answered, slowly and carefully, *"Deux euros vingt, monsieur."* Serge never knew the man's name; he drank his pastis quickly and didn't talk to Canzano or the other clients. When Serge got a job at a nicer bar down the street he wondered about the man. Did he still go, every night? Did he still ask how much it cost, even though he knew it was two euros twenty? Canzano had admired the man — for both his ability to stick to a routine, and for his politeness. "How much will that be, please?" Every night. Did the man have a wife and family at home? Serge got glimpses into peoples' lives, but no more. And that was enough for him. He had left his family in the north when he was seventeen and never gone back.

He glanced at the schoolteacher, who was taking his time with the drink and now writing in a black notebook. Serge noticed that it wasn't prose that he was writing, but stanzas. He must be trying his hand at some poetry, for he had overheard the teacher say that he was now retired. Canzano guessed that the teacher had never married; perhaps he had been heartbroken when he was younger. Canzano was good at guessing people's histories, if they didn't tell him their life story after the third pastis.

The actor was almost finished with his champagne and would soon be nodding in Canzano's direction for another. After spending three days observing and overhearing the actor on Sordou, Canzano knew that what all the gossip magazines said about Alain Denis was true: that he had been a beautiful young man — which accounted for 70 percent of his film jobs — and that he had been good at acting, not brilliant, but good, but that his egomania and bad temper had permanently damaged not only his career but every relationship he had ever had. It didn't take a psychiatrist, nor an observant barman, to see that the actor's marriage was doomed, and that his wife's son was suffering.

As if on cue, Denis looked over toward the bar and tapped three times on the edge of his empty champagne flute. Canzano filled another flute with chilled Ruinart, put some olives in a small bowl, and took both over to Denis, removing his empty glass at the same time. The actor huffed and mumbled a *merci* and the schoolteacher turned around and grinned.

Canzano was thankful that he wasn't busy; Marie-Thérèse was having a break before dinner, and he hoped that she was resting somewhere with her feet up. It pained him to see someone so young already working so hard in the hotel business, but he had started even younger. None of the women on Sordou would be any good for Serge Canzano, he had seen during their first meeting back in May: Marie-Thérèse was too young; Niki Darcette too accomplished and sure of herself, although he suspected she came from an even humbler background than he did; Mme Le Bon was married — happily, he thought; and Mme Poux far too old. But Canzano hadn't come to Sordou to get lucky — Hugo Sammut would be fulfilling that part of the job, as he probably was this very minute, with the mojito-swilling artist. And Canzano was, as appearances go, the opposite of the tanned muscular Sammut: the bartender was tall and too thin, had blond hair that was receding, a long, thin nose and thin lips, and a handlebar mustache that he kept carefully trimmed.

Canzano had come to Sordou because he was tired of Marseille; on the island he was offered the same salary that he had been earning at the Sofitel but with room and board included. On the mainland he would have been paying rent for a dive studio apartment for the rest of his life. Why not live for free? And why live in France's second-largest city if you didn't need to? He didn't go to the opera or plays, nor the cinema. Despite his love of good food, he had never made enough money to go to Marseille's fine restaurants. On Sordou he ate extremely well, more than he ever had in his life. He hadn't been sure of Chef Émile when he first met him: he looked too young, and the long hair in a ponytail had put Canzano off. He thought that Villey should be surfing somewhere near Biarritz, not cooking. But he had been happily proved wrong.

What Canzano would miss of city life were museums and libraries, but perhaps he could do that on his time off. The city wasn't that far away, after all. Dirty and noisy Marseille; it was now almost impossible to get anywhere except by motorcycle, and Serge had broken his leg in a motorcycle accident fifteen years ago and had vowed never to ride one again. So when he had overheard two colleagues at the Sofitel talking about the new hotel opening up on Sordou, Canzano used some of his thirty years' worth of connections to find out who the new owners were. For his job interview he made the Le Bons each a Bloody Mary.

The teacher closed his notebook and Canzano looked at him, putting down his tea towel. "Would you like another drink?" he asked.

Monnier looked at his watch. "It's not long until dinner. I think I'll wait," he said.

*"D'accord, monsieur,"* Canzano replied, taking Monnier's empty glass and putting it in the dishwasher. He hid his surprise, as he had guessed that the teacher was a two-

drink-before-dinner man, and last night he had three.

"That kid's not back yet." Monnier turned around and looked out of the Jacky Bar's windows as if he was looking for Brice.

"He'll be at dinner," Canzano said.

Monnier stared at Alain Denis, who was cursing at his iPhone because there wasn't Internet. Monnier turned back toward Canzano and said, loudly, "Sordou is the perfect place to come to read. *A book.*"

Canzano smiled as he dried and checked a wineglass for spots. "Mme Le Bon is working on starting a small library. We'll have the books here, in the Jacky Bar. She's buying some special editions; books that have to do with the Mediterranean. You know, like Camus's *L'étranger.* The books will be a nice addition to my bar. I think I'll put them over there" — Canzano gestured with his head — "on the rosewood credenza."

Monnier smiled. He liked that the barman spoke of *his* bar; Monnier placed much importance on people who had pride in their work, no matter what their job. He was also impressed that the barman knew of such books; all was not lost in the French education system, at least for people of their

162

generation. "Maybe I will have another," he said. "Please."

# Chapter Fourteen:
# Ode to the Rouget
# and Saint-Pierre

The saint-pierre, with its large, flat oval body and spiky top fin, was one of the ugliest fish Émile Villey had ever seen. He didn't know why the Anglo-Saxons called it a John Dory; Mr. Dory, whoever he was, had nothing to do with Saint Peter. The fish was a bottom-feeder; its large eyes had binocular vision and excellent depth perception. When the fisherman had shown up at the dock that morning with a slew of saint-pierres, Villey was over the moon, for despite its unglamorous appearance, it was one of his favorite fish to cook, and to eat.

The chef whispered to the fish, "You're so ugly."

"Who are you talking to?" Marie-Thérèse asked as she came into the kitchen. Villey stepped aside so that the girl could see the saint-pierres lined up on his work surface.

*"Oh mon dieu!"* she exclaimed.

"Don't worry, it tastes nothing like it

looks," Villey said.

"They're awful looking!" Marie-Thérèse said. She leaned in to get a closer look. "But I do like their glittery-gold color. And they all have a birthmark." She pointed to the round dark spot — about the size of a quarter — on each fish's side.

"That's its evil eye," Villey explained. "Other fish approach it, thinking that they're looking the saint-pierre in the face, and then he swings around and opens his big mouth and, gulp!"

Marie-Thérèse stared in disgust.

"Hey," Villey said, putting a hand on her thin shoulder. "Don't worry, it won't bite you. And besides, some people claim that that spot is where Saint Peter left his thumbprint."

Marie-Thérèse smiled. "I like that story better." She straightened her back and put her hands on her hips. "Did you write tonight's menu yet?"

"Yeah, I gave it to Niki a few hours ago to type up."

Marie-Thérèse sighed, leaning against the counter.

"What's wrong?" Villey asked, taking a knife off of the counter and sharpening it. "Tired?"

"No, it's just that actor . . ."

"Alain Denis? Don't let him bother you. He's a certified idiot."

"He's so mean."

"I know. He's complained about the hotel from the moment he got here. Niki told me. It has nothing to do with you, okay? And Saturday night he didn't like the lamb and complained to Max."

"No way!" Marie-Thérèse exclaimed. "That was one of the best meals I've ever eaten in my *life*! Even reheated!"

Émile Villey laughed and tapped Marie-Thérèse playfully on the head. "Now scram and let me prepare these fish, unless you want to help clean and gut."

"Okay, okay, I'm going!"

"Too Ralph Lauren," Sylvie said.

Marine looked at herself in the full-length mirror and turned from side to side. "I like white in summer," she said.

"At least jazz up those white pants with some color." Sylvie opened the closet and took out a silk halter top of sixties psychedelia in blues, greens, and white. "This one; it matches this hotel," she said, holding it up. "Oh my God, is this a real Emilio Pucci?"

"I'm afraid so," Marine replied, taking off the white linen blouse she had been wearing and throwing it on the bed. She looked out to the terrace where Antoine Verlaque was reading and smoking a cigar.

"A gift?" Sylvie asked, motioning toward the judge.

"Yes, last time Antoine was in Paris he bought it for me."

"Nice boyfriend. Can you take off those bra straps?"

"Yes, if you'll help me," Marine said, turning so that Sylvie could unhook the straps.

"You probably don't even need the bra."

Marine laughed. "Am I that flat-chested?"

"No, of course not!"

"I'm a little too prudish not to wear a bra," Marine said. "Not like you . . ."

"Whooooooa," Sylvie said, handing Marine the Pucci halter top. "Are you referring to this afternoon?"

"No." Marine slipped the thin top over her head and then stared at her friend. She went on, "Yes. Maybe."

Sylvie looked down at the carefully restored terra-cotta floor.

"I'm sorry," Marine quickly said. "It's just that . . . you don't know anything about him."

"Have you forgotten being single?" Sylvie asked. "Did you always ask your dates their life history before having sex?"

"Sounds like you two are having an inter-esting conversation," Antoine Verlaque called from the terrace.

Marine was about to close the French doors leading to the terrace and blow her lover a kiss when a shot rang out. "Oh my God!" she said, sighing.

"It doesn't sound like the recluse listened to Max," Verlaque said, turning the page of his *Economist.* "There will be more bunny on the menu."

Marine laughed and closed the door, look-ing through the glass at her boyfriend of three years, and tried to remember what she knew of him the first few weeks they had started dating. She knew of his spectacular rise through the French judicial system partly through another lawyer friend, Jean-Marc Sauvat, who worked at the Palais de Justice with Verlaque. The first time she had visited Verlaque's apartment she had guessed at family wealth — examining magistrates were civil servants and could not afford sixteenth-century Venetian paint-ings. They had made love, in his apartment, after their third official date, long before Marine had ever met Antoine's beloved grandmother, Emmeline, or his Realtor brother, Sébastien, and she still had yet to meet his parents. And so was Sylvie's afternoon any different? Still, *it was,* but Marine couldn't put her finger on it . . . was it the boat, and the sea? The fact that they were far from the hotel that afternoon? Perhaps it was just Marine's own fear; a fear of the sea and a general malaise at being on an island. "You're right," Marine finally said to Sylvie. "I'm not sure how much I even knew about Antoine before we started sleeping together. Not a whole lot."

"Thank you," Sylvie said, bowing her head slightly. "Now turn around so that I can tie the halter behind your impossibly graceful neck, and we'll go down to the Jacky Bar for a few drinks before dinner."

Marine looked at her watch.

Sylvie said. "It's six p.m. That's a perfectly reasonable time to have a drink."

Emmanuelle Denis was waiting at the doors to the terrace, pacing, when Marine, Antoine, and Sylvie arrived for dinner at 8 p.m.

"No Brice?" Verlaque asked, approaching Mme Denis and carefully taking her by the arm.

"Nothing," she replied. She began to cry and put her head on Verlaque's shoulder. "It will be dark soon," she said to no one in particular, lifting her head up. "Thank you for looking for Brice this afternoon," she went on. "Max Le Bon told me. And he gave me Brice's hat."

"We looked for Brice around where we found the hat," Verlaque said. "But we didn't have much time; Hugo Sammut had to get the boat back."

"I've sent Hugo out again," Max Le Bon said, entering the room. "He's doing a tour of the island, by boat, hoping that he'll see the boy close to the shore." Max looked at Sylvie and then added, "Hugo had the boat out earlier today, but didn't see the boy."

"Thank you, M. Le Bon," Emmanuelle Denis said.

"If he doesn't come back tonight," Verlaque said, "I'm going to call some colleagues in Marseille and demand a search of the island." He thought to himself that he should have done it earlier in the day, but he had been sure that the boy would have been back for dinner, his tail between his legs.

Mme Denis smiled weakly and put her hand on her stomach.

Marine said, "Would you be able to eat a little something? Some fruit, perhaps . . ."

"Thank you," she answered. "I'll try. My husband is eating in his room — or I assume he is — he left me a note not to disturb him. He's . . . stressed . . . about this whole thing."

Sylvie resisted from rolling her eyes and put out her elbow for Mme Denis to take, while Marine and Antoine followed.

Eric Monnier got up from his table, as did the Hobbses, when Mme Denis walked by. Only the Viales seemed not to care about the missing boy, but it looked to Verlaque like they were in the middle of an argument.

Marie-Thérèse appeared with sheets of paper — this evening's menu — and handed one to each of the party.

"Hello there, Marie-Thérèse!" Verlaque said.

*"Bonsoir, monsieur le juge,"* the young woman answered, smiling, but then putting her hand to her mouth. She had forgotten that the judge was on vacation.

"You're a judge?" Mme Denis asked Verlaque, putting a hand on his forearm.

"Examining magistrate," he answered.

"Where?"

"Aix-en-Provence."

"Oh, not Paris . . ." Mme Denis said, sounding disappointed.

Verlaque didn't want to go any further with the conversation; he was on vacation and didn't feel like giving Mme Denis advice on divorce, which he guessed her questions were leading to.

## Menu

*Monday, July 8*

**To begin:** Freshly caught local *rouget* fish (thank you, Mr. Hobbs) prepared cold, in a ceviche style, with mango, tomato, onion, lime, ginger, and coriander salsa

**To follow:** Steamed *saint-pierre* (also freshly caught, delivered to Sordou this morning) with fennel, black olives, olive oil, and orange slivers
Or
*Lapin à Liguria:* Rabbit baked with white wine and green olives in the Italian style

Dessert:
Lavender ice cream made by our chef
Or
Peaches with *chantilly*

"Great-looking menu tonight," Verlaque said, turning the paper over in his hands.

"Although a little on the light side. Do you think there will be potatoes?"

Marine stared at the menu and tried not to laugh. She knew that Antoine was trying to lighten up the evening, and she knew that her boyfriend could eat potatoes at each of his three daily meals.

"What do you think you'll have?" Marine asked, leaning toward Mme Denis.

"Just the first course; the *rougets,*" Mme Denis answered, setting the menu down and folding her hands.

Marie-Thérèse returned to the dining room to take orders, and Verlaque turned around in his chair to face the Hobbses. "Mr. Hobbs," he said in English. "Thank you for the *rougets* this evening."

"My pleasure!" Bill Hobbs replied, beaming.

"We used to have more *rougets* in the Med," Eric Monnier added from the next table. "But with global warming and over-fishing, there are now more in the North Sea." Verlaque translated for Mr. Hobbs, and Bill Hobbs raised his arms up in mock helplessness, his right hand shaking. Shirley Hobbs quickly and gracefully moved his wineglass from the edge of the table.

Marine watched Mme Denis, who seemed thankfully distracted by the conversation among the three tables. Marine looked at the woman, not sure if she thought her to be beautiful or a monster who had had too much plastic surgery. From outward appearances Mme Denis had everything: money, a famous husband, a size 6 waist, education, and grace. But Marine saw in her eyes the sadness she so gracefully bore; although she was smiling while listening to the men talk of fish, her eyes watered, and she played nonstop with her multi-diamond wedding ring.

Sylvie kicked Marine under the table as they saw Hugo Sammut walk across the terrace and into the hotel, alone. Marine excused herself and went into the lobby, where the Le Bons were speaking with the boatman.

"No sign of him, Hugo?" Marine asked.

"Nada," Sammut replied.

"This isn't good," Max Le Bon said as he began to pace across the lobby. "Not good at all."

"Famous actor's son dies on Sordou," Cat-Cat said, folding her arms across her chest and looking out the window.

"Hey, wait a minute," Hugo Sammut said. "Don't jump to conclusions. He's camped out somewhere. No harm can come to him on Sordou; there are no wild animals, and it's warm out so he isn't going to freeze."

"Hugo's right," Marine said.

Hugo continued, "For all we know he's tying one on with old Prosper . . ."

"Hugo, since you no longer work here, you can leave your theories to yourself," Max Le Bon said.

"Max, Hugo did go out looking for the boy," Cat-Cat said. "Hugo, did you talk to Prosper?" Cat-Cat asked.

Hugo shook his head back and forth. "Knocked on his door, and on the lighthouse door, but no answer. He must have been out foraging for his dinner."

Marine looked from Hugo to the Le Bons. "Excuse me," she said. "Are you talking about the recluse? The rabbit hunter?" Marine suddenly thought of the evening's menu.

"Sordou's only full-time resident," Max Le Bon explained. "He was the lighthouse operator, as were his ancestors, until Marseille automated the lighthouse in 1986."

Cat-Cat continued, "Prosper was permitted to stay on the island, with a small stipend from the region, provided he keep the glass clean and check the lightbulbs every week. It's still an important lighthouse, after all."

"We all saw the lighthouse when we came to Sordou, from the boat," Marine said. "This Prosper may have seen Brice, no? Shouldn't we go and get him?"

Hugo Sammut looked at his ex-bosses and bit his upper lip.

"Well," Max Le Bon began. "He's a little special . . ."

Just then the group heard a commotion, and loud talking, coming from the dining room. Eric Monnier appeared in the doorway of the lobby, grinning. "I think you're needed in the dining room," he said, looking at the Le Bons. "We seem to have a . . . guest."

The Le Bons looked at each other and quickly made a move for the dining room. Monnier made a big theatrical sweeping gesture with his hand, as if to usher them in. He was now openly laughing when Marine asked him, "Who is it, for heaven's sake?" She was getting frustrated at the distraction from their conversation of the missing boy.

"I think it's Vincent van Gogh reincarnated," Monnier said, looking toward the dining room. "Yes, it's the mad Dutchman himself . . . only instead of sunflowers he seems to be carrying a dead rabbit."

# CHAPTER FIFTEEN:
## ABOUT THE RECLUSE

Marine stared at Prosper Buffa; he did indeed resemble Vincent van Gogh, although an older version of the artist who had died too young. Buffa's once-bright-red hair — with a matching scraggy beard now streaked with white — looked like it hadn't been combed or washed in weeks. He was extremely thin, his pants being held up by an old leather belt that he wore, oddly, on the outside of a tattered striped dress shirt, not through the pants' belt loops. The pants, once new, and also once navy blue, were filthy, cut off and frayed just above the ankle, making Buffa look like a shipwreck survivor. But the oddest part of his clothing was on his feet: black leather dress shoes with pointed toes that had been fashionable in the 1980s. Buffa evidently had no use for the leather supporting the ankles, so had worn them down by stepping flat on the leather each time he put them on, trans-

forming the shoes into slip-ons, like slippers.

Marine tried to guess his age, but couldn't;
somewhere between fifty-five and seventy
was the best she could do. Prosper Buffa
was in fact sixty-four. He was an only child;
born on Sordou and homeschooled on the
island as well, by his mother, a former
teacher. His father — Honoré — had inherited the job as lighthouse keeper from his
father, Pierre, and Honoré did the job well,
and with pride, until Mme Buffa died of
the flu when Prosper had been ten years
old.

And from there, things went downhill for
Honoré Buffa. Although getting supplies to
Sordou was always difficult, the supply of
vodka was sure to never run out. At the turn
of the century a Russian ship had capsized
in a freak storm, just off the island. Pierre
Buffa, Honoré's father, had managed to
save seven of the sailors, but the rest, including the captain, had perished. The ship's
cargo, much of it vodka, had run up on the
shore on the far side of the island, and
Pierre Buffa found the crates and hid them,
out of sight of his wife, Ginette, who was a
teetotaler. Now and again, on a day of
celebration, or at the end of a long hard
season, Prosper's grandfather would remove

a bottle from its hiding place and bring it to the lighthouse, where he hid it, pouring a little into a glass, savoring it (Ginette Buffa, when she saw the clear liquid in her husband's glass, and the smile on his face, knew exactly what it was, and where it came from). Years later, Prosper's father found his own father's secret, buried in the ground near the orchard that his own wife, before she fell ill, had so lovingly tended. The supply was endless, and Honoré — unlike his father — became addicted to the clear drink, washing away his sorrows in it. Prosper, by then twelve, assumed as many of the lighthouse duties as he could, taking over completely after his father's death in 1979. And when, in 1986, the government sought to automate the lighthouse, Prosper too took to the drink.

*"Mesdames et monsieurs,"* Prosper Buffa said, bowing, *"bon appétit."* Prosper was pleased with himself; he hadn't slurred his words because today, an unusual and surprising day, he had not drunk any vodka. But he would tonight; he deserved it.

"M. Buffa," Max Le Bon said, quickly approaching the recluse. "Let me escort you to my office . . ."

"Not so fast, fancy pants!" Buffa exclaimed.

Sylvie and Antoine laughed out loud, as did Eric Monnier, who had pulled up a chair at their table.

"I have here another rabbit for the chef . . . the boy you hired to cook . . ." Buffa laughed at his own joke and looked at the dining patrons, hoping for more encouraging laughter. He held the dead rabbit up by the ears for the diners to see. "Tell him Prosper can catch as many bunnies as he needs."

Delphine Viale gasped and put her napkin to her mouth.

"Will do, will do," Max Le Bon exclaimed, gritting his teeth. "Come with me, M. Buffa, and our bartender will pour you a pastis."

"Better make that a double," Monnier whispered to the others at their table. "Vincent looks like he likes a tipple. Speaking of that, we need another bottle of wine."

"Hear hear," Verlaque replied, signaling to Marie-Thérèse, who was standing at the far end of the room, her large brown eyes widened to a maximum, mesmerized by the scene. She saw the judge's finger pointing to the wine bottle, and she ran to the bar to tell Serge that he needed to find another bottle of Vermentino.

"Come along, M. Buffa," Maxime Le Bon repeated. "And you're not supposed to be shooting in the late afternoon," Le Bon hissed in Buffa's ear.

"Who was shooting?" Buffa asked. "Certainly not me."

"Come along," Le Bon repeated.

"Not so fast, I repeat, dear hotel proprietor," Buffa said, now walking around the dining room, enjoying the spotlight. Stopping at the Hobbses' table he picked up their bottle of white wine and peered at its label. Shirley and Bill Hobbs looked at each other, frozen. "Good choice," Buffa said. "Oh, the many fine Burgundies I have had in my life. . . . Such memories of Montparnasse . . ."

Monnier slapped his knee and laughed out loud. "He's never been to Paris in his life!" he cried out. "At least I would bet on it," he added.

Buffa carefully set the bottle down and winked at Mrs. Hobbs before continuing his rounds. He slowed down at Clément and Delphine Viale's table. He looked closely at Mme Viale — who still had her napkin up to her face — and then with a wave of his hand said, "You must be the Parisian. Not the person I'm looking for this evening. However, dear madame, if you get lonely, my lighthouse is just —"

"M. Buffa!" exclaimed Max Le Bon.

"That will be enough!"

"I told you," Buffa said, running his hands through his hair, his eyes suddenly looking wild. "I'm *looking for someone.*"

He walked on, stopping before Mme Denis, and, smiling, placed his gnarled, freckled right hand on his heart. He bent down on one knee. "My dear and glorious madame," he said, taking her hand and kissing it.

Emmanuelle Denis closed her eyes, trying to block her nasal passages.

"You would be Mme Denis, would you not?" Buffa asked.

"Yes, how did you know?" she asked, looking down at him.

"Because someone speaks very highly of you," Buffa said. "Not of your dim-witted husband. Him, he hates. And with good reason, might I add . . ."

Mme Denis's eyes widened and she stood up, pulling Buffa to his feet. "*Where* is my son?"

If Buffa was surprised by the woman's sudden strength, he didn't show it, but the other diners stared, open-mouthed. Antoine Verlaque put his napkin down and got up.

"No need for a show of strength, dear gentleman," Buffa said, holding his hand up toward Verlaque. "All right!" Buffa hollered in the direction of the French doors that led to the terrace. "You can show yourself now!"

Brice Dortignac walked in slowly, looking tired and even thinner, if that was possible in one night and one day. Mme Denis ran across the dining room and hugged him, crying softly. "My boy, my boy . . ."

*"Je suis desolé, maman,"* Brice said.

"And now I'll take that pastis!" Prosper Buffa yelled to Max Le Bon. "Delivery of rabbit, and teenager, done. Next: drinks." He turned and gazed around Marine and Antoine's table and stopped when he saw Sylvie. "Saw you out on the rocks today," he said, wiggling his eyebrows up and down.

Antoine Verlaque leaned back, resting his head on the wrought iron chair's cushion, and relishing the taste of his cigar, a Sir Winston. The summer night's air, much cooler on the island than on his terrace in downtown Aix, blew across his face. He could hear his friends — Marine, Sylvie, and Clément (Mme Viale had gone to bed, professing a headache) — discussing Émile Villey's deceptively simple meal, plate by plate. Every time Marine spoke Verlaque's ears perked up; even after three years, he still loved to hear her voice.

During the dessert course Bill Hobbs had sat down beside Brice, and Verlaque had watched them talking, Mr. Hobbs's hand now and again touching the boy's skinny shoulder. Brice hadn't cringed in the way other teenagers would have; instead, his head was bent down, intently listening, and he now and again looked up at the American, smiling. His mother told them that Brice's father lived in New York, and they had lived there when Brice was in grade school.

Some men were so comfortable around children, Verlaque pondered, and if they weren't, it was immediately obvious, especially to the child. Bill Hobbs had that gift, or genuine interest, in the young. Verlaque's father did not, but his grandfather had. His commissioner back in Aix, Bruno Paulik, although from outward appearances looked like some hardened medieval warrior, was a kitten around children; Verlaque had seen Paulik on the job with distressed children, and with his own ten-year-old daughter, Léa. Paulik had sent Verlaque a text message a few hours before they arrived on Sordou. It had said, "Enjoy your much-deserved holiday. Think of me here in Aix with soaring temperatures and hordes of tourists. The grapes will be well on their way by the time you get back; Hélène has done miracles bringing them back to life, and Léa says they look like little green pearls. *Bonnes vacances,* Bruno." Antoine Verlaque hadn't erased the text message as he usually did, but kept it and read it again before coming down to dinner. As the inheritor of a flour fortune, Verlaque had more money than he knew what to do with and had recently bought a vineyard and crumbling farmhouse, giving it to Bruno Paulik and his wife, Hélène. Hélène Paulik was a rising star in the French wine world, but without a family fortune she was destined to make someone else's wine. Verlaque had done enough research that he knew he might never make money on the vineyard, but it would be Hélène's wine, not someone else's, and he had been thrilled to give her that chance. The money was no good to anyone sitting in a Parisian bank, and the funny part of it was, there was still much more.

He thought of Bruno, his father, grandfather, and men like Alain Denis. And where was Antoine Verlaque in this lineup of men? He had little experience with children, and they sometimes frightened him more than hardened criminals; but perhaps it wasn't fear, but merely worry about his own inexperience? Why not learn from others? He could begin to treat children, whose ever they were, as he had been treated by Charles and Emmeline, his paternal grandparents: with attention, intelligence, and kindness. He looked over at Marine and she was staring at him, smiling. She winked and his heart melted.

Serge Canzano came out onto the terrace with a bottle of champagne. "The champagne is on the house," Canzano said, popping the cork. "In celebration of the boy's return." He gently set the bottle down — giving it a twist — into a silver bucket and walked away, looking forward to cleaning up the bar and getting into bed with volume three of his Napoleon biography.

"The champagne is also in hopes that we keep our mouths shut about Prosper Buffa when we get off Sordou," Verlaque said, leaning over and taking the bottle out of the champagne bucket and pouring, beginning with Marine's and Sylvie's flutes. He looked up at Clément Viale, remembering that his old friend had invested in Sordou's hotel. "Sorry, mate. That came out wrong; I was completely amused by the island's resident madman."

"As was I," Viale said, a little unconvincingly.

"Have you ever seen a kid eat so much?" Sylvie asked.

"What's going to become of him?" Marine asked. "His stepfather isn't going to change. It's only a matter of time before he runs off again."

"Where is M. Dortignac, Brice's father?" Sylvie asked.

"Emmanuelle told us that he lives in New York," Marine replied. "He's a commodities trader."

"Ah, that's why the kid speaks such good English," Clément said.

Verlaque pictured Brice's father, yelling down the phone in some Wall Street high-rise. Rotten with kids, he imagined. Alain Denis was obviously in competition with other men and had no interest in children. What made women like Emmanuelle Denis, obviously intelligent and strong — as she had proven this evening with Prosper Buffa — choose men like Denis?

"Bill Hobbs has offered to take Brice fishing," Marine continued. "I overheard them talking about it during dessert."

"Adorable," Sylvie said. "Maybe Brice can give the Hobbses some fashion advice. So, did Brice tell Prosper Buffa *all* about us? I certainly got that impression." Sylvie closed her eyes for the briefest second; she didn't care that old Prosper had seen her and Hugo making love, but she cringed at the thought that the young teen might have also been watching. She prayed not.

"I did too," Verlaque said, puffing on his cigar and looking up at the sky. "And no wonder. We're a pretty odd lot."

"Speak for yourself, Dough Boy," Clément said. The group laughed.

"Was that your first meeting with Prosper Buffa?" Verlaque asked Clément Viale.

"Yes," Viale replied, sipping his champagne. "I knew that there was a former lighthouse keeper on the island, but had never seen him before. And what a name! Prosper! As if!"

"Oh, I don't know," Marine said. "Without wanting to sound corny, maybe M. Buffa *is* prosperous, in a nonmonetary way."

"You're right, Marine," Sylvie said. "You do sound corny."

The group laughed again. "Imagine," Verlaque said. "Vincent van Gogh really did look like that. And nobody spoke to him . . . or very few people. The poor soul. I think of that every time I go to Arles . . . expecting him to appear from around a corner, muttering to himself."

"And to think that he only sold one painting, to Theo, his brother," Sylvie added. She looked down into her champagne glass and reflected on her successful career as an art photographer. Thanks to her representative galleries in Berlin and London she made enough money to have paid for her apartment in Aix and secure her daughter Charlotte's future.

"Surely you don't mean we should befriend our island recluse?" Clément asked, laughing nervously.

"Brice obviously did," Marine said. She picked up the bottle and refilled everyone's glasses. "To recluses, and eccentrics, everywhere," she said, lifting her glass in the air.

# CHAPTER SIXTEEN:
# A CHAMPION SWIMMER

A seagull's scream pierced the morning clear sky, waking Verlaque and Bonnet up at 9:10 a.m. Verlaque moaned. *"Oiseau de merde,"* he said. "What is the seagull's purpose on earth?" He sighed and rolled over.

"Antoine, it's after nine a.m.!" Marine said, looking at her watch and then putting it back on the nightstand. She hugged Verlaque and then got out of bed, putting on the housecoat supplied by the hotel. "We'll be the last ones downstairs for breakfast."

"All right, all right," Verlaque said. "I hate breakfast, anyway." He threw back the linen sheet and then quickly put it back in place, forgetting that he was naked. "You naughty girl," he said, looking at Marine, who was standing at the foot of the bed.

"Great night last night," she said, smiling. "Thank you."

"Thank you too," he said, once again throwing back the sheet and this time getting out of bed.

Marine walked over and hugged him. "I love your smell," she said.

Verlaque buried his head in her curly auburn hair and was about to kiss her when another call rang out. "That was a woman, not a seagull," Marine said, pulling away from the judge and looking toward the terrace.

"Someone doesn't like the coffee here?" Verlaque said.

Marine opened the French doors and stood outside, leaning against the balcony's railing. She couldn't see anything, but she could hear the banging of doors and rushing footsteps.

The scream now sounded like sobbing, and loud voices wafted up to their room, coming from the hotel's terrace. "Let's go," Verlaque said, opening a drawer, pulling out the first clothes within reach, and quickly getting dressed.

Marine did the same, throwing on a beach dress over her head, and jumping into a pair of clean underwear. "We smell like sex, I'm sure," she said. "We'll have to shower later."

"Either no one will smell it," Verlaque said, opening the room's door and letting

Marine pass through, "or everyone will."

Coming down the hall was Eric Monnier, holding his black notebook in his hand. "Did you hear those screams?" he asked.

"Yes," Verlaque said.

"They were coming from outside," Marine added.

"It doesn't sound good," Monnier said. "Stupidly obvious thing to say. Sorry."

On the stairway down to the lobby they ran into Clément Viale, who was still in the process of buttoning up his shirt. "Horrible sounds!" he said. "What's going on?"

The lobby was deserted, and through the dining room they could see that the Jacky Bar was as well. The glass doors leading to the terrace had been propped wide open, and the foursome made their out.

"What on earth?" Verlaque asked. He did a quick take, and it seemed that almost the entire staff, and guests, were present, standing or sitting on the terrace. The tables had been set for breakfast and were strewn with croissant crumbs and spots of jam and unfinished cups of coffee.

Marie-Thérèse was sitting in a chair, sobbing. Émile Villey was kneeling before her, quietly speaking. An older woman, wearing a crisply ironed old-fashioned maid's uniform, and whom Marine had said hello to in the halls, was sitting beside Marie-Thérèse, with her arm around the girl.

Max Le Bon, along with Hugo Sammut and Serge Canzano, was standing off to the side. Max quickly walked over to Verlaque and said, "Marie-Thérèse has just had the fright of her life, I'm afraid."

"What happened?" Verlaque asked.

"It's Alain Denis," Max said, whispering. "Marie-Thérèse went for a walk this morning, along the cliffs on the south side of the island, and found him . . . his body, I mean . . ."

"What?" Verlaque hissed. "Dead?"

Max nodded, and looked in the direction of Marie-Thérèse.

"What exactly happened?" Verlaque asked.

"We don't know," Le Bon answered. "Cat-Cat and Niki have gone to tell Mme Denis, who's still in her room."

"And Brice?" Verlaque asked.

"Fishing," Max replied. "With M. Hobbs. On the other side of the island."

Hugo Sammut came over and said good morning to Verlaque and Marine. "I heard Marie-Thérèse screaming from my cabin. We should go," he said. "To . . . the body."

"Of course," Verlaque answered. Eric Monnier and Clément Viale came and offered their help. "Thank you," Verlaque said.

"We may as well all go, since we don't know what we're going to see when we get there. What did Marie-Thérèse say, exactly?"

"I couldn't make heads or tails out of it," Max replied. "She can't stop crying. I only know that he's on the south shore . . . where the steep cliffs are, on a small beach . . . dead. Mme Poux," he continued, looking over in the direction of Marie-Thérèse. "Could you please . . ."

"Certainly," Mme Poux said. "We'll take care of her."

"I'll stay here too," Serge Canzano said. "I'll clear up the breakfast terrace."

"Come, Marie-Thérèse," Émile said, gently lifting the girl out of the chair with Mme Poux's help. "Let's get you into a comfortable armchair with a cup of tea." Émile nodded in the direction of the judge.

"Very well," Verlaque said. "Let's go, then."

As they walked, Marine thought to herself that if anyone had been watching their group they would have looked very odd as they walked in single file, even though the cliff path was at times wide enough for two or even three people. Hugo Sammut was in the lead, being the most familiar with the walk, with Max behind him, then Verlaque,

194

Marine, Clément Viale, and finally — coughing as he stumbled along the path — Eric Monnier.

Hugo stopped after they had been walking for fifteen minutes and turned around to speak. "In just a few minutes, we'll veer left and descend, on a rough, steep path, toward the south shore and a little cove. I'm fairly certain that's where Marie-Thérèse was. There's a small stone beach there, and some flat rocks that are nice for sitting on. I go there often myself. Oh, Mme Hobbs . . ."

The group turned around to see Shirley Hobbs walking quickly toward them. "I heard the commotion on the terrace," she said. "The bartender told me what happened; his English is quite good!"

"Yes, Mrs. Hobbs," Verlaque replied in English. He didn't like the excitement in her voice. "But this is really not —"

Mrs. Hobbs waved her hand in the air. "I insist on coming," she said. "I'm a trained nurse. That young waitress was in hysterics. . . . I heard her wailing. . . . Perhaps the actor's not dead and needs medical attention?"

"Very well," Verlaque said. *"Elle est infirmière,"* he told the rest of the group.

"A nurse could be useful," Hugo said.

They continued walking and Marine took the opportunity to speak to Verlaque while the path was still wide enough. "Someone will have to go and find Bill and Brice," she whispered.

"I know," Verlaque said. "But since they left so early this morning, I think they'll be back at the hotel at the same time we will . . . around noon. Where is Sylvie?"

"She could sleep through an earthquake," Marine said. "In fact, she once did, when she was in China for a photo conference."

"My question is," Verlaque whispered, "what was Marie-Thérèse doing down here in the early morning?"

The walk down the path, although steep, took less than five minutes. The stone beach that Hugo had told them about was tiny — about twenty feet across — and to the right and left of it were limestone rocks jutting out into the sea. And there in the middle of the beach was Alain Denis, lying facedown, wearing his usual bright-pink linen shirt and white linen shorts. The group instinctively rushed toward the body, stopping short about a yard away, for the gray and white stones surrounding the body were stained dark red. Hugo leaned down on one knee, as did Verlaque.

Eric Monnier stood beside Marine and

said, under his breath, "Dogs the world over will be in mourning." He walked around the body and looked out at the sea, his hands held behind his back.

Marine ignored the teacher's comment and squatted down as well, looking at the actor.

"What a mess," Shirley Hobbs said.

Verlaque smiled slightly; he would have used the word "kerfuffle"; it had been one of his English grandmother's favorite expressions. Mrs. Hobbs started to kneel down and Verlaque put out his thick hand, as if to protect her, but the American took his hand and gave it a tight squeeze. "I was a nurse during the Vietnam War," she said matter-of-factly. "I've seen much worse." Marine and the others, understanding the word "Vietnam," slightly bowed and nodded, showing their respect.

Shirley Hobbs looked down at Denis and said, "He's been shot in the head." She pointed to the right-hand side of the actor's head. "Small gun, I'd say," she continued. "Close range. But I'll take his pulse all the same." She lifted the actor's arm and put her hand on his wrist. "Cold," she said. "And no pulse. I'd say he was here all night."

Verlaque translated for the group, but left

out Mrs. Hobbs's guesswork about the kind of gun and distance of shot.

"The shot," Marine said. "Last night . . ."

"Prosper told me he wasn't shooting last night," Max said. "I didn't believe him."

"The autopsy will tell us more," Verlaque said, his mind racing. He looked around and saw that Hugo was slowly walking around the body, looking down at the stones. "Anything, Hugo?"

"Nada," Hugo said. "No gun, and no footprints, not even his . . . but there are so many stones . . ."

"The gun wouldn't be here, would it?" Max Le Bon asked.

"It would if it was suicide," Marine said.

"Oh," Le Bon said, looking down at the body. "That didn't occur to me."

Verlaque asked, "Hugo, did Propser ever tell you about Alain Denis being here in the old days?"

Hugo shrugged. "He mumbled something about Denis being here, yeah," he replied. "But was typically vague, and when I pressed him, he shut up."

"Was it in the sixties?" Verlaque asked.

"I had the impression it was before that," Le Bon replied. "Before Denis was known."

"I got the same impression," Hugo added.

"I'll talk to Prosper later," Verlaque said.

He made a note to call Paulik and have him find out more about Prosper Buffa.

"Do we just leave him like this?" Clément Viale asked, frowning, looking at the body.

"I'm afraid so," Verlaque said. "But we can cover his body."

"When we go back up to the hotel," Hugo said, "I'll ask Mme Poux for an old sheet."

"Thank you, Hugo," Max said. "And I assume I'll be the one to telephone the police."

"If you wouldn't mind," Verlaque said. "And if someone could be at the dock to greet them when they arrive. . . . They'll need to be brought down here by the path." Using his handkerchief as a glove, Verlaque reached into Alain Denis's shorts pockets, trying not to disturb the body. He pulled out the hotel room key out of the right-hand pocket. There was nothing in the left.

"What in the world was he doing on this secluded beach?" Mrs. Hobbs asked. "He must have been lured out here, by his murderer."

Verlaque nodded and was thankful that Mrs. Hobbs was speaking in English.

"We'll go back up now," Max said. "You're staying here with the body, I assume."

"Yes," Verlaque answered.

"I am too," Marine added.

"Then I'll have someone bring you down your breakfast," Max said.

"That won't be necessary," Mme Poux said. She had just arrived and was carrying a small basket.

"How did you know where we'd be?" Max asked.

"Marie-Thérèse is now able to speak calmly," she answered. "And in full sentences. Émile is with her, so Serge made a thermos of tea and Émile has wrapped up some scones."

"That was very thoughtful," Verlaque said. "I'm going to stay here, with Mlle Bonnet."

"Serge has hot drinks for the rest of you, in the Jacky Bar," Mme Poux said.

"Well," Eric Monnier said, turning toward the path. "I'll be off."

"He's added a fortifier," she added. "In yours too, Judge Verlaque."

"Much obliged," Verlaque said, taking the basket.

"Mme Poux," Max Le Bon asked. "Do you know how Mme Denis is doing?"

Yolaine Poux blinked and nodded. "She's very upset," she said. "Your wife, M. Viale, is with her, and has given her a sleeping pill."

"Delphine has lots of those," Clément said dryly.

"I assume he's dead?" she asked, looking down at the body.

"Yes. He was shot," Verlaque said. "Probably last night."

She looked up at the others, and Marine noticed that the housekeeper's eyes were watery. But it could have been the sea air and breeze, Marine realized. Mme Poux lifted a white sheet out of a cloth shoulder bag she had been carrying. "I thought we might be needing one of these," she said, and she bent over and with Verlaque's help placed it gently over Alain Denis.

"What in the world was he doing down here?" Max Le Bon mumbled, echoing Shirley Hobbs's same question.

"Perhaps he came for a swim," Mme Poux said, staring at the body. "He was a champion swimmer," she continued. "When he was young. Not especially graceful, but a good strong swimmer."

# CHAPTER SEVENTEEN:
# A PRAYER SONG

Bruno Paulik's chest swelled when the director of Aix-en-Provence's conservatoire announced Léa's name. The police commissioner took his wife Hélène's hand and squeezed it. The conservatoire — a former seventeenth-century mansion in Aix-en-Provence's chic neighborhood the Mazarin — wasn't air-conditioned, and Hélène lifted her tanned legs slightly off the wooden chair, whose seat was covered in cheap vinyl.

The pianist, who often accompanied the Pauliks' ten-year-old daughter, turned to the page of his songbook where a Post-it was marked "Léa." Gabriel Fauré's *"En prière"* was one of Bruno Paulik's favorite hymns: a song that Léa had been practicing for eight weeks, and how well — or poorly — she sang it on this hot July day would decide if she progressed to the level of the state-funded conservatoire's choral school.

Léa walked slowly up the stage's four

wooden steps, and Bruno thought of how lucky they were — their only child did well at school and was passionate about music (Mozart above all else). He loved his wife even more than on their wedding day. The Syrah and Cinsault grapes were ripening in the sun in *their* vineyard; they had owned the vines for less than a year thanks to a generous gift from Bruno Paulik's boss, Antoine Verlaque. The judge had made it clear that his was a silent financial partnership — Hélène had total control of the wines — but he remained enthusiastic and eager for almost daily news of the grapes. He had even promised to help in September's harvest. Picturing his boss leaning over the vines in his 500-euro English leather shoes made Bruno grin, but he didn't for a second doubt Antoine Verlaque's stamina and physical strength. Bruno was a farm boy from the Luberon, and his wife, Hélène, was one of Provence's star winemakers, but they could never have purchased their own grapes if it hadn't been for Verlaque's investment (something that the judge insisted on calling it).

The pianist began, and Léa pursed her lips in concentration. Slowly, her young soprano voice filled the room. Paulik's eyes watered; he couldn't believe the sounds that were coming out of a young girl's mouth, and it was their daughter, their love child. He sat as still as possible and listened with every muscle in his body tense.

And so he flinched, bumping Hélène's knee, when his professional cell phone began to vibrate. He slipped his hand into the inside left jacket pocket and slowly took out the phone, turning the vibrating mode off. It was Antoine Verlaque; the week before leaving on vacation the judge had given Paulik the name and number of the hotel where he and Marine would be staying, and the commissioner had registered it into his phone. Sordou: that was the name that flashed on his phone's tiny screen. Paulik tried not to cringe when he saw Mme de Montague looking over at him and frowning. He could just imagine what the posh mother of five was thinking: *quel paysan!* Hélène saw his stricken face and put up a hand with one finger pointing in the air, and mouthed the words "one minute." Verlaque could wait, and Paulik closed his eyes to concentrate, trying to make up for the precious few seconds he missed.

Bruno, who was an opera lover, silently noted that Léa ended on a rather too-high note. But he was thrilled for her, and by the sound of the applause, including that coming from the conservatoire's director, who was now on his feet, he could tell the audition had gone well. Léa had been the last performer, and Bruno moved the chairs out of his way to hug her and then get out of the stuffy room and call Verlaque as soon as possible. Mme de Montague raised an eyebrow when he squeezed his big rugby-player body past her, and he smiled and said, "Wasn't that terrific?" Hélène was right behind him, and they almost ran to meet Léa. He and Hélène gathered Léa in their arms, and he was sure he could feel his daughter's heart pounding.

"How did that feel?" Hélène asked, kissing Léa on the forehead.

"The worst part was walking up onto the stage," Léa replied. "Then, as soon as I began singing, it felt good. Even really good."

Paulik beamed and stopped himself from imagining an adult Léa singing at La Scala in Milan. "*Chérie,* I have a quick, very important call to make. I'll be right back."

"To Judge Verlaque?" she asked, smiling.

Paulik nodded up and down.

"Okay then," Léa said. "Tell him I say hi."

The hotel was eerily quiet. No jazz music came from the Jacky Bar, and the guests all seemed to have gone back to their rooms while the Marseille police examined the cove and the body of Alain Denis. Marie-Thérèse had stayed in the kitchen, watching Émile cut vegetables for lunch, but he was unusually quiet and refused all offers of her help. After an hour of sitting on a stool in the corner she got up and said that she was going to set the tables in the dining room and terrace, and Émile replied with a grunt.

Marie-Thérèse loved the dining room and sometimes pretended that it was her own. Not a dining room in her house, but a dining room in her hotel, one that she would one day share with her husband — someone like Émile, who was talented, hardworking, and kind. She loved the marble floors and white linens, and as she passed a table she flattened down a tablecloth that had buckled. She opened the terrace doors and walked out, setting up the parasols one by one as there was no wind today. As she was cranking up one of the umbrellas she paused and looked down over the edge of the terrace. She could just see Sordou's harbor, where uniformed policemen were coming and going, like ants, she thought. Letting out a big sigh, Marie-Thérèse went back into the dining room to get linen napkins out of the buffet and opened it up to find only five. She'd have to go to the laundry room and get more from Mme Poux. She walked down the hall and as she walked she made a mental note of all she had to do before lunch — ask Niki for today's menu; get wineglasses from Serge and set them on the tables; double-check the salt cellars and pepper mills — there was a fourth thing, and she stopped, thinking that would help jog her memory, when she heard the Le Bons talking.

"I can't believe you'd think of his death in such a way," Max Le Bon said.

"I'm being realistic," Cat-Cat answered. "You're the dreamer in this relationship, remember."

*"Oui, chérie,"* Le Bon replied, sighing. "*I* wanted Sordou, as you remind me of daily."

"Well, we have Sordou now, like it or not," Cat-Cat answered. "And Alain Denis's death will bring us publicity."

Marie-Thérèse leaned against the wall and closed her eyes. She knew — everyone knew — that Sordou was in "Phase One" as Émile called it, and the hotel's investors were waiting to see how this first season went before contributing more money to finish construction on the two remaining wings. But the Le Bons hadn't managed to fill the hotel — only seven of the eight rooms were booked this week, and only six next week. As Émile had told her, Sordou, beautiful as it was, was too close to Marseille, too far from Saint-Tropez, had a limited menu and only eight rooms, and no nightclubs or boutiques. "What about the Jacky Bar?" Marie-Thérèse had questioned Émile.

Émile had buckled over his chopping block, laughing.

She went on, "When I have a hotel . . ."

"Oh yeah?"

"Yes, Émile," Marie-Thérèse had calmly replied. "I'm going to have a bar just like the Jacky, and play nice soft jazz like Serge does."

Cat-Cat Le Bon's voice caused Marie-Thérèse to open her eyes. She knew she should keep moving along the hall, toward the laundry room, but it was as if she were frozen. She also didn't want her bosses to see her.

"He was an awful guest," Cat-Cat said. "And if his death can bring us some notoriety, then I'm thankful."

The telephone rang. "There you go," Max said. "More guests!"

"Don't be daft," Cat-Cat replied. "Nobody even knows yet."

Marie-Thérèse coughed and loudly banged her feet as she walked, hoping she was making an impression that she had just arrived.

"Marie-Thérèse," Max said when he stepped out of his office. "How are you? Are you feeling better?"

Relieved, she stumbled out a *"Oui, merci"* and hurried along to find Mme Poux.

Cat-Cat came out to stand beside her husband. "The commissioner of Aix wants to speak to Judge Verlaque," she said. "He's holding."

"He'll have to call back," Max said. "The judge is down at the cove."

"Did she hear us?" Cat-Cat whispered, looking down the hallway toward the laundry room.

"Every word, I would imagine."

"Small gun at close range?" Verlaque asked, trying not to too obviously stare into Dr. Cohen's dark eyes.

"Yes," she replied, turning slightly to look at the lifeless body of Alain Denis. "There doesn't seem to have been any physical violence, or a fight, but I'll know more when I get him to the lab at La Timone." She looked out to sea and then turned back to Verlaque. "Can a boat get in here?"

Verlaque was about to hazard an answer when Hugo Sammut was at his side. "You'll be able to better answer that than me, Hugo," Verlaque said.

Hugo nodded. "It's too shallow for any kind of proper boat, except a dinghy perhaps," he said. "But a larger motorboat can come into the entry of the cove and stop very close to that cliff to the east." He pointed, and Dr. Cohen and Antoine Verlaque looked. "Do you see that large white rock, touching the water, just below where there's a small pine tree growing out of the cliff?" he asked. The doctor and judge nodded. "That can be used as a step; you'd hop off the boat and then walk toward this beach on a small path that hugs the cliff, just about three feet off the water. It's doable, even for someone not very sporty." He looked at Verlaque.

"I guess that means that M. Denis's body will have to be taken back to the main harbor by that path we came down," Dr. Cohen said.

"I'm afraid so," Verlaque said.

"But the real problem," Hugo went on, "was yesterday's wind."

Verlaque looked at him. "In the early evening the sea was rough, wasn't it?"

Hugo nodded up and down. "Yep. Too rough to get into this cove, and rough enough that a sailor wouldn't risk even leaving the port on the mainland. I sailed more often when I lived on the Atlantic than I do in Provence. People don't realize how windy it is here."

"So a swimmer couldn't get in here?" Verlaque asked.

"What, with the gun wrapped in plastic, taped to his chest?" Hugo asked, laughing.

"Something to that effect . . ."

"No way, José."

Hugo stepped aside as two policemen carefully lifted Denis's lifeless body onto a stretcher and began making their way up the path. Two other policemen followed, to take a turn carrying the body, with the crime photographer bringing up the rear.

"After you." Verlaque gestured to Dr. Cohen. "I'll wait for your phone call from Marseille," he said. "Thank you for coming out to Sordou."

"Don't mention it," she replied. She turned back to look at the sea; today it was as smooth as glass. "I can imagine it's heavenly to spend a week here."

Verlaque nodded. "It was," he replied.

"Fifteen for two points," Marine said, laying a five of hearts on top of the jack Eric Monnier had opened with. She moved her tiny colored peg along two holes in the hotel's wooden cribbage board. *"Merde,"* Monnier mumbled. He then laid down a five on top of hers and said, smiling, "Twenty for two points."

"Twenty-five for six points," Marine said, quickly laying down another five.

*"Merde!"* Monnier said louder this time. "And don't worry, I don't have another five. Go. I can't go any further."

She laid down a six. "Thirty-one for two points."

Monnier groaned. He turned the cards over and reopened, playing an eight.

Marine slapped a seven on top. "Fifteen for two points."

Monnier played his last card, a ten. "Twenty-five for one tiny point. Well played."

Marine had dealt so Monnier counted his hand first. Using the starter card, a four, he had four points. Marine, on the other hand, had a double run, plus two combinations of fifteen using the starter card and the fives and six in her hand. "Fourteen points," she said, pegging.

"And now you get to count your crib," Monnier said, sighing sarcastically.

Marine flipped her second hand over. She had a queen, a king, a two, and a three. "Fifteen for two, fifteen for four, and a run of three makes seven points. Not bad."

"I gave you the two and three," Monnier said. "That was asking for trouble."

"Yes, considering how many ten-spot cards there are in a deck," Marine said, smiling.

"You're ruthless," Monnier replied, leaning back in his chair and folding his arms across his chest. "I'm going to get one of Serge's Bloody Marys. I think the vitamins will do me good. I need some brain power. Would you like one?"

"Yes, thank you," Marine said, shuffling the cards for the next hand. Monnier slowly got up, and Marine turned and watched him walk slowly to the bar; Eric Monnier didn't seem the kind of man who ever rushed. He walked slowly, spoke carefully and slowly, played cards slowly. Monnier and the barman were now laughing as the drinks were being made, and Marine felt lucky to be on Sordou, despite Alain Denis's murder.

Monnier came back carrying the tall Bloody Marys and gave one to Marine with a little bow. "I had no idea I'd be outwitted at cribbage," he said, sitting down.

Marine smiled. "My mother taught me to peg like that," she said. "You can get ahead that way."

"You don't peg *well,*" Monnier said. "You peg ruthlessly. You're a killer. Oops, sorry."

"Are you afraid?" Marine asked, trying to sound casual, and cutting the deck so that Monnier could flip over the starter card. He turned over a queen and set it on the cribbage board.

"You mean being here? After Alain Denis's death?"

"Yes," she said, watching Monnier deal. "Somehow I'm not," she continued, "and I get the feeling not many of us are." She looked at Monnier for an expression, but couldn't see one. "Have we seen too much of this kind of thing on film and are now anesthetized?"

"Perhaps," Monnier said, frowning as he looked at his cards. "Do keep in mind the nice cards I gave you for *your* crib."

Marine smiled and quickly understood that he didn't want to talk about the murder. No one did. Her thoughts were confirmed when Monnier asked, "Were you an only child?"

"Yes. How did you know?"

"I was too," Monnier replied. "So I can usually tell. I picture you sitting at the kitchen table, playing cribbage with your mother, waiting for your father to get home from the university, or law office . . ."

"Hospital." She thought she saw Monnier flinch. "Papa is a doctor."

"I won't pry anymore," Monnier said, staring at his cards. "I'm determined to out-peg you this time."

# CHAPTER EIGHTEEN:
# PAULIK, AND SCORES OF
# JOURNALISTS, ARRIVE

Antoine Verlaque looked out onto the shimmering blue sea, thankful that almost every birthday his brother gave him an expensive pair of sunglasses. "I'm told that a fisherman named Isnard will be coming later with provisions," he said to a young policeman who was standing on the dock, looking at the sea with binoculars.

"Yes, sir," the policeman replied, letting the binoculars fall loosely by their strap around his neck, then looking at the judge.

"Given the celebrity status of the deceased, it won't be long before journalists try to get here," Verlaque said.

The policeman nodded. "We have the dock covered as per your instructions; no one on or off unless they can show their law badges."

"Except the fisherman," Verlaque said, rubbing his stomach. "We need food."

The policeman grinned. "Understood,"

he said. Looking across at the sea, and then up at the hotel, perched on its cliff, its pink surface turning almost red in the afternoon sun, he added, "Beautiful place."

"It certainly is."

A boat with a flashing light sped toward Sordou's harbor then slowed down and stopped beside the blue coast guard's boat that was poised at the mouth of the harbor. After a minute or two's discussion between the captains of the two boats it started up again. The closer it got, the more Verlaque could make out its blue police markings. "Here's the commissioner, right on time," the policeman said. When the boat was within twenty feet the judge could see the top of the commissioner's bald head. Bruno Paulik's sunglasses reflected the afternoon sun and his hands tightly gripped the boat's dashboard.

The boat came so quickly it appeared as if it wouldn't be able to stop in time, but slowed down just feet before the dock. The driver — a rookie policeman who had grown up on the sea — expertly pulled it into place. Paulik quickly hopped off and shook hands with Verlaque.

"How's your tummy?" Verlaque asked.

Paulik peered at the judge over his sunglasses. "Are you teasing me?"

"No, not at all," Verlaque replied with a smirk on his face. "I just know that you get carsick."

"I'm fine," Paulik replied as they began walking up to the hotel. "Now that my feet are on dry land."

Verlaque laughed. "I'm sorry that I interrupted Léa's concert. Thanks for getting here so fast."

"She had just finished."

"How did she do? Fauré's 'Prayer,' right?"

"Yeah, that's it. She did wonderfully, passed with flying colors," Paulik replied. "How did you know what she sang?"

"She sang some of it for me," Verlaque replied, smiling. "Last time I was at your place. We were walking in the vineyard checking things out. Speaking of that, how are the grapes? Do we need rain?"

"Perfect," Paulik replied. He looked up at the hotel and whistled, then said, "We had record amounts of rainfall this spring, so even though it hasn't rained in almost two months, the grapes are fine. They're grooving the hot sun and their rocky soil."

Verlaque shook his head back and forth. "Amazing."

"How is Marine?"

"She's just finished playing cards with a retired schoolteacher from Aix," Verlaque answered. "She no doubt worked her magic on him."

"Marine could sell ice to an Eskimo," Paulik said. "Has she been making the rounds?"

"I think she's befriended almost everyone here. She's chatted up the deceased's stepson and knows what he's reading."

"What, then?"

*"Death in Venice."*

Paulik whistled.

"Marine quickly told me an interesting theory," Verlaque continued. "That the stepson, Brice, may be protecting his mother."

Paulik nodded, looking at the flowers that lined the path. "You told me on the phone that Brice was at the murder scene earlier that day."

"Yes," Verlaque replied. "Marine and I found his hat. But she thinks that he could have planted it there, for us to find."

"Thus leading our suspicions toward him and away from his mother."

"Exactly."

"Sounds heroic," Paulik said.

"That's what Marine said. 'Romantic' was her term."

"Let's carefully compare the mother's and son's statements, then," Paulik said. He stopped and stretched his arms out. "It feels like it's about ten degrees cooler here than in Aix."

"It is," Verlaque replied. "It's paradise." He was getting tired of telling people how beautiful Sordou was.

"Except when film stars are murdered."

"Except when film stars are murdered," Verlaque repeated. "I'm glad you're here," he added, looking at his commissioner.

Paulik paused, as if he didn't know how to reply to his boss's compliment. "Figures that Marseille's two commissioners would be on vacation at the same time."

Verlaque laughed.

Paulik went on, "One of my brothers — the dentist in Carpentras — just moved into a new house with a swimming pool. He called a local pool maintenance company to get someone out to show him the ropes, but they couldn't come for a week and a half. They were understaffed; the boss was away on summer holidays."

Verlaque stopped in his tracks. "The owner of a pool company takes a vacation during their only peak season?"

"Yep."

"God help this country."

"Well, I for one wouldn't want to live anywhere else."

A rumbling of motors, getting louder and louder, stopped the commissioner's defense of his homeland, and both men turned around at the top of the hotel's stairs and looked at the sea. Three boats had appeared at the mouth of the harbor, and seeing the coast guard's boat each one stopped and dropped anchor. More were coming toward Sordou. The young policeman on the dock was speaking to his colleagues via a VHF walkie-talkie with one hand and watching the new arrivals with his binoculars in the other. He then ran up the stairs to join Verlaque and Paulik. "Journalists taking photographs," he said.

"Already?" Verlaque asked no one in particular.

"They got here almost as quickly as I did," Paulik added.

"A leak?" the young officer suggested.

Verlaque suddenly remembered interrupting Marie-Thérèse in the Le Bons' office; she had been whispering on the telephone, quickly hanging up when he had walked into the room.

He looked at Paulik and rolled his eyes. *"Merde."*

"Don't worry," the policeman said. "They won't get on the island." He quickly added, winking, "Except for Isnard."

221

"Thank you."

"Who's Isnard?" Paulik asked.

"Our dinner."

"Good thing we can still drink," Sylvie said, holding her mojito in her hands. "So which one of us do you think did Alain Denis in?" she asked.

"Sylvie!" Marine said.

"Hugo told me that the murderer couldn't have come to the cove by boat," Sylvie said. "Or even swum here, as the sea was too rough."

"I was afraid of that," Marine said. "There's another thing," she went on. "It would have been difficult for an outsider to contact Denis to get him down to that cove at a specific time."

Sylvie looked over at her friend with a puzzled expression.

"No cell phones or Internet," Marine said.

"Now you're freaking me out!" Sylvie said, looking over her shoulder.

Marine made a mental note to ask the Le Bons and Niki if there had been any phone calls for Alain Denis on the hotel's landline, or if he had received any letters.

Sylvie made a loud slurping noise and played with the mint sprig in her drink. "My money is on his wifey."

"I bet on the unhappy stepson."

"Marine! I'm shocked!"

"Hey, two can play at that game," Marine said. She didn't want to tell Sylvie about her new theory. She looked down at her glass of white wine, which was now empty. "Another one?"

"Let me treat you, ladies," said Clément Viale, who was now standing beside their terrace chairs.

"Thank you!" Sylvie exclaimed. "I'll have a mojito."

"And let me guess," he said, looking down at Marine, smiling. "You're drinking a white Burgundy."

"That's right," she answered, shielding her eyes from the sun with her hand. "It's a Mâcon Villages."

"Oh dear," Viale said. "Let me get a splashier Burgundy for you. We need to have some fun around here," Viale said. "My wife won't come out of our room, and Emmanuelle . . . Mme Denis . . . has been given sleeping pills."

"How did Brice take it?" Marine asked, since Clément Viale seemed to be the news keeper.

"Harder than one would have thought," he answered, shrugging.

Sylvie said, "Marine was just saying —"

"Thanks for the drinks offer," Marine quickly cut in.

"One mojito, and one fine Meursault, coming up," Viale said. "Mind if I join you? It looks like Antoine is going to be busy over the next few days." He looked down at Marine's thin tanned legs and smiled.

Marine and Sylvie exchanged quick looks. "No . . . not at all," Marine slowly answered. "That would be fine."

"I'll be right back, then, ladies."

As soon as Viale was out of earshot, Sylvie whispered, "You should tell him that Antoine is a trained killer."

Marine laughed. "I don't think I need to do that," she said. "They knew each other when they were young, and I think that Antoine was, and still is, someone you don't want to cross. Besides, I'd like to spend as much time as I can talking with the hotel guests. Clément Viale has invested money here, and I don't trust him."

The Le Bons were in the lobby to greet Verlaque and Paulik. After introductions were made, Max Le Bon said, "Commissioner Paulik, you're welcome to stay overnight at Sordou; we have one spare room."

"Thank you," Paulik replied. "I'll take you up on that . . ." He stopped, realizing that the phone had been ringing since they came into the lobby.

Niki Darcette came quickly out of the office and stood beside Cat-Cat Le Bon, who took her cue. "Excuse me," Cat-Cat said. "I think I need to help Niki answer the phones."

Cat-Cat quickly left, but before Niki Darcette left Verlaque said, "In case you hadn't noticed, there are about ten boats anchored off of Sordou. The news of Alain Denis's death has been leaked, and the police officers guarding the harbor have been given strict instructions that no one is to be admitted off or on the island, the exception being Isnard."

"But the reservations are coming in . . ." Niki answered.

Cat-Cat returned in an instant. "Commissioner Paulik, this call is for you."

Paulik excused himself.

"When will we be able to start accepting new guests?" Max Le Bon asked.

"When I say so," Verlaque said.

"That's insane," Niki argued. "We need to be able to tell our callers when they can book."

"When the case has been closed," Verlaque replied. "I'm sorry; I don't know when that will be."

"But his body isn't even here anymore!" Niki protested.

"Niki . . ." Max Le Bon said, taking her arm.

"That was Dr. Cohen," Paulik said, returning from the office where he had taken his call. "Alain Denis was shot at close range yesterday, sometime in the late afternoon, early evening. There are no signs of violence or a struggle."

"We all heard a shot ring out at six p.m.," Verlaque said, looking at Paulik.

"Does that mean M. Denis knew his assassin?" Cat-Cat asked.

"Most likely," Paulik answered. "Who is that?" he continued, looking out the hotel's glass front doors toward the front steps. Two men approached, carrying baskets.

Verlaque said, "It's Isnard, with our provisions."

"But who is he with?" Paulik asked. He thought they had given strict instructions who was to come and go on Sordou.

The door opened and the fisherman entered. *"Bonsoir, Messieurs, Mesdames . . ."*

"Hello, Isnard," Cat-Cat said. "You can take the food straight into the kitchen."

"We haven't met your friend," Verlaque said. "You were to come alone."

*"Oh la la!"* Isnard moaned. "I was out on

the sea all day with my cousin Fred. What was I supposed to do, take him all the way back to Marseille, and then come back here? Right, Fred?"

"Yeah," Fred said, finally looking up at the group. "Plus you needed help carrying this stuff." Fred was a good twenty years younger than Isnard, and his nose was bright red, burnt by the sun.

"Go on then," Verlaque said. "And thank you for the food."

"So do we know how Alain Denis died?" Isnard asked, tilting his head as he spoke. "The journalists out in those boats are all buzzing to know." Fred nodded with enthusiasm.

"Did he fall from a cliff? *Un peu trop de . . . ?*" Isnard continued, tapping his finger against his nose.

"Isnard!" Max Le Bon bellowed. *"La cuisine!"*

# CHAPTER NINETEEN:
# FANCY FOREIGN NOODLES

Marie-Thérèse put wineglasses on the last remaining table left to be set and adjusted Mme Poux's carefully ironed napkins at each place setting. She had noticed Mme Poux's hand shake as she gave Marie-Thérèse the pile of napkins, and Marie-Thérèse had smiled gently at the maid, thankful that Mme Poux had been so comforting that morning. The island was now surrounded by police and journalists, their boats bobbing up and down on the sea, and the hairs on her forearms stood up from nervous excitement. The chubby judge had been joined by a bald and muscular policeman — *un commissaire,* Cat-Cat Le Bon had emphasized. He had big brown eyes like her older brother Claude and had smiled as he passed her in the hallway, making him less frightening than when she had first seen him walking up the front stairs with the judge.

"I'm here to warn you that the judge and commissioner would like to speak to all of us before dinner," Niki Darcette said as she walked into the dining room.

Marie-Thérèse swung around. "Where?"

"Here," Niki answered. "There's going to be some kind of announcement."

Marie-Thérèse realized that she was twisting a napkin in her hands and she set it down, trying to flatten it out with her fist.

"Nobody's gonna notice a few wrinkles," Niki said, walking over to stand beside Marie-Thérèse. "Not tonight."

"There are so many police boats out there, and some policemen walking around the island."

"Yeah," Niki said, frowning.

"Who's in charge?" asked the maid. "The judge, or the commissioner?"

"The judge," Niki answered. "Antoine Verlaque is an examining magistrate." Seeing the blank look on Marie-Thérèse's face, she went on, "He has more power than the commissioner, technically. A magistrate can do anything he wants: wiretap, enter a suspect's home without a warrant . . . all kinds of things. The commissioner works alongside the magistrate and is the boss, so to speak, of all of the police in his or her town."

Marie-Thérèse whistled. "You sure know a lot about the law."

Niki laughed. "Yeah, I could go on and on. There was a time in my life when I had lots of free time on my hands, and had free lodging, so I thought of studying law. But it was way too boring."

"So you studied hotel management instead?" Marie-Thérèse asked.

"Yeah, sort of."

"That's what I'd like to do," Marie-Therèse said, straightening her back. "I've just decided. In Lucerne. I've sent in my application."

"Wow!" Niki replied, laughing. "Do you have an extra twenty-five thousand euros lying around?"

"Does it cost that much? They were kind of vague about the costs . . ."

"That's just for one year."

Marie-Thérèse's face fell. "I had no idea. Maybe I could get a scholarship."

"Maybe," Niki quickly replied, feeling suddenly very touched by Marie-Thérèse's bright enthusiasm, and naivety. "But do you really need school? You're getting great experience here, on the job. . . . That's worth its weight in gold. And we're all so happy with how well you are doing at Sordou."

"Really?" Marie-Thérèse asked, her eyes sparkling. "Even when I drank the judge's wine?"

Niki laughed. "If I had a centime for every mistake I've made, I'd be a millionaire." Voices echoed down the hallway and got closer and closer to the dining room. "Here comes everyone," Niki said. She then reached over and touched Marie-Thérèse's arm and gently caressed it. "Look sharp," she added, smiling. Marie-Thérèse saluted, smiling back, and Niki felt a flush of joy. It had been so long since she had made another human being feel good about herself — she had learned that from Claire, all those years ago in Néoules. Niki had worried over the past few years that she had lost her capacity for joy. And here, on this strange day, she found that it was not lost.

"Hello, Niki; hello, Marie-Thérèse," Verlaque said as he entered the dining room. The early evening sun reflected on the blue sea, making it sparkle. It was as flat as glass. "This has to be one of the best views on the whole of the Mediterranean," he added.

"I never tire of it," Niki said.

"And you, Marie-Thérèse?" he asked, smiling.

*Mais oui, oui,* she answered, falling over her words. "But I'm so busy it seems that I often forget to look at the sea." She added, "But I love this dining room."

"It's perfect," Verlaque replied. "Here they come. . . . I've asked that all of the staff and guests come here to meet the commissioner of Aix-en-Provence's police force."

Within five minutes everyone was present and introductions had been made. Bruno Paulik stood with his back to the picture windows and addressed the group. The guests and staff, out of some kind of respect, stood standing in a semicircle, except for Mme Denis, who had been woken and was sitting, slumped forward, in a chair.

"Thank you all for coming so quickly," Paulik began. "As you now know, I'm Bruno Paulik, police commissioner of Aix-en-Provence, and to my left is your fellow guest, and my colleague, Judge Antoine Verlaque. Mme Denis," he continued, "my sincere condolences, and I'm sorry to have woken you."

Mme Denis nodded, and then looked at her hands, twisting her large rings.

Paulik continued, "And the chef . . ."

"Émile," Marie-Thérèse quickly replied.

"Thank you. Émile. I'm sorry for interrupting this evening's dinner preparations."

"No problem," Émile replied. "But I won't be able to stay long."

"Understood. As you all know, M. Denis was found dead early this morning on the south side of Sordou by the hotel's maid, Marie-Thérèse."

Almost each member of the group looked at Marie-Thérèse, and she cringed, looking down at the floor.

"The coroner has just called me, reporting that M. Denis died sometime last night, between four p.m. and eight p.m., from one shot to the head."

The group gasped and Mme Denis tried to stand up.

"We heard the shot then," Marine said.

"It was just before six p.m.," Sylvie added.

Brice quickly took his mother by the arm and sat her back down. "Do you realize what you are saying?" Emmanuelle Denis asked, gasping for breath. "That my, that my . . ."

"Yes, unfortunately," Paulik replied. "Alain Denis was shot in cold blood."

"Who killed my husband?" she spat out.

*"Maman, s'il te plaît . . ."* Brice murmured, sitting down beside her and taking her trembling hands in his.

"So what does the news mean for Sordou?" Cat-Cat Le Bon spoke up.

*"Cat-Cat,"* Max Le Bon protested.

"This is sheer Agatha Christie," Sylvie

whispered.

"I'm afraid that no new guests will be able to arrive until we get this cleared up," Verlaque replied.

"And we intend to do that as quickly as possible," Paulik added.

"Don't fret too much, Max," Delphine Viale said. "There's no such thing as bad news where publicity is concerned. The phone will be ringing off the hook, as I believe it has today."

*"Chérie!"* Clément Viale replied, frowning at his wife.

"*Chéri,* you yourself said so this morning," Delphine continued.

Mme Denis looked up, her eyes swollen. "I can't believe you all. . . . Plus, I asked for a policeman to guard my door. The killer may be after me too. Where is our protection?"

Paulik replied, "There are two policemen guarding the dock, and a boat at the mouth of the harbor, Mme Denis."

Mme Denis began to cry and Antoine Verlaque quickly crossed the room and put his hand on her shoulder. Before he could release it, the widow had reached up and clasped his hand with hers. Despite the summer heat, her hand was cold.

"I can assure you that Sordou will go on

running like before," Cat-Cat Le Bon said, stepping forward.

Niki followed her by saying, "You'll all receive the same attention that you've been getting all week. We promise."

"You don't need to spoil us," Shirley Hobbs replied in English. "We'll be fine."

"I'll keep fishing," Bill Hobbs added, making a fishing gesture with his hands.

Bruno Paulik tried to smile. "Thank you all for your cooperation. Tomorrow morning Judge Verlaque and I will begin interviewing you in alphabetical order. Anything you saw or heard will be of help; anything out of the ordinary, however minor it seemed at the time."

"Is it possible the murderer came ashore via boat, or by swimming?" Serge Canzano asked.

"No way," Hugo Sammut said. "It was —"

"We'll no doubt explore that route," Paulik replied. He and Verlaque had spoken together before the meeting; they had believed Sammut's opinion that the sea had been too choppy for an outsider to have come onto the island, but it was still possible. But more important, they didn't want to alarm the Sordou guests and staff that the murderer was, more than likely, among them. "So until tomorrow morning's interviews, bon appétit."

"Speaking of that, I need to get back to tonight's dinner," Émile said.

"Go on, Émile," Verlaque replied.

"We're all starving!" Bill Hobbs exclaimed in English.

"Bill!" Shirley hissed.

Émile quickly left, and Serge whispered something about opening the wine and followed Émile out. Marie-Thérèse looked at Verlaque, wide-eyed. "You may go and help, Marie-Thérèse," he said.

*"Merci!"* the girl replied, almost running.

"I'm going to retire to my room," Mme Poux said.

"I'll accompany you, Yolaine," Niki said.

"There's no need for that," Mme Poux replied sternly, leaving the room.

"Fine, have it your way," Niki muttered, leaving with the Le Bons and Hugo Sammut.

"Well, bon appétit, everyone," Verlaque said, finally moving away from Mme Denis.

"Brice and I will dine in our suite," Mme Denis said.

"That's fine," Verlaque said. "I'll tell Marie-Thérèse."

Marine walked over and took Verlaque by the arm. "You'd make a fine maître'd'," she said, winking.

"I feel a little like that," he replied.

"Wow, the next few days are going to be interesting," Sylvie said, pulling out a chair at the only table set for four people.

Marine sat down and looked around the room. "It's quiet."

Verlaque looked over at Monnier, who had already eaten almost all of the bread that Marie-Thérèse had just put on his table. Monnier was hunched over, writing furiously. Verlaque envied the poet's undying love for, and dedication to, his art.

"Hey, where was Prosper for tonight's interrogation?" Sylvie asked.

"It wasn't an interrogation, and you know that very well," Verlaque replied.

"Judge Verlaque told me about M. Buffa," Paulik answered. "We thought it best to go to the lighthouse to speak to him. I understand he's a bit of a . . . distraction."

"And how," Marine said. "He's straight out of a novel."

"A nineteenth-century one at that," Sylvie replied.

Marie-Thérèse appeared with Serge, both carrying bowls of soup. "A seafood soup with freshly caught monkfish, Swiss chard, rice noodles, ginger, and cilantro," Marie-Thérèse announced. "With a touch of chili," she added.

"Thank you," Verlaque replied. "The soup will be excellent with the white wine from Cassis, don't you think, Marie-Thérèse?"

Marie-Thérèse beamed. "Yes," she said. "Serge said . . . I mean . . . the fruity bouquet of the Cassis wine will be perfect with the monkfish, and the addition of the . . . um . . . Marsanne! . . . grape will add the touch of Rhône heaviness that the ginger and chili need . . . um, or rather . . . require."

Paulik looked up and smiled. "Sounds perfect," he said.

Marie-Thérèse swung around on her heels and went back into the kitchen to fetch the rest of the soups. Marine saw Serge, who had been standing in the doorway, give the girl a thumbs-up. "She's adorable," Marine said.

"Definitely not the murderer," Sylvie said, leaning toward her bowl. "And this soup smells heavenly."

"Have you been eating like this all week?" Paulik asked.

Verlaque nodded, too busy to reply with words. The smells of the ginger, pepper, and cilantro wafted up to his nose. He twisted some of the noodles around in his spoon, took a piece of monkfish with his fork, setting it gently on his spoon with the broth, and then put it in his mouth and closed his eyes.

"This broth is so delicate!" Marine said. "I don't know how he does it, cooking this well on an island."

Verlaque nodded again in agreement and then opened his eyes. "What the . . . ?" he said, looking out toward the hallway.

"What, Antoine?" Marine asked.

"I just saw Isnard and his goofy cousin," he answered, quickly getting up.

"What?" Paulik asked, setting down his spoon. "The fisherman is still here?"

The two men quickly left, followed by the eyes of all of Sordou's diners.

"Isnard!" Verlaque called out just as the fisherman reached the front door. "What is going on? Why are you still here?"

Isnard shrugged and put up his hand. "I didn't want to bother you," he said. "But Fred here has never seen such a fancy hotel, and I thought I could give him just a little tour . . . since you were all busy having your meeting."

Fred mimicked his cousin with the same shrug, and then looked down at his running shoes. "Fancy kitchen," he finally said, looking up. "I'm a good home cook myself."

"For Pete's sake, Isnard," Verlaque said, sighing. "Get the hell off the island now, before I lose my temper."

"And tomorrow," Paulik added, "you are to come unaccompanied."

*"Oui, monsieur le commissaire!"* Isnard said, bowing. "Let's go, Fred; a fish stew at my place awaits us. And mine doesn't have fancy foreign noodles and weird spices."

# CHAPTER TWENTY:
# THE REST OF US ARE
# STRANGERS

"Even the coffee is good here," Paulik said as he set down his empty espresso cup.

"Illy," answered Verlaque, who had already had three cups for breakfast. That morning Paulik and Verlaque had been set up in the future conference room, which had uninspiring views of the walls surrounding Émile's *potager.* "We purposely planned the conference room here," Max Le Bon had explained that morning as Verlaque and Paulik helped him bring in two small dining room tables and four chairs to create an office. "We figured that if you're hard at work a view would only be distracting."

"It's perfect," said Verlaque.

"The guests are outside or in the hotel, milling around until their names are called," Le Bon said. "It was good of you to give them some kind of estimated appointment time."

"We figured twenty minutes each," Verlaque said. "Although, just like at the doctor's office, by the end of the day we'll no doubt be running late."

"Better that than finishing early, eh?" Le Bon replied. "Let's hope that at least one of our clients can shed some light on the subject."

"Thank you, M. Le Bon," Paulik said.

Max Le Bon took his cue and nodded, leaving the room.

"There are only three places on the island for a boat to pull up: the natural harbor, the cove where Denis was found — and then, a boat can't get in very far — and over by Prosper's lighthouse," Verlaque said.

Paulik asked, "How reliable is Prosper?"

"Despite his eccentric appearance, and affected voice," Verlaque said, "I'm told that Prosper pays a maniacal attention to his lighthouse — even though it's now automated — and to his small dock."

"I still think that a good swimmer could get here from a boat anchored not far from Sordou," Paulik offered.

"Yes, it's still possible; I've seen stranger things before."

Paulik didn't reply but instead looked at the paper laid before him that Verlaque had quickly written up early that morning. "Marine Bonnet," Paulik said, smiling.

"Suspect, and interviewee, number one."

As if hearing her name, Marine knocked gently on the door and let herself in. "Hello, you two," she said.

"Please have a seat, Mlle Bonnet," Paulik said trying to keep a straight face.

Marine sat down and said, "I don't want to take up too much of your time in here. For the life of me I'm stumped. I can't imagine anyone killing Alain Denis, so I'm inclined to think that the killer came in from the sea." She stopped and then added, "How romantic that sounds."

Verlaque repeated the conversation he had just had with Paulik.

"I see," Marine said. "An obsessive light-house keeper and rough sea lessen the chances that the killer came from off the island. I think it best I go back outside and keep my eyes and ears close to the ground."

"Or sea," Paulik added.

"That would be great," Verlaque said. "But if there is a killer among us — and I agree, it is hard to believe — please be careful. They're unlikely to give anything away and may be dangerous."

"I'll make sure to have Sylvie close to me," Marine said.

Verlaque raised his left eyebrow and Paulik laughed.

"I'll send the next person in," Marine said, getting up.

"Serge Canzano?" Paulik read.

"The bartender," Marine said. "I'll see you both at lunch."

"Can't wait," Verlaque said.

While they were waiting for Canzano, Verlaque quickly filled in Paulik on the guests and staff, with brief descriptions of their work and/or personalities. For Canzano he added, "quiet efficiency," for Cat-Cat Le Bon "tigress," for Eric Monnier, "the absentminded poet."

"The hotel manager?" Paulik asked.

"Seductress, with a troubled past."

"The housekeeper?"

"Just plain weird," Verlaque replied. "Plus she may have known Denis when they were young. She told everyone down at the cove that he had been a champion swimmer in his youth."

"Alain Denis was from Marseille, wasn't he?"

"Yes."

"And the boy, Brice?" Paulik asked. "What's he like?"

"Sad, and angry," Verlaque said. "Remember when you were like that, at that age?"

"Like what, sir?"

Verlaque silently noted that Bruno Paulik

had gone back to calling him "sir." "You know," he went on, "weren't you a troubled, angry teenage boy?"

"Um, no."

Verlaque smiled. "And why not, do you think?"

"The pure unconditional love from my parents," Paulik replied, and then frowned. "I'm sorry, sir, I didn't mean . . ."

Verlaque waved his hand. "No worries," he said. "I got that in spades from my grandparents. But they were in Normandy most of the time."

Canzano knocked on the door and Paulik, relieved, called, "Come in!"

"Sit down, M. Canzano," Verlaque said, motioning to a chair.

"Thank you. I'll have your Lagavulin ready for you just before lunch, Judge Verlaque," Canzano said. "As usual."

Paulik coughed. "I'm afraid we have to begin with the most basic of questions," he said.

"Like where was I late Monday afternoon?" Canzano asked, his face poker-straight.

"Yes."

"Where I always am," he said. "I was in the bar during and right after lunch, and then for *apéro.*"

"The bar is closed for a bit in the afternoon," Verlaque offered.

"That's right," Canzano replied calmly. "I, as do most of the staff, take a siesta, usually between three and six p.m."

"Perfectly understandable," Verlaque said. "As you all wake up long before the guests, and go to bed long after. Did you hear the shot?" Verlaque asked. "It was just before six p.m."

"No, I didn't," Serge said. "I was back in the bar, but we were playing music, and I had the blender on, so there's no way I could hear it."

"Blender?"

"Yes, I made a margarita for M. Viale. He was my first customer."

"What was your opinion of M. Denis?" Paulik asked. "Bartenders are known to be good observers of people."

"He was a difficult man," Canzano said. "And unloved."

"By whom?"

"His wife and stepson, for one. Only they could love, or not love, him. The rest of us are strangers."

Paulik wrote down the words "the rest of us are strangers" and added a question mark.

"Did you notice anything unusual in the

Denis family's behavior?" Verlaque asked.

Canzano paused before speaking. "I think that Mme Denis may have . . . no, let me rephrase that. One night Mme Denis left the bar, quite late, and drunk, with M. Viale." He looked at Verlaque and added, "Your old school chum."

"Well done," Verlaque said. "We went to university together."

"What night?" Paulik asked, picking up a pencil.

"Saturday," replied Canzano without hesitating. If the bartender thought it odd, or sordid, he did not let on.

"We've asked Mlle Darcette and M. Le Bon to give us your CVs and contact addresses when you are back on the mainland," Verlaque said. "Is there any other information we should know about you?"

Canzano shook his head. "Not what you can't glean from my résumé. I've been a bartender almost all of my life, for thirty years. I've lived in a studio near the Cours Julien for most of them, but gave it up to take this job. No use paying rent for an empty apartment. I've never been married and never had children. My parents are dead."

"And you love French history," Verlaque offered.

"That I do. You're observant as well," Canzano said, flashing a rare smile.

"We'll see you later, before lunch," Verlaque said, returning the smile.

"Very well," Canzano said, and getting up he gave a slight bow, reminding Paulik of a servant in the nineteenth-century English dramas Léa and Hélène like to watch on DVD.

"This should be interesting," Verlaque said, reading Niki Darcette's name after Canzano had firmly closed the door.

Niki Darcette walked quickly in and sat down before she could have a chance to be offered a seat. She pulled at her tight skirt, wishing she had worn her elegant Max Mara shorts that she had bought on sale when she got the job. M. Masurel had told her, after her desperate phone call from Cannes, never to make herself uncomfortable before the police or lawyers; clothes were important: keep them loose, cleaned, and ironed. In moments of stress she would think of his face. She did so now.

"You began working here in April, correct?" Verlaque asked.

"Yes," Niki replied. "You can see that on my CV. I began early to help Cat-Cat with the bookings, before the hotel officially opened."

Verlaque leaned forward. "I looked at your CV already," he said. "This morning."

Mme Darcette shifted in her chair.

"Would you care to fill in the missing years?"

"The Le Bons didn't tell you?"

"No."

"I've hidden nothing," Niki said. "They know all about it."

"So where were you, after high school in the Var, and before your first job at the Hilton in Bordeaux?"

"In jail," Niki replied flatly.

Paulik stopped writing and looked up.

"But not for murder," Niki said. "Theft. Among other things."

"Why don't you start at the beginning?" Verlaque said.

"Or you can call your colleagues in Cannes and get a more detailed version," Niki said. Before Verlaque could reprimand her, she said, "I finished high school with a fifteen out of twenty on the *bac.*"

"That's a very good score," Verlaque replied, where grades above twelve get a special mention. "Why didn't you go to university?"

"I got fifteen without even trying," she answered. "I had good study habits — not thanks to my parents, but thanks to some

249

friends — but then they moved back to Paris when I was in middle school. I fell in with the wrong crowd and moved to the Côte as soon as I graduated, with my then boyfriend, a real louse named Kévin. Kévin worked in a café for a few months . . . maybe it was even weeks . . . and then quit. The work was too hard. Stealing was easier. I saw how he did it and followed suit."

"What did you steal?"

"Kévin would be stupid about it; he'd grab purses and then not know what to do with them except take the money. So I dropped him and started hanging out with some friends of his who were into breaking and entering . . . mostly high-end stores. The ring-leader was a real creep named Robert, a million times rougher than Kévin. Funny how I end up with creeps. Anyway, we got caught after robbing a jewelry store. . . . I had one phone call to make, and I knew my parents wouldn't care nor be of any help."

"So you called the family friends," Verlaque suggested. "The ones who taught you to study, before they moved to Paris . . ."

Niki tried to choke back the lump in her throat. "Yeah. M. Masurel was a lawyer — a big shot — in Paris. They moved from our village when I was in sixth grade; their daughter and I were best friends."

"Yves Masurel?" Verlaque asked.

"Yes, that's him."

"I've worked with Maître Masurel," Verlaque said. "Brilliant. And entirely honest."

"And he set you up with a lawyer in Cannes?" Paulik asked.

"No," Niki replied, straightening. "He came down to Cannes that day. He represented me."

Verlaque nodded, impressed. "How much time did you get?"

"Six years, three with good behavior."

"Six?" Paulik asked, surprised. It was more than usual, for robbery. He made a note to call the Cannes police.

"And you learned the hotel business while in jail?" Verlaque asked.

"Yes," Niki replied. "They were trying an experiment; training what they called 'exceptional' prisoners in restaurant and hotel work. There are more than enough jobs on the Côte. I flourished."

"I can believe it," Verlaque said, smiling.

"What do you know of Alain Denis?" Paulik asked.

"Absolutely nothing," Niki replied. "I've never even seen one of his films."

"And as a client?" Verlaque asked.

"A pain in the ass," she said. "But that's

251

not telling you anything you don't already know."

"Where were you Monday at six p.m.?" Verlaque asked.

"I heard the shot," Niki said. "I thought it was Prosper. I was in the office, making phone calls."

"Could you give us a list of those, so that we can verify the calls?" Verlaque asked.

Niki shrugged. "Sure," she said. "I kept a list."

"And you didn't see anything unusual on Monday?" Verlaque asked.

"No," Niki answered. "Except at breakfast, I did see a slight smile, and a weak, barely audible 'thank you' come from Alain Denis's mouth."

Marie-Thérèse brought Verlaque and Paulik two more espressos and placed them down on their makeshift desk. *"Émile vient de faire des financiers,"* she said, pushing a plate of small rectangular almond cakes toward the two men.

*"Encore chaud,"* Paulik said, dipping one into his coffee.

Verlaque tried not to be disgusted by his commissioner's spoiling of a delightfully fluffy cake by turning it into a soggy mess. "Please thank Émile for us," he said.

Marie-Thérèse nodded and quickly left, leaving the door open for Brice. The teen walked in, softly closing the door behind him. "Technically, my name comes after my mom's," he said, sitting down. "Dortignac . . ."

*"Financier?"* Verlaque asked, motioning to the cakes.

"Gross," Brice said, wrinkling his nose.

"We thought we'd speak to you before your mom," Paulik said, finally acknowledging the boy's comment.

"You don't like *financiers*?" Verlaque asked, perplexed.

"But Dortignac comes after Denis," the boy continued. "I never had that name, Denis. Never."

"We realize that," Paulik said.

"We'll talk about your food tastes another time," Verlaque said, omitting the word "bad." "So, no desire to carry the Denis name, eh?"

"Prosper says we should only eat things that come from the sky, and sea, and land . . ."

Paulik stifled a yawn, while Verlaque suspiciously looked at his *financier*. "Let's get back to the name Denis," Verlaque said, setting his cake down, "and we'll talk about Prosper later."

"I never wanted the name Denis because I never liked him," Brice said, crossing his arms.

"Enough to kill him?" Verlaque asked.

"What?" Brice cried.

"You were down on the cove on Monday," Verlaque said.

"So were a lot of people," Brice answered.

"You could have been checking the cove out, trying to figure out how to get Alain Denis down there."

"That's crazy!" Brice yelled. "Besides, where would I get a gun? This isn't the U.S."

"In the U.S.," Verlaque suggested. "You're back and forth a lot, no?"

"Yes, but I don't have the desire nor competence to sneak a handgun back to France on an airplane."

"Nicely phrased," Verlaque said, his eyebrows raised. "Do you read a lot?"

"Yeah," Brice slowly replied.

"Poetry?"

"Nah," the boy answered.

"Too bad. Prosper has a gun," Verlaque suggested. "And you were with him on Monday."

"He has a hunting rifle," Brice said.

"I didn't say what kind of gun was used to kill your stepfather," Verlaque said.

"Besides," Brice said, his voice finally

cracking, "I was with Prosper all day. He can tell you."

"All right," Verlaque said. "When did you get there?"

"Around midnight," Brice answered. "I was angry and so I stormed out of the hotel. I didn't know where to go, so I kept walking toward the lights of the lighthouse. When I got close to it, Prosper heard my footsteps and came running out with his rifle. It scared me to bits."

"I can imagine. Continue."

"He invited me in — when he saw I wasn't going to rob him — and made me tea. We talked for a bit — or he talked, and I listened, trying to figure out what he was saying. He must have seen me yawning, because he then gave me this moth-eaten wool blanket and told me I could sleep on a cot in the corner of his kitchen."

"And the next day?" Verlaque asked.

"We ate breakfast out on his pier," Brice said. "And he told me about the fish, and birds, on Sordou. He knows as much about all that as M. Hobbs does. We had a lunch of cheese and bread — I was starving — and then he took me out into the land behind the lighthouse, looking for rabbits. We didn't find any though. We spent the late afternoon playing chess; he won both games . . . and then I told him I thought I should be going back to the hotel . . . and you know the rest."

"Your father lives in New York," Paulik said, wanting to get back to the U.S. connection. "Right?"

"Yeah, in Manhattan," Brice replied. "But I hardly see him anymore. He's married to this young model, and they have twin girls . . . babies."

"I see," Verlaque said more quietly than he meant to. "And M. Denis never took on the role of father?"

Brice laughed. "Didn't even try."

"Did you know that your stepfather was a champion swimmer?"

Brice looked genuinely surprised. "No. When he was a kid?"

"About your age," Verlaque said, lying. Since they hadn't yet interviewed Mme Poux, he really had no idea when.

"Well, he didn't drown anyway," Brice said.

"Right," Paulik said, setting down his pencil.

"Take good care of your mother," Verlaque said. "You can send her in now."

Brice left the room, and Paulik leaned over toward Verlaque. "He's a little too . . . smug."

"He just could be bright," Verlaque said. "He reads."

"Being a reader doesn't automatically make him innocent. You were digging into him, getting some good reactions, but then you let up," Paulik said.

Verlaque shrugged. "I feel sorry for him."

"The sun and heat has . . ." Paulik was about to finish his sentence when the door opened and Brice came in with Emmanuelle Denis, guiding her to a chair with his arm. He helped her to sit down and turned to go, whispering, *"À tout à l'heure, maman."*

Mme Denis looked up at the two policemen, her eyes red and swollen. "How are you feeling, madame?" Verlaque asked.

"Rotten," she answered, blowing her nose. "That's the surprising thing."

"Surprising?"

"Well, yes. I haven't loved Alain for years. So why do I feel so lousy?"

Both men stayed silent, hoping that Mme Denis would elaborate. She did. She went on, "I think it's partly because it's messy, this death. And we're still married, so I'm the one who will have to deal with the inquest, the reporters, the fans. . . . Had we been divorced, this wouldn't have been my job. I don't want to do any of this. . . . I just want to go away and start a new life, with my son."

"Well then, let's try to get this solved as quickly as possible," Verlaque said. He was surprised by Mme Denis's narcissism, and had Alain Denis been a kinder man, Verlaque would have been angered by it. But Alain Denis, although not quite a monster, had been extremely unlikable — and so Verlaque continued, "You can put M. Denis's agent and manager in charge of dealing with the press; that's what they're paid for. Did you see M. Denis after he ate lunch in your suite?"

"No," she replied. "Brice's room has two beds, so I've been sleeping in one of them."

Verlaque leaned forward. "If you and Brice have been sharing a room, how did you not see that he was absent that night he spent down at Prosper's?"

Mme Denis bit her lip. "I was with someone else, in another room."

"M. Viale?"

"Yes," she answered. "There's an empty room at the end of our hall that we've been using . . . until the commissioner came, of course. I had Mme Le Bon make up the room, and I paid for it. Both nights. I hope that doesn't make me sound like a harlot, but I'm lonely."

"It's not our business," Verlaque said.

"Unless it interferes with the investigation. Where were you on Monday evening at six p.m.?"

"I was in my room . . . our room . . . the one I share with Brice. You were out looking for him, and I was upset, so I just went to the room and lay down."

"Did anyone come to your room?" Paulik asked. "Or phone the room?"

"No, why?" Mme Denis asked. "Oh, I see. To establish my alibi. No, no one came by, or called."

"Did your late husband have enemies?" Verlaque asked.

Mme Denis smiled. "Of course; but I can't think of anyone who would want him dead. He was an obnoxious man, more and more so the older he got. There are directors and fellow actors who have been enraged by Alain's selfish behavior on set, but as I said, murder is an extreme way to . . . settle disagreements."

"And you've never considered murder?" Verlaque asked.

Emmanuelle Denis stared at him, wide-eyed. "I can't even kill flies," she said. Verlaque stayed silent; he had heard that before, from murderers.

"Thank you, Mme Denis," Verlaque said, pushing his chair out.

"One last thing," she said, ignoring Verlaque's cue that the interview was finished. "And I'll tell the Le Bons this as well: my emerald and diamond ring has gone missing."

# CHAPTER TWENTY-ONE:
## DREAMING OF UNIVERSITY

"Are you sure?" Verlaque asked.

"Positive," Mme Denis replied.

Verlaque sat back down.

"I keep all of my rings together — especially when I travel — in a small silk Chinese purse," she went on. "I put them on, religiously, each morning, after I have dressed, and take them off — also religiously — just before I get into bed, setting them on the dresser. I love the ritual; so I know I'm not mistaken."

"And Brice?" Paulik asked.

"He looked under the dresser and bed, just to confirm for me that I'm not losing my marbles," she answered.

Paulik said nothing; Mme Denis had misunderstood his question: he had wanted to suggest that the boy had taken the ring. He had seen it before: to buy drugs, or even the latest gadget. Mme Denis's next statement confirmed Paulik's suspicions that perhaps Brice had taken the ring. She said, "I've recently had my jewelry valued, at Drouot in Paris. That diamond and emerald ring was antique; eighteenth century. It was valued at two hundred fifty thousand euros. It was given to me years ago, by . . . well, it doesn't matter."

"This is indeed serious," Verlaque said. "When did you first notice it missing?"

"Yesterday morning," she replied. "I looked for it during the day, but to no avail, and after dinner Brice helped me search the room. I went to bed upset, and I was planning on telling the Le Bons this morning, but —"

"Yes," Verlaque cut in. "Do you think," he said, slowly, "that M. Denis could have taken the ring?"

Mme Denis looked at the judge in amazement. "What for?"

"I don't know . . ." Verlaque's mind raced. *Did Alain Denis need money that badly? Would someone kill for the ring? Or did Denis take the ring because it was given to his wife by a former lover?* "Money, perhaps," Verlaque went on. "Were your late husband's finances in order?"

"His accountant keeps them in order, yes," she replied. "But there's not much to keep in order, as I understand. Hence the television commercials. This week's stay was a splurge, and we got a discount from the Le Bons; they were hoping Alain's staying here would attract business."

"All the more reason for your late husband to take the ring," Paulik suggested. Mme Denis didn't reply.

"Have you seen M. Denis's will?" Verlaque asked.

"Our lawyer is arriving tomorrow," she answered. "Provided you'll let him on the island."

"Of course," Verlaque said, smiling. "We'll leave you in peace now. Try to rest a bit more."

"I'll try. Thank you . . . for your help. I know that you're meant to be here on vacation."

Verlaque considered making a joke that he had been getting bored by the sun and sea, but kept the thought to himself. "It's no problem."

The minute Mme Denis was out the door Verlaque said, "I'm ravenous."

"Coincidence that we just interviewed a hotel employee who was jailed for theft," Paulik noted, seeming not to have heard his boss's declaration, "and then a ring goes missing . . ."

"I don't see Niki stealing anymore,"

Verlaque said, getting up to stretch.

"Oh really?"

"Nah," Verlaque said, not having heard the sarcasm in Paulik's voice. "She's got too much to lose."

"But it would be so tempting," Paulik continued. "I can't believe a ring could be worth that much money."

"I can," Verlaque replied, thinking of his grandmother Emmeline's jewelry, now in a safe in a bank on the Rue d'Opéra in Paris.

"With two hundred fifty thousand euros Hélène could buy one of those new stainless steel grape presses from Italy," Paulik said, "Or even two."

"Does she need a new press?" Verlaque asked.

"No, no, don't worry," Paulik quickly replied. "The old one is fine."

"Who's next on the list?"

"Sylvie, and then Marie-Thérèse Guichard."

"Marie-Thérèse Guichard," Paulik said. "Is she the waitress?"

"A sort of girl Friday," Verlaque answered. "She's one of the sweetest people I've ever met. And no, I don't think she's a murderer, or a thief. Sylvie should have been here by now. I'll pop my head outside the door to see where she is." Verlaque opened the door and looked up and down the hall. He saw Marie-Thérèse and asked if she had seen Mlle Grassi.

"No, sir," Marie-Thérèse answered. "Would you like me to run outside and look?"

"No, thank you," Verlaque answered. "You can come in now, since you're the next person on the list after Mlle Grassi." He ushered her in and put the "do not disturb" sign back on the door.

The girl sat down quickly. "Stop wringing your hands, Marie-Thérèse," Verlaque said.

"Yes, sir," she replied, separating her hands and placing them, palms down, under her thighs.

Paulik leaned forward, his forearms resting on the table. "At what time did you find the body of Alain Denis?"

"Um, just before seven a.m.," she replied, swallowing.

"Are you normally out walking around in the early morning?" he asked.

"No, sir."

"So why yesterday?"

Verlaque looked sideways at his commissioner but stayed silent. He didn't want to upset the girl.

"I start work at seven-thirty a.m. . . . ."

"Yes, but not down at a small cove, no?"

"I went down to . . . think . . ." she answered.

"Really?" Paulik asked, leaning even more forward. "That's a little far, isn't it? For a think?"

Marie-Thérèse bit her lip and her eyes filled up with tears.

Verlaque now leaned forward. "We're sorry to upset you," he said. "Please go on."

The girl stifled a sob and began speaking. "I thought it would bring me good luck. . . . When I got the job on Sordou I had done the same thing . . . in Marseille . . ."

"Went down to a cove?" Verlaque asked.

"Well, I walked to the end of the old port," she said, sniffling. "There were a bunch of us being interviewed the next day, and I didn't think I had a chance to work at such a fancy hotel, so I sat at the edge of a pier, looking at the sea . . . and . . ."

"Prayed?" Verlaque asked.

"Yes," she replied. "Prayed. That's what I wanted to do at the cove yesterday. I wanted to be alone."

"What were you praying for?" Verlaque asked. Paulik looked at him sideways.

She began to cry. "Lausanne . . ."

"The city in Switzerland?" Verlaque said, trying to coax her on.

"Hotel school," she went on, sniffing.

"Oh, I see," Verlaque said. "You've applied to university in Lausanne?"

"Yes, but it's all for nothing, even if I do get in," she said, blowing her nose.

"Why is that?" Verlaque asked, but as soon as the words came out of his mouth, he knew the answer. "Oh, it's a private school, isn't it?"

"It's so expensive," Marie-Thérèse almost wailed. "I was so stupid to even apply."

"What about a scholarship?" Paulik asked, leaning forward again.

"I phoned them," Marie-Thérèse answered. "That's when you saw me," she said to Verlaque.

"Oh, I'm sorry, Marie-Thérèse, if I spoke sharply to you," Verlaque said. "I was trying to figure out who leaked the murder to the press." He looked at Paulik and explained that on Tuesday he had come across Marie-Thérèse in the office, making a phone call but hanging up when she saw him.

"It's okay," she whimpered. "I forgive you," she said, now smiling a tiny bit. "The Swiss secretary I spoke to on the phone was mean and told me that even if I did get a scholarship, it would never cover the costs of living in such an expensive city."

"Don't give up hope," Verlaque said. "Where there's a will, there's —"

"What did you do when you first saw M. Denis's body?" Paulik asked, cutting off his boss.

"I screamed." She looked at the men and realized she was meant to continue. "I ran over to him . . . his body, I mean. . . . He was lying on the beach, facedown. I didn't want to touch him. I screamed again . . . and ran."

"How would you describe M. Denis?" Paulik asked.

"Um . . . not very nice . . . and snooty."

"Was he rude to you?" Paulik asked.

"Yes, but that doesn't mean . . ."

"No one is accusing you, Marie-Thérèse," Verlaque said, glancing at Paulik.

"When was he mean?" Paulik asked.

"Um, most of the time," she replied. "He was fussy, and impatient. I was upset by it at first, but Émile calmed me down. He told me that M. Denis was like that with everyone, so I shouldn't take it . . . um . . ."

"Personally?" Paulik asked.

"Yes."

"You must see a lot of what goes on around Sordou," Paulik said.

"Um, I guess . . ."

"Did you ever see M. Denis and one of the other hotel guests, or staff members, have a fight?"

"Well . . . he yelled a lot at his wife," Marie-Thérèse replied, shifting in her seat. "And we all saw Hugo get mad at him. Plus, M. Denis told Émile that his food was boring!"

Paulik tried to keep a straight face. "Émile must have been upset by that."

"Yeah! He said that Alain Denis wouldn't know a trout from a tuna."

This time both men had to hide their grins. "Anything else, Marie-Thérèse?" Verlaque asked. "Anything at all, even if it seemed insignificant at the time."

"Well, there was this thing he was doing."

"Who?" Verlaque asked. "M. Denis? Go on."

"He, *M. Deni*s, was walking in the garden the other day. Twice I saw him do it that day . . ."

"What?"

"I'm trying to tell you," she said, huffing. "He was walking around, and he pulled out of his pocket . . ." She stared at Verlaque and went on, sitting up straight. "Pants pocket, to be specific . . . I mean *precise* . . . a little piece of paper, and he read it."

Verlaque looked at Paulik and then asked, "And?"

"Well," she said, "I'm telling you this because it happened twice, and both times he read the note he laughed. To himself."

Paulik wrote the information down. "Thank you," he said. "You've been very helpful."

"That means I can go?" she asked. "It's almost lunchtime."

"Yes," Verlaque replied, getting up.

"Thanks!" she said, already at the door before either man could ask her about Mme Denis's ring.

# CHAPTER TWENTY-TWO:
## PAST LIVES AND SO ON

"What in the hell was that?" Verlaque asked.

"I'm sorry," Paulik answered. "I shouldn't have cut you off."

"You're bloody right."

"It's just that . . . you were getting off topic," Paulik said, looking straight at the judge.

"I was trying to make Marie-Thérèse feel better," Verlaque said. "I don't think that someone so young can give us straight detailed answers if they're frightened out of their wits."

"Brice is younger than Marie-Thérèse," Paulik suggested.

*"Oui,"* Verlaque replied. *"Mais Brice est un garçon."*

"So you're tougher on boys?"

Verlaque shifted his weight. "You're right," he finally said. "I think of boys like me. And I'm hard on myself."

"Women can commit crimes," Paulik said.

"Although it's hard for me to imagine."

"As the father of a girl."

"I didn't say that."

"Let's use the hotel phone and call the Palais de Justice," Verlaque said, changing the subject. "Get some officers to dig up Denis's past, especially when he was in his heyday, filming. I've heard that he was trouble on set. Find out if anyone ever threatened him." Verlaque didn't admit that his source was Sylvie's reading of gossip magazines.

"Then you're assuming that the murderer swam here," Paulik said.

"I still think it's possible, despite what Hugo said."

"Or perhaps one of the older guests or staff is a retired film star," Paulik suggested.

Verlaque straightened his back. "That's not a bad idea," he said. "Mme Poux, for example. There you go: a woman. She could have been a behind-the-scenes person on set."

"The script girl."

"Wardrobe assistant."

"Caterer."

"This good brainstorming is making me hungry, and it's going to be more bloody fish," Verlaque said. "Maybe trout?"

"Or perhaps tuna. Let's go then," Paulik

said, getting up. He took the list in his hand and read, "Next up after lunch, the Americans."

Antoine Verlaque and Bruno Paulik closed the conference room door and walked down the hall toward the lobby. They crossed paths with Niki Darcette, who was carrying a champagne bucket. "Lunch will be out on the terrace," she said, gesturing toward the front doors with her head. "It has cooled off a bit, so you won't bake out there."

Verlaque thanked her, noting that she sounded relaxed; almost informal. She must have been relieved to have the interview over with, he noted.

"Is that for us?" he asked, pointing to the bucket.

"Sorry, no," Niki replied, smiling. "Mme Denis has asked for some chilled white wine; I'm taking it to her room."

"Very well," Verlaque replied. "I'll go into the bar and fetch my whiskey," he said to Paulik. "Would you like one?"

"No thanks," Paulik answered. "Maybe later this evening, before I shove off. I'll meet you outside."

Verlaque walked into the Jacky Bar, soothed by the bar's carefully selected vintage furniture and the gentle whirring of the ceiling fans. Eric Monnier was in his favorite corner, writing in his black book. Monnier saw Verlaque and lifted his Bloody Mary in a toast.

"Too hot out there for you?" Verlaque asked.

"The atmosphere among the diners is just a tad too tense," Monnier replied. "I thought I'd eat in here and then do some reading."

"Bon appétit, then," Verlaque said.

Serge Canzano had already poured Verlaque's drink, setting the crystal glass on the bar along with a small silver-plated pitcher of still water.

"Thank you," Verlaque said, pouring a tiny bit of water into the whiskey. "Cheers." He took a sip and then walked over to the French doors that led to the terrace. Before going out he paused and looked at the sea — very much the color of Mme Denis's missing emerald, but much more precious. The limestone cliffs sparkled against the deep-blue sky, and Verlaque looked at the dozen or so scraggy pine trees that managed to grow out of the white rock. He turned his gaze to the terrace, its wrought iron tables beautifully set for lunch with white linen tablecloths, Italian porcelain, and Riedel stemware. But no laughter came from the diners, as it had on previous days. Someone coughed; another diner set down his fork a little too quickly and it rang out when it landed on the plate. It reminded Verlaque too much of formal dinners spent with his parents, in stiff Parisian restaurants that even he knew, as a young teen, were out of fashion. He and his brother, Sébastien, lived for the vacations with their paternal grandparents, Emmeline and Charles, where they would eat in, as Emmeline was a fine, simple cook, or eat out in noisy brasseries. But their favorite vacations with Emmeline and Charles were in Italy, on the Ligurian coast, where they would spend weeks on end in a small family-run hotel.

*That's what Sordou should be,* he thought. The kind of hotel where the service is impeccable, and the food delicious, and yet the atmosphere relaxed, familial. It had been like that, he mused, before the murder.

"Over here!" Sylvie hollered.

"Where were you?" Verlaque asked when he got to their table.

"Sorry," Sylvie replied. "I lost track of time. Marine and I were swimming."

Marine looked over at her friend, angry to have been made an accomplice.

When Verlaque had sat down, Sylvie

leaned in and asked, "Will I still get to be interviewed?"

"Of course," Verlaque said, putting his napkin on his lap. "Why? You didn't *know* the deceased, did you?"

"Antoine!" Marine said, knowing that he was referring to a previous case where Sylvie had indeed known the deceased, intimately.

"I just saw the poet," Verlaque said. "He said that the atmosphere was tense out here."

"Mmm," Marine said, nodding. "The Viales had some sort of argument, and she left. The Hobbses were obviously upset by it and now seem shaken up, and Mme Denis and Brice aren't even here."

"They're eating in their room again," Paulik answered.

"Can't say that I blame them," Marine said. "Before Alain Denis's death, I had the feeling that we were all becoming friends — Eric Monnier hopping from table to table; Bill Hobbs taking young Brice under his wing; Shirley Hobbs showing me her watercolors . . ."

"I was just thinking the same thing," Verlaque said. Marine's description was much like that small Italian hotel.

"I overheard the Le Bons arguing," Sylvie said. "Should I tell you now, or wait until my interview when you have a cheap desk light shining in my face?"

Verlaque laughed despite himself. "Save it for later."

Marie-Thérèse arrived and announced the lunch menu. "We didn't have time to type it up," she said. "Because of the . . . interviews. So, the starter today is a grilled tuna salad . . ."

Verlaque looked at Paulik and winked.

"Um, made with tuna, of course, and avocado, coriander, spring onions, and a chili pepper."

"Sounds great," Verlaque said.

"And the dressing," she went on, "is made with soy sauce, lemon grass, and limes."

"Wonderful," Marine added.

"The main dish today will be crab and Gruyère tartlets," Marie-Thérèse continued. "Chef Émile has made individual puff pastry shells and filled them with crab, Gruyère, and spices. Serge recommends a chardonnay from Burgundy."

"And with the tartlets?" Verlaque asked. "Vegetables?"

"Um, salad."

"More salad," Verlaque said, pouting.

"A light lunch today," Marine said.

"Well, Isnard didn't come," Marie-Thérèse said.

"Oh dear," Verlaque said. "I'm afraid my commissioner may have frightened him."

"What?" Paulik asked, finally joining the conversation. He had been trying in vain to get some reception on his cell phone.

"I'll be right back with the wine," Marie-Thérèse said, anxious to be gone. "That is, if you want some."

"Sounds lovely," Marine said. "And please bring us two bottles of sparkling water." After the girl had left, Marine asked, "How did it go this morning?"

"Fine," Verlaque replied. "But no earth-shattering discoveries. About the most interesting thing to come out of it is that Niki Darcette has spent time in jail for robbery."

"Really?" Marine asked.

"I'll fill you in later," Verlaque said. He wasn't especially keen to talk about the case in front of Sylvie. "And that Alain Denis was unpleasant to just about everyone here."

"It's funny how things come out about people after an awful event like this one," Marine said. "Past lives and so on, or how they react to tragedy. For example, who would have known that soft-spoken Mme Hobbs, who paints watercolors, was also a nurse during the Vietnam War?"

"That's so true," Verlaque agreed. "Some

people get tense, and others — like Niki and Marie-Thérèse — seem more relaxed."

"How is Mme Denis?" Sylvie asked.

"Sad, and angry, but not necessarily about her husband's death," Verlaque replied. Marie-Thérèse appeared with the salads, and he tilted his body to the side so that Marie-Thérèse could set down the starter in front of him. "That reminds me," he went on. He waited until the girl had gone and then told Marine and Sylvie about Mme Denis's missing ring.

They discussed the ring, and expensive jewelry in general, while eating their first course. "The food is wonderful here," Marine said, finishing her salad. "But I have a craving for . . ."

"A steak," Verlaque said. "Rare."

"Gummy bears," added Sylvie.

"I was going to say potato chips," Marine said. "Those English ones that you buy, Antoine, at Monoprix . . ."

"French ones are just as good," said Paulik. "Especially the handmade chips from Allauch. I have a cousin . . ."

Conversation stopped as a gray-haired, uniformed man came bounding up the terrace steps. Despite the warm July day he wore a jacket, whose multiple medals and stripes could be seen from yards away. He stood at the edge of the terrace and it didn't take long, as there were few diners, to spot whom he was looking for. The *"merde"* that he whispered could be heard by everyone on the terrace, which was followed by a long sigh. He then walked over to Verlaque's table.

Paulik set his napkin down and quickly got up. "Général Le Favre," he said. "Hello . . ."

"Welcome to Sordou," said Verlaque, who was also on his feet. Sylvie and Marine looked on. "May I present Dr. Marine Bonnet, and Sylvie Grassi."

*Le général* nodded briefly in their direction and shook their hands.

"Do you have news for us?" Paulik asked, perplexed.

"News?" *le général* repeated. He reached into his jacket and pulled out a folded newspaper, throwing it on the table. "Gentlemen, do I have news for you."

Verlaque grabbed the newspaper and opened it up. *"Merde,"* he said, handing it to Marine.

*"Merde* is right," Le Favre said. "And more expletives were said this morning at the precinct. The phone has been ringing off the hook."

Marine said nothing and passed the paper

to Paulik. He looked at it, then said, "*La Provence.* Figures."

"Granted, it doesn't have a circulation like *Le Figaro* or *Le Monde,*" Le Favre said. "But, it means we've lost a few days of investigation without the whole world knowing where — and how — Alain Denis was murdered. Plus . . . *that photo!*"

"Let me see," Sylvie said, taking the newspaper from Paulik. She looked at it and then laughed.

"The journalist obviously had a front-row seat in the dining room," Le Favre continued after he had glared at Sylvie.

"I have no idea how," Verlaque said, shaking his head back and forth.

*"Les hublots,"* Marine suggested. Marine looked at the photograph again and said, "The photo was taken from the kitchen. I went in there yesterday, looking for Marie-Thérèse, and I saw that some of the round mirrors in the dining room and bar are actually windows, so that the chef can observe the diners."

"The cook took these photos, and wrote the article?" Le Favre asked, the sarcasm in his voice heavy.

Verlaque thought of Niki Darcette. "The cook . . . unlikely . . . more probable one of the hotel staff; they are desperate to fill up the rooms."

"Antoine," Marine said. "I can't imagine . . ."

"Commissioner," Le Favre said, looking at Bruno Paulik. "Outsiders were strictly forbidden to come onto Sordou."

"And they didn't," Paulik replied. "There were two policemen on the dock, and a boat at the mouth of the harbor."

"So no last-minute hotel clients?" Le Favre asked. "No plumbers? Electricians?"

"No," Paulik replied. "Only one delivery . . . of food."

*Le général* raised his left eyebrow. "Who delivers the food?"

"Isnard," Verlaque replied. "He's harmless; a local fisherman. He came last night with baskets full of food, along with his cousin . . ."

The four friends looked at each other and Paulik slapped his forehead.

*"Merde!"* Verlaque bawled.

# CHAPTER TWENTY-THREE:
## 3 RUE VALOIS

Officer Jules Schoelcher had a book with him — one that Magali had given him, about a policeman in Glasgow — and although he liked the book, he couldn't stop staring out of the TGV's window. He was amazed how the blue sky of the south turned gray somewhere around Valence. He took a photograph out the train's window and his cell phone indicated the nearest village: Saint-Vallier. He had never been to Saint-Vallier, nor was ever likely to go, but he was fascinated and amazed that his Black-Berry knew where the TGV was, speeding along at more than three hundred kilometers an hour.

Alain Flamant, a fellow officer, had driven him to Aix's TGV station, fifteen minutes to the south of the city, and Jules had jumped on the train, his ticket in hand, almost missing it. Flamant made a "call me" gesture with his hand up to his face, and Jules saluted back.

Commissioner Paulik had called Jules from Sordou's phone, telling him to ask a secretary to book a return trip on the first class train; Jules had begun to object and Paulik stopped him, saying, "You'll be glad of the extra space, especially on the way back. . . . You may have some paperwork to go through." Jules Schoelcher was Paulik's favorite police officer, and one day he might well be a commissioner. Schoelcher's fastidiousness had helped enormously in a multiple-murder case a few months back, and Paulik knew that no one was better to do research than Schoelcher, the Palais de Justice's Alsatian-born keen observer and careful record keeper.

Jules was suddenly hungry and made his was to the bar car, holding on to the luggage racks above the passengers' heads as he was bumped along. He got to the bar car, two cars down, only to find a line of about fifteen passengers. He stood in line, trying to decide what to do. He could wait and pay too much for a mediocre sandwich, or hold off and get a quick bite in Paris. Either way, Paulik told him to keep the bills for any expenses, as he'd get reimbursed. But Jules didn't like charging the state for something overpriced. He shifted his weight and realized that he wouldn't have much time; he'd get to the Gare de Lyon at 12:45 p.m. and then have to make his way to his first stop in the first *arrondissement:* the Ministry of Culture. The line was barely moving, and he remembered that Magali had thrown an apple in his backpack before he left the apartment that morning, before he knew he'd be going to Paris. He shrugged and turned around and made his way back to his seat. He sat down, pulled the apple out of his backpack, and took a bite, thinking of Magali, and wondering how many espressos she had made that morning at her job.

The flat, industrial land north of Lyon gradually morphed into green rolling hills, some of them covered in vines. Jules grabbed his phone and snapped a picture. It was blurry, but he sent it to Magali anyway: "In Burgundy," he wrote. The phone told him where he was, so he added: "Cluny. On my way to Paris for some digging around . . . getting back to the Aix TGV station sometime after 10 p.m. I'll take the shuttle home. OXOX Jules." He knew that he could take a taxi back to Aix and charge it as an expense, but why, when the shuttle took exactly the same route and cost less than 4 euros?

By the time the train arrived in the sub-
urbs of Paris, Jules was very hungry. He
looked at his watch and knew that they
wouldn't be arriving at the station for fifteen
minutes, but some of the passengers were
already quickly gathering their bags and
suitcases and leaving their seats. He turned
around and watched them go through the
automatic doors and stand in the narrow
entryway. He shrugged, and the businessman beside him, now slowly packing up his
computer, smiled. "They do that every
time," he said. "Just watch, it will be backed
up, with people standing in the aisle, any
minute." The train slowed down, but was
still ten minutes from central Paris when
the aisle was now full of passengers, some
of them leaning on the backs of seats.

"You're right," Jules said.

"Told you," the businessman said. "I take
the TGV every week. You ride often?"

"Oh no," Jules replied. He didn't want to
say that he was a policeman, nor that this
was only, perhaps, his fifth or sixth time on
the fast train. He looked out the window,
which had water spots streaking against its
glass. "Rain," Jules said.

"Welcome to Paris."

"Well, Provence is too hot for me in the
summer," Jules said. "I don't mind the rain."

The businessman laughed. "Where you from?"

"Alsace," Jules said. "Near Colmar."

"Provence is different than Alsace, that's for sure."

Jules thought to himself: *yeah, cheaper housing, it's cleaner, and people are polite.* As if reading Jules's mind, the man said, "It's nice and orderly up there, and the real estate sure is less expensive, but I love the warmth and joie de vivre of the Provençaux." Jules thought of Magali and smiled. The train slowed down as they pulled up along the platform of the Gare de Lyon. "Have a nice day," the man said, standing up. "Enjoy the rain."

Jules smiled and said, "You too."

Ten minutes later, after making his way through the throngs of vacationers shuffling in the Gare de Lyon — many of whom it seemed to Jules had two large suitcases each — he was sitting on the Line 1 metro, making his way to the Ministry of Culture. He looked at a red-covered map book that Mme Girard — Judge Verlaque's impossibly well-organized secretary — had thrust into his hands before Jules had left. "You can't depend on your smart phone all the time," she had said. "You may be out of Internet range; Judge Verlaque already told me that the phones don't work on the RER. You never know with these things." Jules happily took the book, as he preferred paper; he had been raised reading maps with his parents while on vacation. He easily found the Rue Valois, squeezed in between the Jardin du Palais-Royal and a huge Bank of France building. Knowing that he had five stops to wait, he set the book on his knee and looked at his fellow passengers, enjoying the variety, especially compared to safe and smug Aix-en-Provence. He wondered what they thought of him. . . . Did he look like a university student? A young urban professional? He had worn good slacks, and a white shirt and tie, and was glad that he had a jacket.

He looked up at the metro map and saw that the Musée du Louvre/Palais-Royal stop was approaching, and he tried to remember the last time he had visited the Louvre: it was a school trip, when he had been fifteen or sixteen years old. He thought of that trip, and how half the class had been in awe of Paris, and the Louvre, and the other half thinking of their next cigarette. He had been among the first group. The *Mona Lisa* had been disappointing, as their teacher had warned, but Jules had fallen in love that day with the high realism of the Flemish Renaissance. He remembered trying to get as close as he could to the paintings, to see the artists' brushstrokes, and then being embarrassed by a guard who had yelled at him across the vast room. The doors to the metro opened and Jules quickly got up, realizing that he was at the Louvre.

It was only a three-minute walk to 3 Rue de Valois, and the rain was now a light drizzle. Jules remembered enough of high school history — *thank you, M. Mandar* — that he knew what Valois meant: it was the name of the kings and queens of France during the Middle Ages, almost up until 1600. He thought of Albert, one of his classmates — the smokers — whose standard comeback line when someone was displeased (which was often the case, especially for Albert) was "Let them eat cake!" Albert had loved the French Revolution, especially the gorier bits.

"Actually, it was brioches she said," Jules would correct him.

"If she even said it at all," M. Mandar would add.

The Ministry of Culture was easy to find, as the entire building was wrapped in a tarp, the kind they put on buildings that are under construction, or being renovated. The ministry's name was written in large letters along the side, along with a line drawing of what the renovated building would look like. The entrance was blocked off, surrounded by a ten-foot-high temporary wood fence, and construction workers came and went through a tiny opening. Jules stood there, collecting his thoughts. "Excuse me," he asked a worker going in, who was carrying a hammer. "Could you please tell me where the temporary entrance is?"

"Farther up the street," he said, motioning with the hammer. "But they'll all be at lunch now."

Jules looked at his watch; it was 1:15 p.m. "You're right," he said, and thanked the worker. His stomach growled. He hadn't come across any restaurants or food shops between here and the metro; it was unlikely that he'd find a kebob shop in the immediate vicinity. He turned around and, where the Rue de Valois met another street, saw a furniture shop with a curved white leather sofa in the window, and beside it, a bistro. He quickly walked across the street and looked at the menu, written on a chalkboard. The prices weren't as dear as he had imagined, and he had a quick look around at the terrace, which was packed, protected from the drizzle by an awning. He walked in, trying to look as Parisian as he could, and motioned to the barman with his thumb that he was a solo diner. Jules loved this kind of small bistro; the only sound was the laughter and chatter of the diners and the clanging of dishes and glasses. A harried waitress, but one who had the time to smile, showed Jules to a small wooden table in a corner where he could eat and watch the crowd outside. He was now starving; he quickly ordered a goat cheese crème brûlée with caramelized onions to start, and a classic steak tartare to follow. *"Salade ou frites?"* the waitress asked.

Jules decided to be bold and asked if the French fries were homemade.

*"Certainement,"* she replied.

*"Frites, alors,"* Jules said. *"Et de l'eau, s'il vous plaît."* He felt like he was cheating, in a way — having a big lunch before he had even got any work done — but what else was he to do until the ministry reopened? He took out one of the little notebooks that he always carried and flipped through it until he got to the Sordou case. He was to go through the records at the ministry's cultural monuments division and research anything to do with Sordou's lighthouse, and the family of lighthouse keepers, the Buffas, especially Prosper Buffa. Bruno

Paulik had filled Jules in as much as he could: Prosper, Verlaque had reported, was non-communicative and spoke half the time in incoherent riddles.

The goat cheese crème brûlée arrived, and Jules regretted not having a glass of Riesling to sip. He tried not to eat too quickly, but wanted, at the same time, to be inside the ministry as soon as it opened. A very smartly dressed elderly couple sat at the table next to him. Normally, that would have bothered Jules, as their table was almost touching his. But they didn't speak. The man, who wore a tweed jacket, even though it was a warm, rainy July day, had a silk handkerchief poking out of his pocket. He was obviously enjoying the goat cheese starter as much as Jules was, as after each bite he set his fork down and closed his eyes. His wife, with dyed blond hair (or so Jules assumed), ate cold salmon, but picked at it. She too was elegantly and carefully dressed, but it was her purse that caught Jules's eye. Even he knew — thanks to his sisters, and to Magali — what a 4,000-euro Hermès purse looked like.

Jules looked at the diners on the terrace; most of them, judging by their expensive sunglasses and black clothing, seemed to be locals. He wondered how many of them worked across the street. They were civil servants, like him, but their world seemed miles away from his own.

While Jules was in Paris, Alain Flamant began to go over the records of every film Alain Denis had ever been involved in. There were more than he could imagine: fifty-four to be exact. There were also two recent unauthorized biographies of the actor, and Flamant was able to get ahold of both authors when he got back from the train station. The first author confirmed that Denis was "a royal pain in the ass on set" but wasn't willing to elaborate. "Buy the book," he said before hanging up. The other biographer, a certain Franck Martini living in Toulouse, was more than willing to talk, perhaps due to alcohol — Flamant could hear the clinking of ice cubes while they spoke. "A number of people have threatened Denis over the years," Martini said, taking a loud sip. "But everyone I spoke to confirmed that the most hated enemy of Denis was the director Jean-Louis Navarre."

"The guy who made the Inspector Pernety series in the seventies?" Flamant asked. "I used to watch reruns of those on TV."

"Same man," Martini said. "Navarre said that Denis couldn't act, and that he was too pretty to play a cop. They once even had a fistfight. He hated Denis on the set and hated him even more when Denis had an affair with Navarre's wife."

Flamant whistled. "Is Navarre still alive?"

"Oh yeah," Martini said. Flamant heard him light a cigarette. "Lives in Paris, and still makes films for TV."

Flamant thanked the author and hung up. "Sophie," he said, turning to one of the junior officers enlisted to help with the research. "Find out what you can about Jean-Louis Navarre, a film director, and possible connections to Alain Denis," he said. "Does mostly stuff for television."

"Yes, sir," she replied, sweeping her jet-black hair away from her face. "I'll start with newspapers and magazines," she said. "Should I call him?"

"Not yet," Flamant replied. "Let's first see what we can dig up. We don't want to alarm him."

# Chapter Twenty-Four: Vernacular Architecture

The steak tartare had been perfectly seasoned — just enough capers and Tabasco — and Jules paid the bill and asked for the receipt, the first time in his life he had ever had an expense account meal. He carefully tucked it inside his Moleskine and left, thanking the waitress and barman, who shouted, *"A la prochaine!"* Jules grinned at the thought that the barman assumed he was Parisian and worked — or, even more improbable, lived — in this neighborhood. Jules knew, through work gossip, that Judge Verlaque came from mind-boggling wealth — flour mills, Jules had been told — and had grown up in Paris, in this *arrondissement.* What Jules didn't know was that the Verlaque family mansion — where the elderly M. and Mme Verlaque still lived — was just around the corner. And they too had been eating that day at the Valois bistro, at the table next to Jules.

Inside the Ministry of Culture's temporary entrance a sheet of paper had been taped to the wall listing the divisions and their locations. Jules saw that Historic Monuments was on the second floor, and he walked up the wide stone stairs amid hammering and sawing. A young woman sat at a small glass-topped desk at the top of the stairs and didn't look up when Jules approached.

"Excuse me," Jules said. "Sorry to bother . . ."

She looked up at him, put her pen down, and crossed her arms.

"I have an appointment," he went on. "I'm here to examine the records of a lighthouse, on —"

"Just a minute," she cut in. She got up and walked through a wooden door behind her. A few seconds later she came back, and Jules purposely went on where he had left off.

"Sordou," he said.

"Down the hall." She pointed as a jack-hammer started up. *"Oh mon dieu,"* she moaned, sitting back down.

"Thank you," Jules said. He thought of the friendly businessman on the train, and the train conductor who had joked as he punched Jules's ticket, and the waitress and barman across the street. Here was a girl who had a job that any recent graduate would die for, a job easier and more prestigious than waiting tables or pouring drinks, and yet she was miserable.

As he passed through a set of new, modern glass doors he met another worker, this one older, and smiling. Perhaps the glass doors insulated her from the construction noise, he thought. She showed him a desk, looked carefully at his police ID, and then minutes later was back with a stack of files and books on the lighthouses of France.

"I hope you're not researching all one hundred forty-eight lighthouses in France," she said, smiling.

"Oh no," Jules replied. "Just one. There are that many?"

"One hundred twenty on mainland France," she replied. "And nine in Corsica and nineteen in the *outre-mer.* There used to be a lot more, but one hundred and eighty were destroyed during World War II. . . . Some were rebuilt, others weren't."

"You know a lot about them," Jules commented.

"A few years ago we undertook a huge study of our coastal buildings," she replied. "I was on the committee that did the research. I was lucky to travel around and visit almost all of them, until my second child was born, so I missed out on the Caribbean lighthouses."

"Too bad," Jules replied.

"Which lighthouse are you interested in?"

"Sordou," he replied.

"Ah, the tall skinny one off the coast of Marseille. I remember it." She reached into the stack of books and files and pulled out a yellow file folder, and then two books. "Begin with these; the other books won't be much help. That's where Alain Denis was just murdered, no?" she then said.

"Sordou's great, isn't it?" Jules said, reaching for one of the books.

"Lovely island," she replied, understanding that she was to ask no more questions, and that he was indeed here to investigate the actor's murder. "Although I prefer other — smaller — lighthouses, ones that fit in more with the vernacular architecture."

"Mmm, indeed," Jules said, having no idea what she meant.

She flipped through one of the books she had set before Jules and found, almost instantly, the page she was looking for. "See this one," she said, pointing. "It's near Toulon. . . . This is the kind of lighthouse I like."

Jules bent over and looked at the small color photograph. "I get what you mean. It's very . . . small, and cute."

She laughed. "Yes, it is cute, and it's built in the same style of the houses and barns in that region."

"Oh," Jules said, filing away the word "vernacular" in his memory bank. "Thanks again for your help," he said.

"No problem," she said. She looked at her watch and then added, "I'd love to help you more, but in ten minutes I have to go downstairs for a meeting with the architects and engineers who are renovating the building. We're understaffed at the moment . . . holidays and illnesses. . . . Will you be okay on your own?"

"Oh sure!" Jules said with a wave of his hand.

For the next two hours Jules plowed through the file, and then the pages on Sordou's lighthouse from the books he had been given. He wrote down anything he thought important, including these facts:

the island's first lighthouse (13 meters high, built in 1326)

1774 burnt down

1825 rebuilt, now 40 meters high in cut stone

1829 it is lit by a new system of kindling with mineral oil

1881 electrification

Destroyed 1944 (WWII)
Rebuilt 1959 by architects Arbus and Cril-
lon, 71 meters high
1986 automated

The Buffa family had been guardians since 1868. There were no details given, only birth and death dates, and those only for the male members of the family, possibly because they were given the task of the lighthouse's upkeep. Prosper's great-grandfather, Honoré, born 1868, the year the Buffas came to Sordou, died in 1938, aged seventy. Jules noted that the importance of lighthouses during wartime guaranteed that the Buffa men stayed at home. They seemed to live long, healthy lives. Prosper's grandfather, Pierre, born in 1890, died in 1973. His son, Prosper's father, another Honoré, born in 1918, died in 1979. And Prosper, still very much alive, was born in 1937. Jules put his pen down and stretched, unsure of how to continue. The helpful librarian wasn't yet back, but he turned when he heard the glass doors open, and the surly young woman from the front desk appeared.

"You're still here?" she asked.

Jules wasn't sure if he wanted to reply or not. He knew that she didn't care one way or another. He finally said, "I'm just about to go. I think I've got all the information I can get from these files." He sighed, and the young girl seemed to relent.

"What are you looking for?" she asked.

"An event, that may or may not have happened, on an island near Marseille," he said. *Why not?* he thought. *I've got nothing to lose.*

She sat down, making it obvious that she was more interested in Jules Schoelcher's well-defined arm muscles than in his task.

"Well, you're only going to get facts about the architecture of the island here," she said. "We're *monuments,*" she added.

"What do you mean?" he asked.

"For historical events, on an island, you need to go to the Ministry of Ecology and Energy."

"Really?" he asked. "What floor are they on?"

She laughed. "They're on the twenty-sixth floor, I think."

Jules looked at her and then said, "Oh, not in this building I take it."

"No," she replied. "In La Défense."

"You're kidding," he moaned.

She looked at her watch. "You have time," she said. "Walk over to Châtelet and take the RER A. Don't take the Line 1 metro."

■ ■ ■ ■

Jules had never been on the RER trains that ran beneath Paris; as he looked at his watch — it was just after 4 p.m. — he was thankful that this particular train was fast. He had also never been to the newly constructed business center to the west of Paris, La Défense. He had seen photographs of it, of course, and had seen, standing in the middle of the Champs-Elysées with his parents, a hazy Grande Arche floating in the distance. The Grande Arche contained the ministry he was now racing to, and at 4:25 he was walking out of the train station and across a windy plaza that seemed to Jules to be something belonging more in a futuristic city than in centuries-old Paris. The rain had thankfully stopped, as he couldn't imagine an umbrella staying open in this windy square.

He crossed the plaza as quickly as he could, his head bent down just enough to break the wind but not so much that he would bump into anyone. His stomach was taut; he knew he should have called first, or looked up the hours of the Ministry of Ecology (and Energy!), but he hadn't had time and had wanted to escape what had become

302

a leering stare from the young assistant at the Ministry of Culture. He went through the Grande Arche's front doors and ran to the information desk.

"Hello," he stammered out. "I'm hoping to visit the Ministry of Ecology and Energy."

"You could," the information officer, a middle-aged man with incredibly greasy hair, replied. "But not today."

Jules rested his elbows on the counter that separated him and the man. "Are they already closed?" he asked.

"They're always closed to the public on Wednesday afternoons," he replied. "I'm sorry."

"I'm from the Aix-en-Provence police," Jules explained.

The man opened his hands. "Even if you were the Président de la République, they wouldn't let you in."

"Thanks," Jules said. He turned to leave and then said, "Surely they'd let the president in?"

"Well," the man said, chewing on a pencil end. "I guess."

Jules slumped over on his RER seat, checking his phone messages while there was a bit of Internet. There was only one, from Magali: "Have fun in the capital! OXOX,

M." Fun, yeah. The only thing he had accomplished was to find out a few facts and figures about the date of the lighthouse, and Prosper Buffa's birth date. He looked at his watch; it was just a little before 5 p.m.; he seemed to remember seeing that the Ministry of Culture was open until 5:30 p.m. If he ran he could make it back and perhaps be able to ask help from the friendly librarian before she went home. He kicked himself for not asking for her name and direct phone number. He remembered that she had visited Sordou, and he realized he should have asked her more questions about its history; perhaps this Prosper character had been chatty? On the other hand, he could just head straight to the Gare de Lyon and have a beer while waiting for his train. Jules looked at his watch again and jumped off at Châtelet, ran west along Rue Berger, backtracking on the path he had taken just an hour ago to get to La Défense. He walked into the ministry's temporary entrance at 5:25 p.m. and paused at the bottom of the stairs until he caught his breath. The construction workers had gone home, and the building was now as quiet as it had been noisy at 2 p.m. When he got to the top of the stairs the assistant was standing at her desk, putting a small umbrella in a cloth bag.

"Not you again," she said. "We're closed."

Jules walked up to her so quickly that she stepped back, stumbling, and bumped into her swivel chair. He reached into his jacket pocket and flashed his badge in her face, about three inches from her nose. "Police business!" he yelled. "And now, I'm going back into the Monuments office." In fact, this is what he imagined doing. But he couldn't bring himself to do it, no matter how many times he had rehearsed it while on the RER. Instead, he showed her his badge, said nothing, and then quietly walked toward the library, not looking back.

He walked over to the impressive glass doors and swung them open, walking quickly into the carpeted library. The lights were still on, and he called out, "Hello?"

"Over here, at my desk," the librarian answered from behind a small bookcase. She held her hand up and waved.

"Hello again," she said, smiling. "I thought you might have still been here after I finished my meeting."

"I went on a wild-goose chase."

"Where to?"

"La Défense," he answered. "The young woman at the entry told me I should be doing my research at the Ministry of Ecology and Energy."

"What? That would be useful if you were looking for information on birds, or the rock formations of the islands. Besides, they're closed on Wednesday afternoons."

Jules mustered up a smile. "I know."

"What do you need to know?" she asked. "I didn't want to ask before, but I think you're looking for something more than the history of the lighthouse. Something about Alain Denis and Sordou."

Jules leaned forward. "The current lighthouse guardian, Prosper Buffa, hinted that Alain Denis was around Sordou in the late 1950s," he said. "Did you meet this Prosper? From what I understand, he speaks in riddles."

"What a character," she said, slapping the desk. "I remember him."

"Did M. Buffa show you around the lighthouse, and Sordou?"

"Yes, he did," she replied. She leaned in and whispered, "And do you think he's linked to Alain Denis's death?"

"Perhaps," Jules said, lying. *How do I know?*

"You don't think that that poor old soul M. Buffa did it, do you?" she asked.

"No," he replied, lying again. "But he's

difficult to get information out of, as you know. Did he ever tell you stories, of the lighthouse?"

"He was strange, that's for sure," she said. "My name is Anne-Sophie, by the way."

"Jules." They shook hands.

"He rattled off lots of facts about the lighthouse," she said, sitting back now. "And we had a nice sandwich lunch that I had prepared in Marseille . . . and he told me about all of the buried ships around the island."

"Jacques Cousteau kind of stuff."

"Exactly," she answered. "The underwater ships are protected by the Ministry of Ecology and Energy, by the way. Back at La Défense."

Jules laughed.

Anne-Sophie went on, "And he did talk about deaths, strangely enough. His mother who died young, a younger brother who died of the flu, like his mother, fishermen going out to sea and never returning, storms . . . and a drowning."

"Drowning?" Jules asked.

She bit her lip, concentrating. "M. Buffa was about twenty when it happened," she said, sitting forward and getting flushed. "Yes, I remember now, because he was playing with me, the old flirt, and said that at the time of the drowning he was as old as I was, even though at the time I was well over thirty, and he knew it." She paused and then went on, "He was saddened by it, and he said there were two girls who died . . . no, wait a minute . . . a girl and an older woman."

Jules thought to himself that Prosper would have been twenty in 1957. "And that's all he said?" he asked. "No mention of Alain Denis?"

"Oh no, he didn't mention any names. My assistant had finished taking some measurements and photos, and our boat had arrived," she said. "So we said goodbye, and he told me to come back anytime, and he winked."

"Do you have records of deaths, on the islands, here in the library?" Jules asked.

"Not here," she answered. "Do you think there's a connection?"

Jules shrugged. "Never leave a stone unturned."

"Archives," she said, pointing to the ceiling. "Upstairs."

Jules looked at his watch; it was almost 6 p.m. *"Ils sont déjà fermés, non?"*

Anne-Sophie opened her desk drawer and pulled out a set of keys, jangling them.

# CHAPTER TWENTY-FIVE:
## BILL'S BUSINESS

"Général Le Favre looks like he just stepped out of the Franco-Algerian War," Marine said, breaking a bit of baguette and dabbing it on a plate where she had poured pungent green olive oil.

"He did," Verlaque answered. "He was a young officer stationed in Algiers; he was decorated various times, each medal for some act of bravery or another."

"Same thing in Vietnam," Paulik added. "I heard he once went into the jungle driving a helicopter that he had taken, without permission, from a French military base; he went deep into enemy territory to pick up some wounded soldiers who were stranded."

"Did he get them out?" Marine asked.

"Yes, just barely," Paulik replied. "They were shot at. As soon as he landed the helicopter, it basically fell into pieces. He's been retired for years, but they can't keep him away from police headquarters. He's an eccentric . . . lives by himself in some *cabanon* in the *calanque* Callelongue." Once fishermens' cabins, *cabanons* dotted Marseille's coast, especially on the fjord-like *calanques;* the one-room stone huts now sold for a small fortune. Because of this, Veraque whistled. He had dreamed of owning one for years, but despite his wealth he didn't have what it took to buy one: family connections in Marseille.

"Maybe he knows Shirley Hobbs from Vietnam," Sylvie whispered.

"They wouldn't recognize each other after all these years," Paulik pointed out.

"I was joking, Bruno," she replied.

"The baskets," Marine said, setting down her fork.

"Yes," replied Verlaque. "Isnard's cousin hid his camera in the baskets."

"If it's even his cousin," Marine replied.

"After lunch I'll go and tell Émile and the Le Bons that they'll have to find another way to get food here," Verlaque said.

"Well, I wouldn't be too upset if I were you," Sylvie said, looking down at the front page of *La Provence.* "You look quite good in the photo . . . 'cause cameras add about ten pounds, right? You look genuinely svelte."

Marine broke into laughter and Verlaque

put on his reading glasses. "Let me look at that again," he said.

The remainder of the lunch was uneventful, except for the dessert that Émile had managed to make: raspberry sorbet, ginger cookies, and chantilly.

After lunch, Verlaque reported the missing ring to the Le Bons and showed them the newspaper. Max and Cat-Cat seemed to Verlaque to be surprised, and as angered by the article — and photo — as he was.

"This certainly wasn't the kind of press we were hoping for," Max said, folding the paper in half and handing it back to Verlaque.

"Any publicity is good publicity," Velaque said. "No?"

"I hope you aren't suggesting that we set this up," Cat-Cat said.

Verlaque hesitated before answering. "No. If you *had* wanted this kind of thing, I assume you would have approached a larger newspaper."

The Le Bons laughed.

"I'll arrange for provisions to be brought to Sordou by a police boat, for now," Verlaque said. "Until you find another deliverer."

"Thank you," Cat-Cat said. "I'll have

Émile give you a list of what he needs food-wise for the next few days."

"About Mme Denis's ring," Max Le Bon said. "Did she accuse any of our staff?"

"No," Verlaque replied truthfully. "But she claims to have thoroughly searched her room too."

"I suppose you know about Niki's past?" Cat-Cat asked in a hushed voice.

"Yes," Verlaque replied. "Does she have keys to the room?"

"Yes, we all have access to the keys," Cat-Cat said. "But only four of us really ever use them: Niki, Marie-Thérèse, Mme Poux, and myself. And I trust all of them, as much as I trust my own husband."

"Well, if you could talk to them about it and have them keep an eye out," Verlaque said, "as the ring isn't our chief concern at the moment. When you ask Émile for his list," he went on, "maybe you could . . ."

"Yes?" Cat-Cat asked.

"I was going to suggest that Émile vary the menu a bit, with some meat."

"I'll second that," Max quickly added.

"Oh really?" Cat-Cat asked, looking at both men with a perplexed expression.

"The food on Sordou is fantastic," Verlaque said. "It's just to change it a bit."

"Émile does do this great thing with chorizo," Cat-Cat said.

"Chorizo?" Verlaque asked. "That would be great."

"Good," Cat-Cat replied. "I'll tell Émile that you'd like to try it. Of course, it all depends if he can get his hands on some good monkfish to go with it."

"Oh," Verlaque said. "It's a fish dish. I have to continue the interviews; I'll see you both later."

After Verlaque had left, Cat-Cat said to her husband, "The judge could use more fish in his diet, if you ask me."

Max Le Bon, married to his wife for over twenty years, didn't argue. Besides, whenever he got off the island, to visit their bank, or do other business in Marseille, he went to La Côte de Boeuf, a restaurant specializing in grilled meats.

"Hello, Mrs. Hobbs," Verlaque said in English as he saw Shirley Hobbs sitting on a chair in the hallway. "I'm sorry to have kept you waiting."

"My husband's in there now," she replied.

"Oh," Verlaque said, perplexed. Mr. Hobbs didn't speak French, and Bruno Paulik spoke very little English. He opened the door and went in; Hobbs and Paulik were laughing, bent over Mr. Hobbs's iPhone.

"My kids gave me this gadget," Bill Hobbs said to Verlaque, holding up his phone. "I use it mainly for photos. The commissioner and I were having a little bit of a communication problem, so I thought I'd regale him with some family photos."

"Their dog is hilarious," Paulik told Verlaque in French.

*"J'imagine,"* Verlaque replied. He was already hungry, and they had just eaten lunch. There was also a murder that needed solving, but they seemed no closer to an answer than they had been yesterday morning, down at the cove. Verlaque sat down, and Hobbs took his cue, putting his phone away.

"The Le Bons both saw you down on the dock on the afternoon of the murder," Verlaque began. "Do you remember anything odd, anything at all?"

"No," Hobbs replied. "I mean not in the sense that there was nothing odd out there, but I could see that the water was churning up a bit."

"No boats?"

"Not a one."

Verlaque translated for Paulik, who replied that he had understood most of it.

"You've been around the sea a lot," Verlaque said. "Bellingham is on the coast, no?"

"Yes," Hobbs said. "Although the Pacific Ocean is quite different from this big swimming pool you call the Med."

"In your opinion," Verlaque went on, "could someone have swum to shore early that evening, coming by boat from the other direction?"

Hobbs reflected for a moment before replying. "It would be a risk; they'd have to be a strong swimmer. Very strong. But I guess anything is possible, if you want something bad enough. That's what we used to tell our sons, anyway."

"And only Eric Monnier was on the dock with you?" Verlaque asked.

"Yes," Hobbs replied, holding still his shaking right hand. "Sorry, the Parkinson's flares up when I'm nervous," he explained. "Eric and I were trying to communicate, and then he went over to the bench opposite and smoked his cigar."

"Did you leave first?"

"No, he did. About five minutes before I did. . . . I got back to our room at six-forty-five p.m."

"Did you hear the gunshot?" Paulik asked in passable English.

"Yes," Hobbs answered. "When I was on the beach. Um, has it occurred to you that this beachcomber . . ."

"Prosper?"

"Yes, Prosper. Is it possible that he may have been hunting, and accidently . . ."

"Shot a man at close range, on a beach?" Verlaque asked. "While hunting rabbits?"

"Well, it sounds stupid when you put it like that. But there are lots of birds there."

"And your wife?" Verlaque asked. "Was she in your room when you got back?"

"Yes, she was painting," Hobbs answered. "She touches up her watercolors in our room, at the desk."

"What time did you get up the next morning, for fishing?" Verlaque asked. "It must have been early."

"Six a.m.," Hobbs replied. "Brice and I had agreed to meet in the Jacky Bar at six-twenty a.m. He was waiting for me when I got there."

Paulik nodded, so Verlaque knew that he was following the English.

"And you didn't go near the cove, obviously," Verlaque said.

"No, we walked down the steps and turned left at the harbor, so to speak, and made for the cliffs on the north side of the island."

"What did you talk about?"

"We did talk a little about Alain Denis, if that's what you're getting at," Hobbs said.

"That is what I'm getting at."

"Well, if you don't mind me saying so, I think our conversation is private."

"Please," Paulik said, and then stopped, as he couldn't find the English words to continue.

"The boy's stepfather was murdered," Verlaque said. "You'd be helping Brice by telling us what you talked about; you wouldn't be accusing him."

Bill Hobbs bit his bottom lip. "I'm not sure about that."

"Oh?"

"I can't, and won't, tell you," Hobbs said. "I'm sorry."

Mrs. Hobbs's interview went quickly. She confirmed that Bill Hobbs had come back to their room just after 6:45 p.m., and then they had dressed for dinner and played a game of gin rummy on their terrace. No, she and her husband hadn't discussed his fishing expedition, as that was "Bill's business." Just before she got up to leave, Verlaque asked her about Vietnam. She explained that she had been fresh out of nursing school, and had lost a brother in the war, and because of that, she signed up to volunteer. She wanted to help other soldiers who needed medical care (her brother had died not in the jungle, but on a hospital bed in an army base, of an infection). She stayed in Vietnam on and off for five years, and then worked in a hospital in Seattle, where she met Bill, who worked across the street at one of his family's hardware stores. They married late, for those days, she said: she was thirty-two and Bill was thirty-four.

Sylvie Grassi kept so serious throughout her interview that Verlaque almost thanked her. As funny as she was, he found her constant wisecracks draining. Her bit of revealing news was that she had overheard the Le Bons arguing; she had been using the guest toilets beside their office and had overheard — either through the vents, or the thin walls — their conversation. "Max accused Cat-Cat of being heartless," Sylvie told Verlaque and Paulik. "She said that the murder would bring the hotel some publicity, and clients. He seemed disgusted by the thought, and she sounded non-plussed. Very practical and matter-of-fact. And then Cat-Cat reminded Max that the hotel was his idea, and that the investors were getting edgy. And then the weird thing was, after their argument I could hear them talking to Marie-Thérèse, who must have overheard but who was pretending not to, and after she left the Le Bons commented that she had most likely overheard every word they said."

After Sylvie had left, Verlaque doodled on a scrap piece of paper, listing the hotel's employees' and guests' names, and at the top of the page wrote "motives." Paulik leaned over and looked at the page as Verlaque wrote. Beside Mme Denis's name he wrote "inheritance, and hatred." Paulik nodded in approval. Next to Brice's name, "hatred."

"Niki?" Verlaque asked.

"Hatred of men?" Paulik suggested. Verlaque wrote it down.

"Serge, the bartender?" Verlaque asked.

"They're both from Marseille," Paulik said. "Perhaps some old vendetta. Seems far-fetched, doesn't it?"

Verlaque put a question mark after Canzano's name.

"Marie-Thérèse has no motive," Verlaque said. "But she was protecting her bosses from us. . . . She didn't tell us about their argument."

"Well, the Hobbses are definitely out of the picture," Paulik said. "And Eric Monnier, as he was with Bill Hobbs."

Verlaque said, "I know what you're saying. . . . The Hobbses can't possibly have any reason for killing a French film star whom they've probably never heard of, Eric neither, for that matter. I can't imagine him ever going to the cinema. But they're here for a reason. They are here to shed some kind of light on the story."

# Chapter Twenty-Six:
## Le Buzz

"I may not seem very friendly at times," Cat-Cat Le Bon began her interview. "But I'd like to say how thankful I am that you are both here, on Sordou, right now."

"I've been thinking," Verlaque said. "Is it easy for one to phone the hotel, for example, and find out who will be staying here during a certain week?"

"Certainly not," Cat-Cat said, frowning.

"Let's say I was to call and pretend I was a cousin," Verlaque said, thinking of Isnard. "And I wanted to double-check when my cousin was booked in here."

"Well, we'd have to be pretty thick to fall for that," Cat-Cat replied.

Bruno Paulik smiled.

"Do you think that whoever murdered M. Denis would have wanted an examining magistrate here? For kicks?" Cat-Cat asked.

"Something like that," Verlaque said.

"That just seems . . . stupid."

"Was it kept fairly quiet that Alain Denis would be on vacation?" Paulik asked.

"Oh no!" Cat-Cat laughed. "Didn't you know? Now I understand why you keep asking these questions. Alain Denis announced it on *Le Buzz* sometime in late spring."

Verlaque looked at Paulik, who was busy writing. They would check the date that the television show aired against the dates of bookings.

"I would have told you," Cat-Cat went on, "but I thought you knew."

"I've never seen that show," Verlaque said. He hated French television; he had only recently figured out how to watch his favorite television show — where an English architect visits couples who are building or renovating homes in the English countryside — on his computer.

"I haven't seen it either," Paulik added.

"That must have helped your bookings," Verlaque said.

"Only marginally, from what we can tell," Cat-Cat replied. "M. Denis was fairly vague when asked about his vacations, so you'd have to know Sordou, or do some research, to figure out where he was talking about. There are dozens of islands between here and Nice."

"What exactly did he say?" Paulik asked,

pen ready.

"That he was going *home,*" Cat-Cat said. "To the sun and sea, to an enchanted, unvisited island."

"And he didn't mention Sordou?" Verlaque asked.

"No, unfortunately for us," Cat-Cat said. "If one didn't know Provence very well, they would probably mistake his hint for another island. We'd only just opened the hotel: there hasn't been a hotel running here since 1966. Speaking of bookings . . ."

Verlaque braced himself; he knew that the Le Bons were anxious to reopen the hotel. "I'm afraid it's impossible until we solve this crime," he said.

"And we're just supposed to sit here and lose clients, and lose money?"

"We're working as fast as we can," Paulik offered.

"When are your next bookings?" Verlaque asked. "Saturday?"

"Yes," Cat-Cat said.

"That gives us three more days," Verlaque said. "If we aren't done by then, perhaps we can move the investigation to the mainland, in Marseille."

Cat-Cat drew in a big breath and then sighed with relief.

"The afternoon of the murder," Verlaque

said. "Were you in your office, or room?"

"Room," Cat-Cat replied. "We have a small apartment at the back of the hotel, next to Mme Poux's. I was lying on the bed reading when I heard the shot, and Max was in the shower, so he didn't hear it."

"What did you do?"

"Nothing," she replied, "since I assumed it was Prosper. But I was angry, because our clients could have gotten hurt. I had seen Mme Hobbs earlier in the day, painting by the sea, and her husband and M. Monnier sitting together down by the dock."

"What time?"

"Well, it would have been before five-thirty p.m., because that was when I came up to our apartment to rest."

"Were you worried when you hired someone who had spent time in jail?" Verlaque asked.

Mme Le Bon smirked. "It was Max's idea, not mine," she said. "He's the more benevolent of the two of us." Verlaque thought of their argument, as described by Sylvie. "He had read a newspaper article about how well ex-convicts can do in the restaurant and hotel business, if given a chance and properly trained," she continued. "That young chef in England started it."

"Jamie Oliver," Verlaque offered.

"Yes, that's him. But I'm glad, now, that we hired Niki."

"She seems very dedicated," Verlaque said. "And efficient. How did she get on with M. Denis?"

"I was afraid you would ask that," Cat-Cat replied.

"Oh?"

"Niki didn't like him, let's just put it that way."

"I'm afraid, Mme Le Bon," Paulik said, "that you'll have to be more specific."

"He . . . made a pass at Niki," she said.

"Just once?" Verlaque asked. "Mlle Darcette didn't tell us."

"More than once," Cat-Cat said flatly.

"She told you, then?"

"Yes, she was livid," Cat-Cat said. "I've never seen her so upset."

"Upset-sad, or upset-angry?" Verlaque asked.

"The latter."

Max Le Bon seemed more nervous than his wife. In fact, Velaque had commented to Paulik at the end of the day that Cat-Cat Le Bon hadn't seemed the slightest bit nervous, which they both knew was rare. "I've seen even police get nervous under police questioning," Bruno Paulik had said.

Max Le Bon had confirmed that both he and his wife were in their apartment when the gun went off, and when pressed admitted that Niki Darcette had been furious over Denis's unwelcome flirtations. What he was able to add had to do with the hotel, as if he wanted to release some of the tension: "We weren't able to book all of the rooms, even this week, even with Alain Denis here," M. Le Bon said. "It's that single that you are in, commissioner."

"Why do you think that is?" Verlaque asked.

"Any number of things, none of which we thought of when we naively bought this hotel," Le Bon said. "Proximity to Marseille . . . or is fifteen miles too far out? Too expensive, or not expensive enough? Too quiet? Who knows . . ." His voice fell off.

"And since Denis's death?"

"I don't like to admit this," Le Bon said. "But we're now fully booked until the second week of September."

"So his death helped, in some weird way."

"Who knows?" Le Bon repeated. "But Niki has been working really hard over this past week; she's been sending out press releases daily, and harassing journalists . . .

before M. Denis's death, I'd like to add. We also splurged and put a small ad in *Madame Figaro* magazine. It came out last Sunday. We're waiting to ask clients, when they get here, if they saw the ad. If they telephone to reserve, we ask them outright how they found out about Sordou."

"And what do they say?"

"Niki tells me about a third saw the *Madame Figaro* ad, and a few have seen our website, and one or two have admitted they'd like to come to pay homage to Alain Denis."

"Only one ot two?" Paulik asked.

"Truth be told," Max said, "there are probably more than that who booked because of Denis, but . . ."

"But they won't admit it," Verlaque suggested.

"Exactly," Le Bon said. "It doesn't put anyone in a good light if they say they'd like to come to see the island where a famous actor was murdered."

"Good afternoon, gentlemen," Eric Monnier said as he sat down, setting his Panama hat on the table.

"Hello, M. Monnier," Verlaque said. "You were by the dock, having a cigar, on the afternoon of Alain Denis's death."

"Yes indeed," Monnier replied. "An Up-mann forty-six. My last one."

"Last cigar?" Verlaque asked. "Or last forty-six?"

Monnier laughed. "Last forty-six; don't worry!"

"How long were you there?" Verlaque asked.

"For over an hour," Monnier said. "As long as it took me to smoke the forty-six. I got there just before five p.m. and left sometime after six-thirty p.m."

"Did you see anything unusual?" Paulik asked.

"No, or I would have told you," Monnier replied. "Bill Hobbs was reading some self-help book that Yanks go for, on the bench opposite me. We tried to talk, but there was an issue with the languages."

"But you knew what he was reading?" Paulik asked.

"I can read English fairly well," Monnier said, "but get all tongue twisted when I have to speak it."

"And out on the water? Was there anything?"

"Nothing," Monnier said. "It was getting rough, even I could see that. Not a soul was out there."

"You're from Marseille, right?" Verlaque

asked. "The commissioner did some digging around before he got to Sordou."

"Well done," Monnier said, winking. "And I would imagine you have a team of policemen researching our files right now."

"We do."

"I was born in Marseille on June 12, 1940."

"Alain Denis was born in Marseille in 1940 as well," Verlaque said.

"Marseille is a big city," Monnier replied.

Verlaque said, "Mme Poux, the housekeeper, told me that Alain Denis was a champion swimmer. Did you know that?"

"Not in any kind of detail," Monnier said. "He swam at the club, I believe . . . Le Cercle des Nageurs. Again, like his prestigious high school and family mansion overlooking the Corniche Kennedy, Le Cercle was way out of my league."

"You've been to Sordou before?" Verlaque asked. "You told me on the boat."

"A few times, yes, when it had a roaring hotel. We didn't go near the hotel, mind you. Stuck to the other side of the island. But I mostly vacationed on Frioul, at my uncle's cabin. Sometimes when we were kids we would get a boat ride over here and swim around Sordou's shore, hoping to get a glimpse of the rich and famous staying at the hotel."

"Oh, so you swam too," Verlaque said.

"My dear boy, we all swam in those days," Monnier said. "There wasn't television — unless you were rich — or video games, or those awful cell phones."

"So you didn't know each other?" Verlaque asked. "Denis went to Thiers High School."

"I know that," Monnier said. "When he became famous, which was soon after high school, if I remember correctly, all of Marseille claimed some responsibly for Denis's talent and stardom. Alas, I can claim nothing. I never met him. In 1953 I was awarded a scholarship to study with the Jesuits in the Vaucluse."

"The boarding school?" Paulik asked. "In Avignon? Saint-Joseph?"

"That's the one," Monnier said. "Best thing that ever happened to me."

"Why do you say that?" Verlaque asked.

"Because they taught me poetry, dear boy."

Yolaine Poux walked silently into their makeshift office and sat down, smoothing her apron.

"I'm sorry to take you away from your work," Verlaque said.

"It's not a problem," she answered.

Verlaque had a hard time not looking at Yolaine Poux; her gaze — especially her light-blue eyes — was intense. Marine had commented on what a handsome woman Mme Poux was, and Verlaque now agreed. He had never seen her this close; her complexion was radiant, even if she too was born in 1940. Her cheekbones were prominent, showing off not only her olive skin but also her full lips and wide mouth. But it was her statuesque physique that so impressed him; her legs were long and still thin and shapely — he could see this as her black dress fell just to the knee — and her shoulders wide. "You told me something very interesting yesterday," he began. "That Alain Denis was a champion swimmer. Did you know him growing up?"

"Yes, I did," she answered slowly but clearly. "Marseille is a village."

"Ha," Verlaque mused. "M. Monnier just referred to it as a big city."

"He lives in Aix," she replied. "The Aixois always think that Marseille is a big city."

Verlaque could see Paulik writing, and he could imagine what it said: "No apparent connection between Yolaine Poux and Eric Monnier." Unless she's a good liar, thought Verlaque.

"Would you care to tell us how you knew

Alain Denis?" Verlaque asked.

Mme Poux looked at her watch, and both men saw that she caressed its face. "Do you have a while?" she finally asked.

# CHAPTER TWENTY-SEVEN:
# LE CERCLE DES NAGEURS

Paulik reached into his briefcase and pulled out a small tape recorder. "Do you mind?" he asked.

"Not at all," Mme Poux replied.

She began:

"Whenever I hear classical piano music, especially Bach, I close my eyes and imagine myself floating, on my back, in seawater, with the blue southern sky above me. The higher piano notes sound to me like the delicate ripples of water: like sparkles of light.

"The staff could swim in the club in those days; I doubt that they can today. Le Cercle des Nageurs — that's Marseille's elite private swimming club — was opened in 1921 by a Spanish architect who was obsessed with swimming. Even back then the club trained Olympic swimmers and water polo players, but it also gave bourgeois Marseillais a place where they could swim and socialize. All the same, I had to defend the club when I spoke to my parents about it when I got the job; 'It's not a club for the rich,' I would tell them. They were Communists, as were most of our friends and neighbors. I told my parents: 'The rich have vacation houses. Members of Le Cercle do not; Le Cercle is their residence secondaire.'

" 'Then it should be open to all!' my father would yell, banging the kitchen table with his fist. 'And free!'

"I had to bite my lip; I liked the club's members. They were friendly, and chic, and well educated. I don't know how much the membership fee was back then, in 1956, when I got the job, but I've seen this year's rates published in *La Provence:* the initiation fee, after two members formally sponsor you, is sixteen hundred euros, and after that, twelve hundred fifty yearly.

"I got the job my last summer of high school — I skipped two grades in elementary school. I'd help launder the pool's towels, and sometimes serve light snacks and drinks in the small members' lounge. When I graduated I stayed on full-time. There weren't a lot of jobs in postwar Marseille, and at Le Cercle you felt like you were with a family.

"In the early days, the members dove off

the low cliffs at the base of the club into the sea, but in 1932 a *bassin d'été* was built — a long and sleek outdoor pool, overlooking the Mediterranean and eastern Marseille, full of sea water. I'd never seen such a beautiful pool. . . . When I had finished my shift I'd quickly put on my bathing suit and step carefully into the pool. I tried not to make myself noticed.

"I was a good, natural swimmer, and I knew it. I had my father's wide shoulders and narrow hips, and I could glide through the water just as well as any of the semiprofessional swimmers. Even then there were Olympic swimmers at Le Cercle; nowadays there are so many that I lose track of their names, when I get the chance to watch the Olympics on the small television in my room. In 1951 our own Joseph Bernardo broke the world record in the four-by-two-hundred-meter free swim. He went on to the Olympics in 1952 and in that *La Provence* article I mentioned earlier the journalist interviewed Bernardo; he still goes daily to the club, to swim, and then he reclines on a chaise longue and soaks up some sun, and he talks with the younger Olympic hopefuls. There were photos.

"In 1956, the year I came, an indoor freshwater pool was built, and years after, an Olympic pool was installed. In 1967 I went back to Le Cercle with my husband, to show him my beloved seawater pool, jutting out over the cliffs, but Rémy seemed nervous, and we didn't stay long. Rémy didn't want me to work; he thought that married women should stay home, especially to look after the children. But we didn't have any children, and then Rémy died of a heart attack in 1977. That's when I finally regretted listening to Rémy, and my father, who didn't want me to apply to university, even though all of my teachers wanted me to.

"1956 was a magical summer — it was dry and hot — and I felt thrilled to be alive. The club members who were my age had seen my skill at swimming and made me one of their own. For that summer, anyway. I haven't been swimming since then; I wonder if I'd remember how. I can't remember many of the faces of my friends from that summer — all wealthier than I was — but I can remember some names: Roger, Alice, Claude, Xavier, Marie-Pierre . . . and Alain, of course. Everyone loved him.

"I distinctly remembered the first time I saw his face up close; I was carrying a stack of fluffy white towels into the woman's change room and he was walking down the hall, toward the *bassin d'été,* humming. I almost ran into him, and he caught the towels before they slid one by one onto the floor, and he laughed. *'Fais attention, ma belle!'* he cried. Be careful, my beautiful!

"I told my best friend the next day how beautiful he was. 'He's beautiful enough to be in the pictures,' I said. We laughed, and my father banged on my bedroom wall because we were making too much noise. He was reading Karl Marx.

"Years later I ran into my friend on La Canebière. 'Fancy that!' she had said, shaking my arm. 'You were right all those years ago! Alain Denis was beautiful enough for the movies!' I was Mme Poux now and had never told her what had exactly happened during that summer of 1956.

"Alain Denis — he was the son of a wealthy doctor and a ballet dancer — seemed to glide, not walk, around Le Cercle. A string of young men and women usually followed him, each one vying for his attention. His was a beauty almost feminine: high cheekbones, full lips, and piercing steel-blue eyes. The boys would jump around Alain, trying to be funny. The girls would pout. I immediately noted — this was a pool, after all — that Alain's body was hairless. It fascinated me. That was a contrast to the hair on his head, which he wore longer than what was the fashion in those days; it was parted on the side; it fell elegantly in front of his face. He hardly ever bothered to flick it back out of the way!

" 'Hey, towel girl,' he whispered to me one afternoon when I had finished my shift. I had just swum four laps in the seawater pool and was resting, with my elbows propped up on the pool's edge. I had been looking out at the sea. 'You're a lovely swimmer,' he said.

" 'Thank you,' was all I replied.

" 'What's your name, towel girl?'

"I told him.

" 'See you around, Yolaine,' he said, and dove back under the water.

"I grabbed my towel and got out of the water as quickly as I could; my legs were shaking. I could feel him watching me as I walked around the pool's edge, toward the door that led to the changing rooms. The next day I went straight home after work, not wanting to run into him again. But four days later, after I had I finished my shift on a suffocatingly hot August day, I swam again, almost forgetting about the bold beautiful boy. I swam some laps and then floated on my back — always with that piano music playing in my head — and I lay there, looking at the sky with its fine white clouds racing by. All of a sudden a dark spot appeared in the water just by my right shoulder, and I glanced at it while I floated. It grew out of the water, slowly, and Alain's face appeared. 'Hello, Yolaine,' he whispered. 'You need to teach me how to swim like you.'

" 'Don't be silly,' I told him, and I quickly reached for the pool's bottom with my feet. I didn't want to be lying on my back so close to him. 'You're on the swim team. There's nothing I could teach you,' I said.

" 'I have speed, but not grace,' he said, smiling.

"I'll never forget those words. Years later, after reading about his fall from cinema, those words would come back to me. I have speed, but not grace. Did he become a star too quickly?

" 'Let's lie in the sun,' he suggested.

"So we got out of the pool and lay on our stomachs, propping up our heads so that we could talk, but also look out at the sea. He made me laugh with stories of the swim team; how Aimé always jumped in a second before everyone else, or how Roger had to be forced into the water every morning. We began swimming, and sunning, together almost every night after my shift, for four weeks. His friends never seemed to be around then; I sometimes finished late, and most of the kids left the pool in the late afternoon. Or were they giving Alain some space, knowing that he was wooing me? I never knew . . .

"And then, on the fifth week, I stopped seeing him. You see, the previous Saturday we had swum together, and I felt comfortable enough to tell Alain about my family. He did the same. I even made him laugh. We stayed until I said that I would be needed at home, to help with dinner, and Alain had looked genuinely saddened to say goodbye. We walked down the long hallway toward the change rooms, and just before I was to go into the wooden door marked *femmes* Alain took me by the waist, held my gaze with his blue eyes, and kissed me. To my surprise I kissed back. I have never, before or after, even with Rémy, felt so thrilled to kiss a man. I'm ashamed to say that, but I want you to know everything. 'You're so —' Alain began to say, but a cough down the hall cut his sentence short. We both swung around to see Thierry, the swim-team coach, standing at the end of the hall, his hands on his hips. Alain let go of me and I fled into the change room, trembling.

"At the end of the summer, Alain won the club's four-hundred-meter crawl, and when he stood on the makeshift podium, surrounded by friends and club members, I was almost certain that he caught my eye, and slowly, for two or three seconds, closed his own eyes, as if to apologize. I can understand why we couldn't go on seeing each other; he was a member, I an employee. He was a doctor's son; my father drove a tram.

"The following April a friend of Alain's — he too was well connected; I had seen him at Le Cercle and never liked him — invited Alain to the film festival in Cannes. Alain had been a stylish dresser — this I didn't know, as I usually saw him in a black bathing suit, or in shorts. It was only when I saw photos of him in newspapers and magazines that I realized how smart a dresser he was. His fashion flair — elegant with a haphazard look was how it was described — and beauty caught the attention of at least two film directors in Cannes, as you know. I always respected the fact that he didn't sign the contract with that flashy Hollywood director, but instead agreed to star in a small movie being filmed in Paris that summer. We all know the story, but I'll repeat it anyway. His next film was with that avant-garde Italian director; and for his third film he was back in Cannes, this time to accept the Palme d'Or for best actor."

# CHAPTER TWENTY-EIGHT: DEFENDING MARSEILLE

"That was the last time I ever saw Alain," Mme Poux said.

Verlaque shifted in his seat, realizing that he hadn't budged throughout the telling of her story. His feet were asleep. "Until this week," he said.

"Until this week," she repeated.

"Did he recognize you?"

"No," Mme Poux replied. "I was extra careful to avoid him. I had Marie-Thérèse deal with him. Poor girl."

"Your name has changed too," Verlaque said.

"Yes. I was Yolaine Ségonde then; on Sordou I'm Mme Poux."

Verlaque told Mme Poux about Mme Denis's missing ring. "I haven't seen it," she replied. "It sounds like it might be worth a lot of money, although I've always thought that the sentimental value of jewelry outweighs any monetary price."

343

Verlaque nodded, impressed by how well spoken she was; it reminded him of Serge and his passion for history. "You can never tell a book by its cover," Emmeline had always said. And each time her grandsons Antoine and Sébastien would follow with the line that they knew would come next: "from *The Mill on the Floss* by George Eliot." It had been Emmeline's favorite book. "George, who was really a girl," Sébastien would add, smiling from ear to ear, and Antoine would roll his eyes.

He noticed that the maid was once again rubbing her old-fashioned watch with its tiny rectangular face and thin leather strap.

"Do you always clean the rooms?" Paulik asked.

"No," she replied. "I take turns with Marie-Thérèse."

Paulik and Verlaque got up and stretched after Mme Poux had left. A knock sounded, and Verlaque said, "Come in, Hugo." But it was Marie-Thérèse who opened the door, balancing on her hip a tray holding a pot of tea and a plate of cookies.

"Thank you," Paulik said.

"*C'est l' heure de goûter!*" Marie-Thérèse sang out.

"Snack time, indeed. That's so kind of you

344

to remember us in here," Verlaque said, taking the tray from her and setting it down on the table.

Marie-Thérèse said, "It's my job! I like to see that everyone is taken care of."

"Thank you," Verlaque said. "And if you see Hugo out there, you can tell him that we're ready for his interview."

"I saw him out on the terrace," she replied. "I'll go and get him." And she left.

"That was an amazing story that Mme Poux told," Paulik said, biting into a cookie.

"I wasn't expecting it," Verlaque said. "It was beautifully sad; a classic story of a young love that couldn't be realized due to outside pressure."

*"Romeo and Juliette,"* Paulik offered.

"Marseille style," Verlaque added. "But one wouldn't kill for that, would they?"

"Lust, love . . ."

*"Money,"* Verlaque said. "When we're through here let's see if that lawyer has arrived; my bet is that Mme Denis will inherit."

"According to her there's not much left," Paulik said.

"If we believe that —"

A loud knock cut off Verlaque's sentence, and Hugo Sammut came in.

"Hey," Hugo said, walking across the

room and sitting down opposite the two men.

"Hello, Hugo," Verlaque said. "Let's begin with the afternoon of the murder; what did you do when we got back from the north shore of the island?" Paulik looked at Verlaque, puzzled, and the judge quickly explained that he and Marine had gone for a walk and got a boat ride back to the hotel with Hugo, who had been out with Sylvie. "Did you hear or see anything strange?"

"Nada," Sammut replied. "I pulled the boat up with you guys just after five p.m. and went to my cabin. A little later I looked out my window and saw Bill Hobbs sitting on a bench by the dock."

"With Eric Monnier," Paulik suggested.

"Mmmm, he was alone," Hugo said.

"Are you sure?" Verlaque asked.

"Yep."

"Can you see the whole dock from your cabin window?" Verlaque asked.

"Both benches?" Paulik added.

Hugo reflected. "Um, come to think of it, no. I can only see the north one; the south one is blocked from my view by the gazebo."

"Thank you," Verlaque replied. "Do you remember what time you looked out the window?"

"Nah, sorry," Hugo said. "I was beat."

346

"And the gunshot?" Paulik asked. "Did you hear it?"

"Nope," Hugo replied. "I had a long nap and woke up a little after six-thirty p.m."

"And so you saw nothing suspicious?" Verlaque asked.

"No," Sammut slowly replied. "But on Monday morning, after the breakfast when I lost my temper, I saw Denis down by the cove."

"Go on," Verlaque said.

"Well, I walked down there to cool off, and he was standing on the farthest rock out, staring down into the water."

"Okay," Verlaque slowly said. "And you found that odd?"

Hugo shrugged. "It's just that he stayed there for more than fifteen minutes, just staring, and not moving. That's all. I found it weird. I got bored and turned around and came back to my cabin."

"It *is* strange," Paulik said after Hugo Sammut had left. "That story of Alain Denis looking down into the water."

"And more strange that Hugo didn't hear the gunshot," Verlaque said, "given that his cabin is closer to the cove than the hotel is. But I agree," he went on, "that Alan Denis didn't seem like the kind of man who would be interested in examining sea urchins and fishes. It's almost as if *he* was the murderer, checking the depth of the sea, knowing that he would throw the pistol in there."

"Maybe he *was* planning something nasty, and someone beat him to it."

"Such an odd thing," Verlaque said. He was about to speak again when the door opened and Clément Viale breezed in.

"Hello, old chum," Viale said, sitting down.

"Hello, Clément," Verlaque said. "I'm going to get right to the point: just how big is your share in Sordou?"

"Too big, unfortunately," Viale replied. "I own a quarter; Max and Cat-Cat own half, and some private investors own the remaining quarter."

"And they're worried," Verlaque said.

"We all are," Viale answered. "It came as a total surprise that we couldn't fill the hotel this month."

"But now it's full?"

Viale smiled. "Yes, but if you think —"

"If I think what?" Verlaque asked.

"Dough Boy, you're being a smart ass, like you were when we were in university."

Verlaque stayed silent.

"If you think that I — or Max or Cat-Cat for that matter — killed some has-been actor just to fill this place . . ."

"It is full, *now.*"

"It would have filled up."

"You said you were worried," Verlaque said. "But let's move on to another subject. Mme Denis."

Viale laughed nervously. "I suppose the barman told you he saw us leaving, late, together?"

"Yes," Verlaque said. "But I had been there too, remember? Anyway, Mme Denis told me of the spare room at the end of the hall."

Viale frowned, as if Verlaque were the guilty party. "Okay, we had a little tryst, in that room. Good detective work," he said. "Bravo." Viale made a gesture of clapping, without touching his hands together. "It was only two nights," he added.

"We've only been here for four nights," Verlaque said.

"Hey, you weren't exactly a saint back in university!" Viale quipped. "You were the least faithful person I knew."

Paulik coughed and said, "Let's stick to the present investigation, M. Viale."

"Did she hate her husband?" Verlaque asked.

"We didn't even talk about him!" Viale said, his voice getting hoarse. "We had *other* things to do."

■ ■ ■ ■

Verlaque was intrigued to finally spend a moment with Delphine Viale. Up close her face was somewhat softer; her eyes looked tired and her skin was pale compared to the other clients who actually spent time outside, but it glowed. She looked happier than she had when they first got to the island. She sat still, and upright, her hands folded on her lap. She wore her usual outfit of beige linen pants and a white, close-fitted blouse that showed off her thin waist. "I'm not sure what you said to Clément," she began. "But he sure stormed out of here."

"We were talking about his investment here on Sordou," Verlaque replied, half-lying.

"Oh, that *would* make him angry," she said.

"He was worried, no?"

"Yes," Mme Viale replied. "I was never for this idea, investing in an old hotel, on an island too far off the coast, and near Marseille of all places."

"I can see the risk," Verlaque said. "But also the attraction," he quickly added. Something in him wanted to protect his old school chum, even if Clément was an ass.

And to stick up for Marseille, even it was a mess.

"It *is* beautiful here," she said. "But it was such a risk. The children, their future . . ."

"I understand," Verlaque said. *Now I'm on her side,* he thought to himself. *I'm like a bloody yo-yo.*

"And you didn't hear anything? See anything unusual?" he asked.

"No, I've been taking sleeping pills."

*The poor woman,* thought Verlaque. He had never needed sleeping pills and couldn't imagine using them when on a vacation.

"It's the financial situation," she went on. "Clément invested *our* money, but it was *my* legacy. My father's hard-earned money."

"You didn't talk about it, before he signed on the dotted line?"

"Yes, and no," she replied. "I wasn't given the full details. I was in the hospital at the time when he came with the proposal. I was drugged, half-out of it."

"Hospital?" Verlaque asked.

"Yes, in Neuilly," she replied. She looked him straight in the eye and replied, without flinching, "I tried to kill myself."

# CHAPTER TWENTY-NINE:
## AMORE

"If I lived by the sea," Sylvie said, holding on to the mossy cliffs by her toes and floating on her back, "I'd do a series of photographs, one taken every day, always at the same hour, treading water with my camera. Maybe large format; dig out my Hasselblad."

"Does anyone hand-print these days?" Marine asked, also floating and looking up at the blue sky.

"Yeah, a guy in Marseille named Nicholas. He does the printing for all the photographers around here; well, the ones still taking pictures with film."

Marine's toe lost its grip and she let go, doing a backward somersault in the water. "Dizzy," she said when her head surfaced. "Those were easier to do when I was a kid." She swam to the rocks and held on to them with her fingers, floating on her stomach. "It's funny that I'm more frightened by the sea than the fact that there's a murderer on Sordou," she said, looking at Sylvie.

Sylvie let go of the rock and began treading. "At least they can't get us here, swimming," she said, looking around.

"Are you afraid?" Marine asked.

"I wasn't until now."

"So you aren't afraid either," Marine said. "I get the feeling that few of us are. I saw Mme Hobbs happily going off to paint; and Clément Viale told me he was going to try to walk around the island. Does our nonchalance in the face of murder mean that the killer was only after Denis, and somehow we sense this? Or are we being naïve?"

"I think you're right," Sylvie said. "We're not afraid. And that would mean the killer knew Denis, probably very well. We all sense that."

"Mme Denis was closest to him," Marine said.

"But she's the only one among us who *does* seem afraid."

*"Seems,"* Marine said. "She could be faking it."

"What if she really is afraid for her life?" Sylvie asked. "Why?"

"Because she and Alain were involved in something together?" Marine suggested. "Something crooked? Drugs?"

"They really loved each other," Sylvie said, swimming beside Marine and holding on to the rocks. "What if they were acting at hating each other? I saw that on a *Miss Marple* once."

"You watch *Miss Marple*?"

"Yeah, with Charlotte," Sylvie answered. "It's dubbed into French on Sunday nights. She loves it. So, think of it: most of the time their fights were out in the open, where we could all see."

"Oh, you're good," Marine said, placing a foot on the rocky ledge and heaving herself out of the water. She slipped on the moss, scratching her knee, and fell down on the wet rocks, laughing.

"You don't have the technique right," Sylvie said, lifting herself out of the water and also slipping on the moss.

The women, still laughing, half-crawled to a dry patch on the rocks, where they had left their towels and books. "You know," Marine said, shifting her weight to try to find a comfortable flat bit of rock, "Antoine told me that Mme Denis was really upset during her interview."

"See," Sylvie said. "That goes with my theory that they were faking their hatred, and your theory that they were into something shady. Together. Maybe they were trying to cheat their crime partners, and so Alain was bumped off. And that's why Mme Denis is frightened."

"So that means the killer had to swim here."

"Or they're one of the staff."

"Now *you're* freaking *me* out," Marine said.

"That's why the Denis picked Sordou," Sylvie said excitedly. "Because their contact was already here."

Marine fumbled in her beach bag that she had bought on sale at Monoprix. "I need to write this down," she said. She pulled out a weathered notebook with a marbled cover.

"Florence," Sylvie said. "You bought that book on our last trip there."

Marine nodded and began writing. She said, "Your theory of the killer being already here works with Hugo's opinion that the sea was too rough that evening for someone to swim in." She wrote this down as well.

"Hugo may be full of maritime facts," Sylvie said, "but I'm not so sure he's correct all the time."

"Hugo," Marine said, looking at Sylvie.

"What?"

"I doubt he has an alibi, and he told you that he slept through the gunshot."

"So?" Sylvie asked. "I did too."

"Perhaps that fight at breakfast was staged."

"You mean Hugo was also acting?" Sylvie said, immediately realizing what she had said. "The actor Alain Denis, getting everyone to act. *Merde.*"

"But it did seem genuine," Marine said. "Hugo was livid. And so was Denis."

"Were they trying to cheat Hugo?" Sylvie asked, pulling her legs up to her chest and wrapping her arms around them.

Marine lay back on her side, propping her head up on her elbow. "I think we're getting carried away."

"Let's hope so," Sylvie said. "For Hugo's sake. I'm going to do a bit of serious fashion-magazine reading to get my mind off this. My God," she said, looking at a page in *Elle.* "Whoever thought of these high-heeled running shoes is going to make a mint."

"Hideous," Marine said, glancing at the photograph and then flipping over onto her stomach. She picked up her Florentine notebook and wrote down the names of the staff and guests on Sordou. She read over her list, thinking of each person, possible motives, and their ability to point a gun at someone and pull the trigger. This was the hardest thing to do, and why she preferred the theory that the murderer had swum into the cove. She looked at the female names, knowing that a woman could physically shoot someone; Antoine had told her that one of the best shots at the Palais de Justice in Aix was a female officer named Sophie. But what kind of rage would lead to a premeditated murder? Marine stared at the names. *"Amore,"* she whispered in Italian. Sylvie looked over and smiled, and continued reading. "That's what you'd kill for, wouldn't you?" Marine asked her friend. "I mean, as a woman."

Sylvie set down the magazine. "Love," she said. "That's about the only thing that I'd kill for," she said. "Especially if someone threatened or hurt Charlotte."

Marine looked at Emmanuelle Denis's name. Defending her son. Had Alain Denis hurt Brice? Denis could be violent; they had a glimpse of that at the hotel. Marine took her pencil and drew a line between the names "Emmanuelle" and "Brice." She wrote: "Brice? Brice had been at the cove; we found his hat, and he admitted to being there. Could he be defending his mother? Did he really place his hat at the cove, hoping it would be found, by either us, or the police, to take the suspicion away from Emmanuelle?" Marine put her pencil down and rested her chin on her hands, thinking about the boy. Although dishonest, it seemed a heroic thing to do, and it suited the character of a young boy who was a self-professed romantic, and who read Thomas Mann while on holiday.

# CHAPTER THIRTY:
# PROSPER HAS MORE GUESTS

"My grandfather always said 'never trust a skinny chef,' " Verlaque remarked as he watched Bruno Paulik gather up his papers and slide them into his leather satchel. They had just finished interviewing Émile Villey; throughout their meeting the chef had made a valiant attempt to stifle his yawns.

Paulik grunted. "Émile seems honest to me," he replied, "just very focused on cooking."

"Oh, I agree with you there. He wouldn't shut up about his monkfish with the ginger and chili."

"Don't forget the noodles and cilantro," Paulik said, keeping such a straight face that Verlaque thought he might be serious. "And I don't see Émile having the time to think up a murder, contact Denis, rush down to the cove, and then make it back in time to cook," Paulik continued. "He doesn't have a motive either."

"Alain Denis complained about the lamb on our first night."

Paulik laughed this time. "I mean, the meals are fairly simple here, and he's only cooking for ten people plus staff, but all the same, he's a busy guy."

"Yes, I agree: Émile is solo in the kitchen; he even makes the hotel's bread and jam," Verlaque said. "Then would he kill for someone else? Is he sweet on Emmauelle Denis? Or was he defending the honor of Niki Darcette?"

Paulik shook his head back and forth. "It was a premeditated murder," he said. "I know that Émile claimed not to have heard the shot because he was too busy banging pots and pans around, and no one came into the kitchen at that time to give him an alibi, but I think that our murderer knew Denis well and planned this."

"Then that even puts Hugo Sammut lower down on the list."

"Exactly," Paulik said. "From what you told me about that outbreak at breakfast, Hugo is strong, but doesn't think before he acts. And to shoot someone, you don't have to be strong. You just have to know how to handle a gun and have decent aim."

"But Hugo, unlike Émile, has a motive. He got fired because of Alain Denis. Let's check the public shooting ranges," Verlaque said. "In Marseille, and the Paris region. Especially for someone who fits Hugo's profile, and for women who have recently signed up."

"I'll put someone on it tomorrow," Paulik said, putting on his sunglasses. "Okay, I'm ready to face the sun and boat."

"Say hello to Hélène and Léa," Verlaque said as he and Paulik shook hands on the dock.

"I will," Paulik said, gently stepping into the speedboat that awaited him. "I'll start the research tomorrow morning, and will call you ASAP."

Verlaque saluted and the boat backed quickly up and sped off. He turned around and saw Marine standing just a few feet behind him. "You're a beautiful sight," he said, kissing her. "What are you up to?"

"I wanted to say goodbye to Bruno," she said. "I've been swimming, and then working."

"Working?" Verlaque asked as they walked on the path that led up to the hotel's front steps.

"Yes, it's getting my mind . . . elsewhere," she said. "And Sylvie's off somewhere with Hugo."

Verlaque bit his tongue; although he liked Sylvie Grassi more and more, he also knew that she was the kind of woman who prioritized things, and her comfort and happiness came first. "Care to take a trip to the lighthouse?" he asked.

Marine looked at her watch. "Dinner isn't for another couple of hours," she said, knowing that they could show up on the terrace anytime before 9 p.m. "I'd love to."

"We need to interview Prosper," Verlaque said. "I'll fill you in on the other interviews as we walk. The housekeeper had one humdinger of a story."

They walked along the north side of the island, on a path that Hugo Sammut and Max Le Bon had worked at clearing. The smells of wild thyme and rosemary surrounded them, combined with the briny smell of the sea that seemed to come in waves. The *cigale* noise was almost absent here; there were fewer trees. They walked most of the path in single file, but when they could walk side by side they did so holding hands. "So, no people can be linked to Alain Denis except his wife and stepson," Marine said after Verlaque had filled her in on their sessions with the hotel's staff and guests.

"So it would seem," Verlaque said. "Except Mme Poux, from way back when. Bruno will begin tomorrow with more detailed research into every guest's and staff's background. We can't possibly do that from here."

Marine laughed. "I'm amazed the hotel's phone even works. Did you meet with Mme Denis's lawyer?"

"Yes, very briefly," Verlaque said. "He showed up just as we were finishing our interviews. He met with Mme Denis alone for about a half an hour, then spoke with Bruno and myself. She's to inherit."

"Everything?"

"Yep."

"And the lawyer has gone?"

"Yes. It was like he couldn't wait to get off of Sordou."

"Don't tell me our lovely island has become sinister," Marine said, pulling at some rosemary and rubbing the stalk between her palms and then smelling them. "All the same, I can't see Emmanuelle Denis shooting a gun."

"Nor can I."

"A hit man?"

"A hit man who's a champion swimmer?" Verlaque asked. "Why not?"

Marine told him of her conversation with Sylvie, and the idea that Alain Denis was involved in something not quite legal.

"Mme Denis could be involved too," she added. "That's why she asked for protection."

"And she was faking hating her husband?"

"That part was Sylvie's idea."

"Not bad."

"Mme Poux could have hired the hit man," Marine said, grinning. "At Le Cercle des Nageurs . . . that was quite a story she told you two."

"There may be something there," Verlaque said, slowing down. "She is the only person, outside of his family, that has a link to him. A swimming link. Come to think of it, Eric Monnier told me he swam too."

"When he was young," Marine said. "I can't imagine it now. It's funny, but I have a hard time imagining certain people with wet hair."

"I know what you mean," Verlaque replied. "Mme Poux, for instance."

"And you say they're all the same age?"

Verlaque said, "Yes. Bill and Shirley Hobbs are a tad younger, born in 1945 and '47. I saw their passports."

"Senior discount week at Sordou," Marine said, laughing. "I still think that Mme Denis is hiding something. She's a strong woman. We were all surprised at that, the night Brice came back, remember?"

"Yes, I think Prosper was quite taken aback."

"Could a hit man have camped out overnight?" she asked. "Swum here from a boat? Or got dropped off, even Sunday, and then waited. Near the cove."

"Interesting theory," Verlaque said. "Let's ask Prosper about any boats hovering near Sordou over the past few days."

"Does Prosper know about Alain Denis's death?"

"Yes," Verlaque replied. "Max Le Bon told him."

"What was his reaction?" Marine asked. "Did Max say?"

"Max said that Prosper rolled his eyes and snickered."

"How odd. And was Prosper born in 1940 as well?"

"We don't know," Verlaque said. "I asked the Le Bons but they had no idea, so we'll have to ask Prosper that question."

"If he even knows," Marine said.

"Bruno sent an officer to Paris to study the lighthouse archives," Verlaque said. "I'm hoping we'll be able to fill in some of the missing details, like Prosper's birth date, when he gets back."

The path narrowed and they walked on in single file, sometimes stopping to look out at the sea. The coastline of Marseille and Cassis was off in the distance, but too far to make anything out; it was just a hazy gray smudge. The lighthouse, however, got bigger and bigger the closer they got. "You don't realize how tall the lighthouse is when you're out at sea, on the boat coming," Marine said.

Verlaque looked up, shielding his eyes from the sun. "It must be sixty meters high."

"Yes," Marine said. "It's not as charming as other lighthouses I've seen, like those in Britanny."

"No, this one is meant for business," Verlaque said. "It's a serious structure; it's as if it's soaring right out of the sea."

"Look, there's a boat pulled up to his dock," Marine said. "Is that Prosper's?"

"No, I don't think so. It looks too big to be his, but I can't imagine him entertaining."

"Prosper did well enough with Brice."

"You're right," Verlaque said. "Brice was even quoting him earlier today."

Marine laughed.

"It's nice to hear you laugh," Verlaque said, stopping and taking her in his arms.

"The atmosphere isn't exactly jolly," she said. "Whenever someone walks into the dining room or bar, we all jump."

"And people aren't telling us everything," Verlaque added. "Sylvie said that Marie-Thérèse overheard that same argument between the Le Bons," he said. "But Marie-Thérèse didn't mention it. And Bill Hobbs won't tell us what Brice divulged when they were out fishing; I'm sure it was something about Alain Denis."

"How can we break the ice?" Marine asked. "It's not like we can have a party."

Verlaque stopped walking again. "Why not?"

"Listen," Marine said, holding her pointer finger to her mouth. "It sounds as if Prosper is having his own party."

The closer Marine and Verlaque got to the small stone house that stood at the foot of the lighthouse, the louder the laughter. The house's small multipaned windows were open, but from what they could tell no one was inside.

"It's coming from the side of the house," Marine said. As they rounded the corner there appeared a pair of filthy bare feet resting on an old wooden stool. It was clear that Prosper had company as two men were laughing, and Prosper's right foot twitched in time along with his laughter.

*"Bonsoir, mes amis,"* Verlaque said.

"Well hello, dear judge," Prosper said,

quickly getting up, bumping the wood table. Marine lunged forward and grabbed an almost empty bottle of rosé before it fell over.

"Good reflexes, my dear," *le général* said, flashing a smile at Marine.

"Do sit down," Prosper said, motioning to two empty chairs. He picked up the bottle and waved it at his friend.

"I'll be right back," *le général* said. "Emergency trip to the cooler on the boat is needed."

"The jacket looks nice on you," Verlaque said.

Prosper looked down at his upper chest and touched *le général*'s medals with his fingers.

"Have you two always been friends?" Verlaque asked.

Prosper shrugged. "Depends what you call friends . . ."

"Come off it," Verlaque said.

"We've been friends for about ten or twenty years," Prosper said.

"Good," Verlaque replied dryly. "Very precise. I'll get right to the point; where were you Monday evening around six p.m.?"

"Monday? What happened Monday night?"

Verlaque sighed and looked at Marine.

"It's the night of Alain Denis's murder."

"I mean what was the sky like that night?" Prosper asked. "Dates and days of the week don't mean anything to ol' Propser."

"The sea was rough," Verlaque said. "It had been calm all day, and at the end of the afternoon it was rough. I don't remember the sky."

"Ah, you should always pay attention to the sky."

"It was the day you saw the couple on the rocks," Marine added. "And Brice was here with you."

Prosper slapped his knee. "And there was a gunshot by the cove," he said. "And it wasn't me."

*Le général* returned, opening a new bottle of chilled rosé as he walked.

"So where were you?" Verlaque repeated.

Prosper shrugged. "Here, where else?"

"And Brice was with you?"

"Why does it matter?" Prosper asked.

"Because," *le général* said, leaning over to pour wine in his friend's glass tumbler, "you need an alibi."

"As does Brice," Verlaque said. "You two showed up at the hotel late that night, re-member?"

"What night was it again?" Prosper asked, scratching his flyaway red hair.

"Monday," Marine said.

Verlaque leaned his elbows on the table and put his head in his hands.

"The sea, and sky, were . . . busy," Marine continued. "And you may have heard a shot, sometime in the late afternoon."

*Le général* set the glasses down and Marine looked on, amazed at how dirty they were. "I was here!" Prosper said. "I did hear the shot, with the boy." Relieved, he grabbed the empty glasses and the bottle of rosé.

Verlaque quickly took the tea towel off the back of *le général*'s chair and wiped the glasses before their host had a chance to pour.

"Prosper's housekeeper is on leave," *le général* said, winking.

Prosper poured Marine and Verlaque each a full tumbler of pale rosé. "Thank you, Prosper," Verlaque said, taking the still-smudgy glass in his hands and smiling at Marine. "Did you know any of the kids from Marseille when you were growing up here on Sordou?" he asked.

Prosper stared at Verlaque.

"I'm sorry if it's a tricky question," Verlaque said, rolling his eyes. "A simple yes or no will do."

"I didn't know any of them," Prosper said, taking a gulp of his rosé.

"So they were around?" Verlaque asked.

"Who?"

"The kids from Marseille," Marine said. "Alain Denis?"

Prosper shrugged. "They didn't have anything to do with me." He looked away, and then added, "You're like that pretty woman from Paris, asking questions . . ."

"Who's that?" Marine asked, leaning forward.

"A civil servant who was researching the islands," *le général* answered for his friend. "Prosper just wants to be left in peace. Isn't that right, my friend?"

Prosper lifted his glass and toasted *le général*. He then set his glass down and tugged at the sleeves of *le général*'s jacket. "I think this is a perfect fit," he said.

# Chapter Thirty-One:
## Antoine's Feast

Marine and Verlaque got into Général Le Favre's boat, Verlaque taking the steering wheel.

"I don't see why you insist on driving," Le Favre said, falling into Prosper as they got into the boat.

"I'm thrilled by the opportunity," Verlaque said. "I haven't driven a boat in ages."

"Where did you grow up?" *le général* asked, hiccuping.

"Paris, but also Normandy," Verlaque answered. "Where there are real waves."

Prosper laughed and hit his knee.

"I don't like the look of that sky," *le général* said.

"It never storms in July in Provence," Verlaque said.

"The sea was pretty rough on Monday," Marine said, leaning back on the boat's wooden bench and holding on to the boat's sides.

"True," Verlaque said, pulling the boat away from the dock and taking a quick look at the sky, which was blue above them, but black over Marseille. He wished he could telephone ahead to the hotel and warn the Le Bons that there would be two extra guests for dinner.

"I should head back," Le Favre mumbled, also looking toward Marseille.

"Prosper," Verlaque shouted over the sound of the engine and waves hitting the small boat. Marine and the general were talking, and so he had Prosper's full attention. "Who do you think killed Alain Denis?"

Prosper Buffa lifted his head back and laughed. "Not the boy."

"Well," Verlaque pressed on. "Who? And why?"

Prosper shook his head back and forth. "It was so long ago," he began.

"What happened?" Verlaque shouted.

"I wasn't there, you busybody!"

"Here we are!" *le général* shouted, tapping Verlaque on the back. "Be careful pulling her up to the dock."

Hugo Sammut was standing at the dock when they arrived. Verlaque steered the boat in while *le général* threw Sammut a rope. Sammut quickly tied it around a post, and he reached his hand out to Marine. "It's gonna blow!" he said. "Did you look at that sky?"

"Like Normandy," Prosper said, smiling, to Verlaque.

"They've all been waiting for you," Sammut said, holding out his hand.

"Thanks, Hugo," Verlaque said, grabbing his hand and jumping out.

"Thanks, Hugo," Prosper mimicked.

"Nice jacket, Prosper," Sammut said.

*Le général* rubbed his arms, suddenly realizing where his jacket was.

"What have you guys been doing?" Sammut asked, seeing the red faces of Prosper and Le Favre, and the bright shining eyes of Marine and Verlaque.

"Having a little aperitif," Verlaque repeated. "And the gentlemen will be staying for dinner. I have to run up and tell Émile and the Le Bons."

Sammut said, "You need to call your commissioner. He's been trying to get ahold of you."

"I have to get back to my *cabanon*," *le général* said, looking at the sky.

"Not tonight, you aren't," Sammut said.

"We'll arrange for you to stay here," Verlaque said. He hoped that the Le Bons could set up the extra room, now that Paulik had gone. He had no idea where Prosper would be able to sleep if he couldn't walk back to the lighthouse.

"Should I bring my cooler up?" *le général* asked.

"No, you can leave it here," Verlaque said, hiding his smile. "There's lots of very good wine in the restaurant. Tonight is my treat."

Prosper rubbed his hands together.

Verlaque stayed and thanked Hugo while Marine, Prosper, and *le général* made their way up the steps to the hotel. "I want to thank you for staying on the island, even though you've been given your dismissal," he said.

"You're welcome," Sammut said, making sure that *le général*'s boat was securely fastened down. "I really have no other place to go," he added. "I'm too embarrassed to show up at my parents' small apartment in Cassis, although when this is all over I suppose I'll have to."

"Would it help if I put in a good word for you, with the Le Bons?" Verlaque asked.

"That would be awesome," Sammut replied. "Thank you. See you around."

"Ciao," Verlaque said, running to catch up with Marine.

Max Le Bon saw the foursome arriving and opened the front doors as the rain began to fall even harder. Max looked just as puzzled as Hugo had at the two new guests, and Verlaque pulled him aside and said, "I'd like to throw a party this evening. I'll pay for *le général* and Prosper's dinner." He looked at them and added, "And their drinks."

"A party?" Max asked.

"It's what we need," Verlaque said, trying not to sound desperate. "Don't you see? It will loosen everyone up."

"Well, I don't know . . ."

"What's going on, Max?" Cat-Cat Le Bon said as she walked toward the men.

"Judge Verlaque thinks we should have a party tonight," Max began. "To . . ."

"Marvelous," Cat-Cat said.

"Really?" her husband asked, looking at Prosper, who was sitting in an armchair, his legs crossed, reading *Le Monde.*

"Of course," she replied. "We've all been cooped up here; the guests are unhappy and our staff are frazzled. And with this storm tonight . . ."

"Great," Verlaque said. "The guys may not make it back, with the storm."

Cat-Cat sighed. "I figured as much," she said. "They may have to share the spare room, but we have a folding bed we can add. At least Prosper appears to have had a shower recently."

"He dressed up for the occasion," Verlaque said, smiling, and making a gesture with his fingers alluding to Prosper's pink bow tie.

"Oh, heavens!"

"Hugo met us at the dock," Verlaque began.

Cat-Cat looked at Max. Max said, "I get your hint, judge. Actually I've been rethinking Hugo's position here," he said. "I'm going to ask him if he'd like to stay on."

"That sounds wise, considering how well he knows this place. I'll go and tell Émile about tonight's party," Verlaque said as Niki Darcette came running in.

"Serge is closing all the shutters in the bar," Niki said. "And I'll start here." As if on cue the wind blew one of the shutters in the lobby closed. The hotel phone began to ring and Niki cursed, running behind the desk to answer it.

"I'll help with the shutters," Max said. He walked over to the large French doors that led out to the terrace and opened them to close the shutters. The wind almost blew him off his feet, and rain came into the lobby, hitting the marble floor.

"Max!" Cat-Cat screeched.

"I'm trying to close the shutters as fast as I can!" Max hollered back.

Verlaque grinned, amused that the usually calm and professional Le Bons were now acting like a normal married couple. He was about to go off to find Émile in the kitchen when Niki reappeared. "Phone call for you," she said. "You can take it in the office."

"Thanks, Niki," he answered. He left the lobby to the sound of people arguing and shutters slamming shut, walked into the office closing the door behind him, and sat down in a leather office chair, picking up the phone. *"Oui."*

*"Salut,"* Bruno Paulik said. "I've been trying to get ahold of you. I have news," he added. "Jules Schoelcher is up in Paris researching Sordou, but in the meantime I've been talking to the police in Cannes."

"And?"

"Niki Darcette only gave us half her story," Paulik continued. "They were caught on the night of the robbery around the corner from the jewelry store. But they weren't caught because of the robbery; one of Niki's accomplices — that guy Robert she told us about — called out for help, and an undercover policeman who was off duty came to his rescue."

"What happened?" Verlaque asked, flipping through the piles of paper on Niki's desk.

"Robert had what he referred to as 'made a pass' at Niki," Paulik said. "She claimed it was attempted rape; she had a knife and had cut his cheek."

Verlaque said, "That's why she got six years."

"Yeah, I'm told her lawyer was sharp and had dug up all sorts of dirt on the guy. Otherwise she would have done more time. The undercover policeman reported that she screamed that Robert had it coming to him, and she would have kept going had he not showed up. The cop told the judge that it took all his might and five years of martial arts training to hold her down until reinforcements came."

Verlaque held a piece of paper in his hand and as he looked at it said, "A good-looking woman could have enticed Denis down to the cove."

"Yep."

"And Niki is about the only woman here who could have done that," Verlaque continued. "Marine and Sylvie are out of the picture; Mme Poux too old; Marie-Thérèse too young; Cat-Cat Le Bon and Shirley Hobbs not at all his type; and Delphine Viale too prudish looking."

"Emmanuelle Denis would have had to make up some outrageous excuse to get him down there," Paulik added. "And since they no longer sleep together, she couldn't have used her sexual powers to tempt him. But Mme Poux . . . I think that she could have got him down there to meet her. When he found out who she was, that they once were sweethearts, he might have even wanted to rekindle their old love, for whatever reasons. Guilt?"

"I hardly doubt guilt," Verlaque said, "but curiosity I'd go with. Thanks for this, Bruno. You'll call me when Schoelcher gets back from Paris?"

"Yes," Paulik said. "Wait a minute; hold on." Verlaque could hear the commissioner speaking to someone else. "Flamant wants to speak to you," Paulik said.

*"Bonsoir, Juge Verlaque,"* Alain Flamant said, after taking the phone from Paulik. "We've been researching Denis's films and have come across something really interesting," he said.

"Go on," Verlaque said.

"Alain Denis and the director Jean-Louis Navarre hated each other. Openly."

"The Inspector Pernety director?"

"Yes." Flamant told the judge about the threats, the affair with Navarre's wife, and the fistfight on set. "But it seems that a lot of people who worked with Denis hated

380

him," Flamant continued. "So I was getting discouraged, until our junior officer Sophie Goulin came across a photo in the archives of *Télérama*."

"I'm all ears."

"It was a fund-raiser for disenfranchised youth in Paris," Flamant said. "And Navarre was among the celebrities raising money for the cause."

"How were they doing it?" Verlaque asked.

"Swimming," Flamant said.

Verlaque sat down. Flamant continued, "It says in the photo's caption that Navarre swims every day. He even swam the English Channel a few years back. We have a call into Navarre's home and his office, but no one's answering. Hopefully we'll have better luck tomorrow morning."

"Thanks for this, Alain," Verlaque said. "And pass my thanks onto Mlle Goulin."

Paulik came back on the phone. "We'll phone you ASAP tomorrow morning," he said. "I sure wish you had a cell phone that worked over there."

"Me too."

"And Léa says to tell you that the grapes are bigger than they were last week; they're no longer pearls, but marbles."

Verlaque laughed. "I can't wait to see them." He hung up and looked at the piece of paper; Niki Darcette had been making rough notes for a press release announcing Sordou as an oasis, the island once a vacation spot for Elizabeth Taylor and Richard Burton, Marcello Mastroianni, and the late Alain Denis.

Verlaque folded the paper and put it in his pocket; was Niki Darcette's rage reason enough for murder? He thought not; she might have attacked a thug from Cannes — someone she knew well — but Verlaque couldn't see Alain Denis's tawdry harassment as something that would cause her to shoot him. Emmanuelle Denis, and Brice, were the only people on Sordou who knew Denis well enough to hate him, as his murderer obviously had. Mme Denis had no alibi, and Brice's alibi was very shaky. Paulik had suggested that Prosper could have taken a nap at any point during their day together on Monday, giving Brice ample time to run down to the cove.

But now they had someone who openly hated Denis and was a strong swimmer. *Why would anyone ever swim the channel?* thought Verlaque. Madness. He didn't even like going under it on the Eurostar from Paris to London. He thought about swimmers as he left the office, carefully closing the door behind him. Was swimming the common thread? Is that why the murderer chose an island to carry out the deed? He thought of Mme Poux; had an old rage resurfaced when she saw her old — as Bruno had called him — sweetheart? Or had Jean-Louis Navarre somehow swum here, hid out, and then swum back to some boat anchored offshore? But why wait all these years?

He saw Marine walking down the hall and they embraced. "I told Émile about the party," she said.

"Thank you!" Verlaque said. "I was going to but got sidetracked." He filled her in on his phone call with Paulik and Flamant.

"I wish we had better phone service here," Marine said.

"That's what we said."

"Well, Émile thinks the party is a great idea," Marine continued. "We talked about the film *Babette's Feast*. Émile said he saw it with his parents when he was young, and it was one of the things that made him want to be a chef. We're calling tonight's party 'Antoine's Feast.' "

"Except I won't be able to buy everyone a forty-year-old Clos de Vougeot," Verlaque said.

"Is that the wine that Babette offers her guests?"

"It was cheaper back then," Verlaque said, smiling.

Marine put her arm through his as they walked into the Jacky Bar. "I can't believe you remember which wine they drank in the movie," she said.

"Like Émile, it was one of my favorite films for a long time," he answered. "And one of my last memories of my grandfather, Charles, who, in the middle of the screening, cried out when he saw the Clos de Vougeot. When we got home from the film, guess what bottle he brought out from the cellar? And it was forty years old."

Marine smiled. "How wonderful that old Bordeaux must have been . . ."

Verlaque stopped, and she laughed. "Oh, you're teasing me, aren't you?" he asked.

"Yes," Marine answered. "I know it's a Burgundy."

Serge gently released the cork from a champagne bottle, and Max Le Bon clapped his hands together. "Excuse me, everyone," he said, looking around the room. "Now that everyone is here, I'd like to, once again, offer my apologies that your vacation has been interrupted by an investigation." Cat-Cat nodded; she had told Max not to say "murder," and he had thankfully remembered.

"Given this evening's storm," Max went on, "we're all housebound — or hotel bound as it were — and Judge Verlaque has generously offered to throw us a party."

The staff and clients politely clapped, with Clément Viale and Shirley Hobbs both hollering "hooray."

"I'd also like to welcome our illustrious guests, Général Le Favre, and Sordou's only native, Prosper Buffa."

Serge and Marie-Thérèse walked around the room, serving champagne, and Émile Villey appeared from the kitchen carrying a platter of canapés. Cat-Cat took the platter from the chef and began to serve, and Émile spoke. "*Salut,* everyone. I'd like to tell you about tonight's menu, which I'm calling 'Antoine's Feast.' " Laughter broke out and to Verlaque's surprise Niki Darcette toasted, *"Merci, Juge Verlaque!"*

Émile continued, "I'd like to thank Marie-Thérèse and Niki, who pitched in with some very important last-minute help. I've made a summer menu, so let's just forget about the storm out there: we'll begin with cucumber and melon gazpacho and then red snapper ceviche shooters, followed by vegetable spring rolls. Once we're sitting we'll eat roast bass with olive oil, mussels, and cherry tomatoes, and, finally, in honor of our meat-loving host, a rack of grilled lamb with stir-fried summer vegetables, wasabi purée, and a cilantro-mint vinaigrette."

A loud round of applause rang out. "And not to forget dessert," Émile said, holding up his hand. "A chocolate cake served with fresh strawberries and vanilla bean ice cream, surrounded by a concoction I call ginger and lavender drizzle."

Serge had turned up the Brazilian jazz, so even if Émile had wanted to keep speaking he couldn't have. Émile walked to the bar, took a glass of champagne, waved to Verlaque, who waved back, and went into the kitchen.

The dinner was a rousing success, with various guests, including Marine and Sylvie, taking turns in the kitchen, helping the chef prepare the food or helping to serve. As it had with the Danish puritans in *Babette's Feast*, the good food and wine cheered everyone up. The Viales looked like they were having a good time, at a table with the Le Bons. Niki and Marie-Thérèse took turns serving and sitting down to eat, and even Serge helped himself to a few glasses of the Krug champagne that Verlaque had ordered.

"The party is a success," Marine whispered in Verlaque's ear. "The silence of the past few days has been unbearable," she went on. "And look, our loners have found good company."

Verlaque squeezed her hand and looked around the room. Niki Darcette was sitting at the bar, chatting with Serge; Mme Poux was sitting with Marie-Thérèse and Sylvie, the three of them laughing; and Eric Monnier had ended up with Prosper and *le général.* Marine looked at their table and said, "Prosper and Général Le Favre are having the time of their lives. But Eric Monnier doesn't seem as happy."

"He's a poet," Verlque said. "I can't imagine poets ever being really happy."

"And your man from northern England?" Marine asked.

"Philip Larkin?" Verlaque asked. "No, I doubt he was that happy, but I'll know more after I've read his biography; I just ordered it from that English bookshop in town," he went on.

"Why do you think all poets are sad?" Marine asked.

He thought of Frank O'Hara's poem about Billie Holiday. "Because they're trying to sort out the human condition and put it down on paper using rhythm and the most appropriate and beautiful words they can find?"

"Say no more," Marine said, smiling.

"Reminds me of Vietnam," Shirley Hobbs said to Verlaque as she was finishing dessert, licking the ginger and lavender drizzle with her finger. The guests had once more changed places and tables, and Verlaque was now sitting with the Hobbses.

"Really?" Verlaque asked.

"Not the food. Everyone pitching in," she said. "It reminds me of the mess halls and makeshift operating rooms. It brings out the best in people."

Verlaque smiled and was about to ask her more about her experience in Vietnam when Clément Viale appeared, holding a deck of cards. "Poker," he said. "Are you guys in?"

"I'll come later," Verlaque said.

"Brice, buddy," Clément called. "You're in."

"The boy's too young," Verlaque said. "That's unfair."

"Oh, Brice is as sharp as a whip," Bill Hobbs said in English, hiccuping.

"Whip?" Clément asked.

*"Cravache,"* Verlaque and Bill Hobbs replied in unison.

"Bill, you know the word for a whip?" Shirley said to her husband.

Hobbs laughed and then shrugged. "I do

listen to those language tapes you brought along," he answered. "Guess I'm picking it up! *Vive la France!*" he cried with an accent that made Shirley laugh and Verlaque cringe. "I think I'll play a few hands too!"

"Thank you for showing me those poems the other day, Eric," Verlaque said. He had helped clear the tables, giving Marie-Thérèse and Niki a break, and Émile had given him a tour of the state-of-the-art kitchen. The storm seemed to be getting louder, but so did the music. The men at the poker table were now teaching Emmanuelle Denis how to play, and Mme Poux was sitting in an armchair, with her stocking feet resting on a footstool, a tiny glass of Serge's homemade Limoncello in her hand, listening to *le général* and Prosper tell stories. Verlaque could see that she was laughing.

Eric Monnier poured the judge another glass of whiskey. "I'm glad to have shared something with you," he said.

"Marine and I were talking about poets over dinner," Verlaque said. "I have the impression that poets are a sad lot. Is that true?"

Monnier tried to smile. "You may be right."

"I'm sorry," Verlaque said. "I don't mean

to pry." He changed the subject. "What was Sordou like in the fifties?"

"Oh, dear boy, we didn't dare step foot on the island. The hotel was for the very wealthy, a smaller version of those Mediterranean hotels on the Côte, or in Italy. Capri, say. We'd swim by, though . . ." He took a sip, smiling at the memories. "Trying to get a glimpse of someone famous."

Verlaque smiled, imagining the skinny but tanned and healthy boys from Marseille, swimming along Sordou's rocky coast. "Did you ever? See anyone?"

"I may have seen Melina Mercouri's breast once," Monnier said. "Falling out of her swimsuit. At least that's what I told my buddies."

"Eric!" Bill Hobbs called, holding up his hand of cards. "We need you," he called out in English.

"I'm needed at the poker table," Monnier said to Verlaque.

"Yes, so it seems. Go along then."

Monnier got up, touching his glass once more to Verlaque's. He bumped into the table as he walked away, and Verlaque laughed and relit his cigar. *Les nageurs,* he mumbled to himself. "Damn swimmers," he repeated in English.

"Excuse me," Brice Dortignac said. "May

390

I sit with you a bit?"

"Sure, Brice," Verlaque said, pulling out a chair and trying not to sound too eager. A chance to have Brice alone was one of the things he had hoped would happen at the party, if anyone would be able to remember, or make sense of it, tomorrow.

"Thank you, judge," the boy said, sitting down with a flop. Verlaque smiled: Brice was as well spoken as a university-educated adult, but his body was that of a teenager, all lanky awkwardness. "You said 'damn swimmers,' " Brice said.

Verlaque puffed on his cigar. "Yes," he answered.

"Given the weather," Brice said, nodding toward the banging shutters, "I assume you're not going for a swim."

"No. I was thinking that the mystery surrounding your stepfather's death may very well have to do with swimming." He stared at the boy, looking for a reaction.

"Not a bad theory," Brice said.

"You're not curious?"

"Nope." Brice set his glass carefully before him, holding on to it with both hands. Verlaque leaned over it, feigning curiosity.

"Apple juice," Brice said. He looked at the half-empty bottle of Lagavulin and added, "In a clear glass it looks very much

391

like your single malt."

"You know about single malts?"

"Sure I do," Brice said. "It's the favored drink of the moment among spoiled rich kids from Neuilly."

"Times have changed," Verlaque said. "I was a spoiled rich kid from the first *arrondissement,* but our fancy drinks were those awful sweet things like Frangelico and Drambuie."

Brice laughed, sticking a finger in his mouth. "Drinks aside," Brice said. "I wanted to admit something to you. I don't want to get M. Hobbs in trouble."

"He wouldn't tell me what you spoke about when you were fishing," Verlaque said.

"I knew he wouldn't," Brice said. "He's a good guy. That's why I really opened up to him; it was as if here was this man, a stranger but a very kind one, who was listening to me. Who understood me and wouldn't judge. Because he didn't know me. Do you understand?"

Verlaque nodded.

"And so I told Bill that I hated Alain. I told him how awful Alain was, in graphic detail. The big fights mom and Alain would get into, usually about me. The nights he wouldn't come home and mom would cry. Their financial worries. I was blubbering by the end of it, especially when I got to the part when Alain struck my mother."

Verlaque leaned forward and then stopped himself. But it was too late; the boy realized that he had possibly incriminated himself, and his mother, and stopped speaking. They sat in silence, listening to Clément Viale trying to get Delphine to dance; Prosper trying to help himself to another drink and getting whisked away by Serge; and Shirley Hobbs trying to get Bill to stop playing poker. Marine and *le général* danced by, arm in arm, to the sounds of a waltz.

"Is that Strauss?" Verlaque asked.

Brice smiled weakly and shrugged. "Not up on my Viennese music," he said. "I'm going to hit the sack. Good night."

"Good night, Brice," Verlaque said. He resisted adding "sleep tight" as Emmeline would have. Brice was far too old for that.

Brice hadn't been gone for more than thirty seconds when Sylvie sat down, carrying a mojito. "Mind?" she asked.

"Not at all," Verlaque said. "Marine is busy being Maria Von Trapp."

Sylvie laughed. "You can be funny sometimes, Antoine."

Verlaque looked at her and smoked a bit of his cigar. "We didn't exactly get off on the right foot when we first met," he began.

"But I know you were looking out for Marine's best interest."

"I thought you were a conceited prick."

"Thanks," Verlaque said. "I probably was. You see, a conceited prick makes a good judge. A good detective."

"What's the matter, then?" Sylvie asked. "Shit, I wish they'd change the music."

Verlaque leaned forward. "I'm getting all soft." He shrugged and took a drink.

"Maybe that's a good thing."

Verlaque looked at Sylvie, suddenly feeling his fatigue. "It's not good for an examining magistrate."

"Right." The music changed into a Caribbean song, *le général* cried out in protest, and Sylvie smiled.

"The thing is, I don't see any of these people as killers," he said, looking around the room, his eyes resting on Clément Viale, who was now dancing the limbo with Marie-Thérèse, under a broom being held up by Niki and Max. "Clément should watch out for his back," he muttered.

"Well, I'm going to go down to Hugo's cabin, despite the rain," Sylvie said, finishing her mojito. "Niki told me that the Le Bons are going to offer him his job back, but because of the storm he doesn't know that yet."

Verlaque said, "Is that why he isn't here tonight?"

"Yeah," Sylvie answered. "His pride is hurt."

"You shouldn't go down," Verlaque said. "It's too windy."

Sylvie got up. "Thanks for the party. I wouldn't worry about going soft; maybe the murderer is a softie too."

"What do you mean?"

"Perhaps even a nice person can kill someone," she said. "If they want to bad enough."

And then, with a flicker and a loud thump, the lights went out and the music stopped.

# CHAPTER THIRTY-TWO:
## RACING TO CATCH THE TRAIN

Jules could see his train on the tracks, and a conductor standing beside *voiture 1,* the first of the first class cars. The red door slowly closed and the conductor put a whistle to his mouth. Jules ran, and for the second time that day, he pulled out his badge. "Police!" he cried.

The conductor yelled something along the track and held up a hand to another conductor who was looking out of a door farther along the train. "What is it?" the conductor asked. "Do you want to pull someone off the train? It's about to leave."

"No," Jules said, panting and bending over putting his hands on his knees. "I need to get on it."

The conductor reached over and pressed the automatic release button and the doors slid open. "Why didn't you just say so?" the conductor asked.

"Thanks," Jules said. He got on; the doors

closed, the whistle blew, and the train lurched and slowly started down the tracks. Jules sat on the steps and pulled his ticket out of his pocket. His seat was upstairs, in *voiture 3,* but he could find his seat in a few minutes: what he needed to do now was make a phone call. He knew that cell phone conversations were frowned upon in the first class cars, but he also wanted this one to be as private as possible. He took out his black book, and his cell phone, and punched Bruno Paulik's name.

"Hello," the commissioner answered.

"Hello, Commissioner," Jules said, trying to breath normally. "I'm on the train."

"Was it worthwhile?" Paulik asked. "Going up there?"

"Yes," Jules answered, pressing the phone to his ear with his right shoulder while he flipped through his book. "I would have called you earlier but it was a race to get to the Gare de Lyon, and I couldn't get decent reception on the metro," he continued. "Can you hear me all right?"

"Perfectly."

"Okay. In 1957 there was a double drowning at Sordou," Jules said. "A girl of seventeen years, and an older woman. The girl's name was Élodie."

"Go on," Paulik said.

"The woman was thirty-seven years old, and her name was Cécile-Marie."

The train made a squealing sound, and Paulik asked Jules to repeat the woman's surname. Jules did.

"Are you kidding?" Paulik asked.

"No."

"Spell it for me," Paulik said.

Jules slowly spelled out the name and wiped his brow with an old Kleenex he had in his pants pocket. He was so thirsty he could barely speak.

"I can't thank you enough, Jules," Paulik said. "Now, stop panting and go and get yourself a cold beer in the bar car, and then a hot meal."

"But that's too ex—"

"It's an order, Jules."

Bruno Paulik hung up the phone and ran out of his office. He saw Roger Caromb two-finger typing at his desk. Caromb was an officer not known for his investigative skills but more for his muscle. He was also a spectacularly fast driver.

"Let's go to Marseille, Roger," Paulik said.

# CHAPTER THIRTY-THREE: AN OLD STORY

"That didn't sound good," Max Le Bon said in the dark.

"Thank you for stating the obvious, my dear," Cat-Cat answered.

"I don't like this!" Emmanuelle Denis cried. A banging noise sounded against the wall. "What was that?" Mme Denis asked.

"A shutter," Verlaque said. With the music off they could now hear the force of the wind and rain, beating against the hotel.

Verlaque took his cigar lighter out of his pocket and lit it. "Everyone, please stay where you are," he said. "Serge, do you have candles behind the bar?"

"I'm trying to find them," the barman answered, pulling open drawers. *"Voilà!"*

Verlaque walked across the room and lit the three tea lights that Serge set on the bar. "Do you have a backup generator?" Verlaque asked.

"That *was* the generator," Max answered.

"All Sordou's energy comes from one generator?" Clément Viale asked. "I've never heard it running."

"It's to the southeast of the hotel, down a small hill," Cat-Cat said. "Out of the way, because of the noise. We bought the best one, or so we were told. It's in a specially built stone hut."

"And the lighthouse has its own generator," Max added.

"There are two flashlights in the office," Niki said. "I'll take one of those tea candles and get them."

"I have more candles," Mme Poux said. "If someone would help me get back to the laundry room."

"Allow me," Eric Monnier said, flicking on his cigar lighter and taking her arm.

"We'll have no hot water, right?" Delphine Viale asked.

"No water at all, I'm afraid," Max answered. "The generator pumps the hotel's water."

Delphine groaned.

"I'll be able to cook on my gas burners, though," Émile Villey happily offered.

"When Mme Poux and Eric come back with candles, I suggest you all go to your rooms," Verlaque said. "It's late anyway. I'll go and look at the generator with Max."

Marie-Thérèse gasped, covering her mouth with her hand. "Oh my gosh!"

"What is it, Marie-Thérèse?" Cat-Cat asked.

"There was a phone call for Judge Verlaque," she cried. "About halfway through the party! I forgot to tell you!"

"That's all right," Verlaque said. "Who was it?"

The girl cringed. "The commissioner," she said in a small voice.

"Well, it will have to wait," Verlaque said.

There was something else about the evening's festivities nagging Verlaque, but he put the thought away in the corner of his mind. The generator was the more pressing issue.

"That was a ripping party, judge." Prosper Buffa spoke up. Verlaque had almost forgotten he was there. Verlaque held up his lighter to see Prosper, who was sitting at a table drinking champagne. Behind Prosper was Général Le Favre, lying across a sofa, fast asleep.

"I'll get a blanket for *le général,*" Cat-Cat said. "He may as well stay there. Prosper, I'll show you to your room."

"The presidential suite?" Prosper asked, refilling his champagne glass on the way out.

Mme Poux and Eric Monnier returned

and distributed candles. The party dispersed, amid good-nights and thank-yous directed at Verlaque.

"You know," Shirley Hobbs said to Verlaque, taking his arm. "After tonight, you'd think that we were all good friends, and that nothing horrible had ever happened here on Sordou."

Verlaque smiled and nodded; he didn't know how to reply. Perhaps his plan of a Babette's Feast had backfired, and the murderer was now too comfortable, and the judge too soft.

The wind howled and blew so strongly that Verlaque and Max Le Bon had to hold on to each other. Cat-Cat had found them coats to wear, and they left the hotel via the laundry-room door and walked along a stone path toward the generator. "We thought we were being smart putting the generator so far away," Max hollered as they walked.

"You were," Verlaque shouted back. "They make an awful noise."

"Almost there," Max said, shining his flashlight ahead. "Just be careful walking down this path. It's at the foot of this small hill." The generator was stored in a rough-hewn stone building, and they lit up its walls as they got closer. Max shone his flashlight all over the building, then slowly tilted the light up to the top of the building.

"There's the problem," Verlaque said. "The roof has caved in."

Max shone his flashlight up the steep hill that lay behind the building. "I bet a rock rolled down the hill in the storm," he said. "I don't know what the architects, or we, were thinking putting it here at the bottom of the hill. The door's around the back," Max yelled. "Follow me!"

The wind was calmer behind the stone building, and the men froze as they approached the door; it was open, and a light shone inside. The beam of light shone on their faces. *"Merde!"* Hugo Sammut hollered. "You scared me!"

"Likewise, Hugo," Max Le Bon answered. "What happened?" he asked, entering the cabin.

"My lights went off at home, and I saw that all the lights were off at the hotel," Hugo replied. "So I grabbed my flashlight and came down."

"Thank you," Le Bon said. "Was it a rock?"

Hugo shone his light down into a corner of the room, lighting up a boulder about half a meter in diameter. "Yep, slid down the hill in the rain and came in through the roof."

"What's the damage?" Verlaque asked.

"We dodged a bullet," Hugo answered. "If the rock had fallen any closer to the generator, it would have been out of commission for a while. But I think I'll be able to fix it in the morning. I have some spare parts in the boathouse."

"Okay then," Max Le Bon said. "Let's hope you're right. Will you be able to make it back to your cabin, Hugo?"

"No problem," Hugo said. "The wind sounds like it has calmed down, and I think I have the most powerful flashlight on the island. Good night, men." They walked out, closing the door behind them, and shook hands before Le Bon and Verlaque made their way back up the hill to the hotel.

Verlaque walked slowly up the marble stairs toward their room. He opened the door with his room key and walked in, bumping his toe up against an armchair and cursing.

Marine rolled over and whispered in the dark, "How did it go?"

"A rock crashed through the roof of the generator room," Verlaque whispered. "Hugo thinks he can fix it."

"There's a candle in the bathroom,"

Marine said. "On the counter."

"Thanks," Verlaque said. "I'll be right back."

When Verlaque came back he slid into bed and leaned his head against the padded linen headboard. "The two policemen who've been guarding the dock were in the bar when we got back," Verlaque said.

"You just missed them when you left to check the generator," Marine said. "They saw the hotel lights go off and came right up. They were soaked, poor guys. They accompanied each of us to our rooms."

"Good."

"I'm not tired," Marine said.

"Me neither," Verlaque said. "I got a second wind from that walk."

"There's a bottle of water on your side of the bed," Marine said. "Cat-Cat was handing them out."

"Sounds like a good idea," Verlaque replied, reaching for the bottle. "After all that champagne, I'm parched."

"Is it possible that someone knocked the generator out?" Marine asked.

"No," Verlaque said. "That's one of the reasons why I wanted to go out there and look at it."

"This is a dumb question," Marine said. "But will the hotel phone still work?"

"Not a dumb question," Verlaque said, reaching for her hand. "The phone line is separate; Max told me it's run via an old underwater sea cable that they installed in the early sixties."

"Imagine," Marine said. "A cable that lies under the water and extends from Sordou to Marseille. All those decades and years of conversations and stories, under the water."

Verlaque squeezed her hand again. "I love you."

"I love you too, Antoine," Marine replied. "Those cables under the water — that reminds me of a book that Charlotte has. It's a story about an American village that was flooded in order to build a dam for Boston; the residents are moved, and new houses built for them miles away. But every now and then the family rows out in a boat onto the new reservoir, and they look down into the water to where their house once was, and the school, and the church. The girl has a hard time forgetting her village, and her old friends who were also dispersed. Her father tells her to let go. Sylvie always cries when she reads that bit. He says, 'You have to let them go.'"

"Say that again."

Marine moved closer to Verlaque and held him, rubbing his stomach. She whispered,

"You have to let them go."

"It's an old story we're dealing with," Verlaque said, throwing off the covers and jumping out of bed. "The one that Prosper hinted at."

"Mme Poux?"

"I don't know, I don't know," he answered, opening one of the desk drawers. He pulled out a manila envelope and got back into bed. "Let's look at every one of these by candlelight," he said, pouring out a stack of passports onto the blanket.

"The murderer is a contemporary of Alain Denis. You wait until old age to carry out the murder," Marine said, looking at Verlaque. "Because when you're young, you have too much to live for. A family. A job. Life."

"But doesn't that all increase — the desire to live — when you're elderly? Or even middle-aged?" Verlaque asked. "Every day is precious, so why murder now, and risk going to prison the last ten or so years of your life?"

"Because you're sick," she slowly replied. "Dying, perhaps."

Velaque nodded. "You may be right."

"Damn, I wish it wasn't the middle of the night. I need to call Papa."

"Are you worried about your parents,

because of the storm?"

"No, no," Marine replied, leaning back against the headboard. "It's true, I usually call them every other day. But tonight I want to ask Papa about his patients. It's just a hunch. It will have to wait until tomorrow morning."

Verlaque looked down at the passports but remained silent, not questioning Marine's hunch but thinking of his parents: if he called them every other month it was progress. "During tonight's party," he asked, his voice suddenly raised with excitement, "were you within earshot when Clément was getting people together to play cards?"

"I was at the bar," Marine said, "chatting with Marie-Thérèse and Serge. Serge gave us a crash course on making the perfect martini." She rubbed her head. "The first one was a good idea . . ."

Verlaque flipped through the passports until he got to the one he was looking for. *"Voilà,"* he said, opening it. He looked at the photo, and date of birth, and pointed to the person's name.

Marine said, "So what? Lots of people go by their second name."

Verlaque continued pointing to it. He told

her about their conversation during the party.

"Oh my," Marine said. "You don't think?"

# Chapter Thirty-Four:
## Swimming

Antoine Verlaque left Marine in the Jacky Bar, where Émile and Marie-Thérèse had made coffee for everyone. Verlaque assured Marine that Bruno Paulik was on his way; Paulik and another officer from Aix had spent the night at a hotel in Marseille, because of the storm, and he had called Sordou at 8:30 a.m., confirming what Verlaque and Marine had guessed. Verlaque ordered the staff and guests to stay in the bar until he returned. Marine tried to argue but he assured her that there was no danger, believing it himself. Alain Denis had died for a specific reason — "you have to let them go" — and there would be no more deaths. And swimming would have something to do with it, of that Verlaque was almost certain.

"What do I say about the two people who are absent?" Marine asked looking around. "And you?" Marine asked.

"You'll think of something," Verlaque said,

gently brushing her cheek with the back of his hand. "Thank you for thinking to call your father this morning," he said. "You were one step ahead of me."

"No, we were side by side," Marine said.

"Like Sartre and Beauvoir."

Verlaque walked out of the hotel and stood at the top of the steps, looking out at the sea. He could see the police boat speeding toward the mouth of the harbor. Bruno would be on board, grasping at the railing trying not to get sick. Verlaque smiled — although he knew he was being mean-spirited — and he turned right and began walking along the path that led to the cove. They would be there, waiting for him.

As he began the walk down the steep hill he could hear the boat come into the harbor and its engine turn off. Small white stones popped out from under his feet and about halfway down he almost slipped, swearing under his breath. He didn't know why he was rushing; only a knot in his stomach told him to hurry. He got to the stony beach and saw a figure sitting on the flat rocks to the west. Verlaque crossed the beach and hopped up on the first, lowest rock making his way over a succession of rocks until he got there. From the back he couldn't tell who it was, and then the man turned around and said hello. Verlaque stood beside Bill Hobbs and looked down. A neat pile of clothes was folded on the next rock over, topped with a black Moleskine and the Frank O'Hara book of poems. Verlaque fell to his knees. "How long has he been out there?" he asked.

"Long enough," Bill Hobbs replied in accented but very good French.

"Poor Eric," Verlaque said. "I was worried he might do this. He was a cancer patient of Marine's father, at the hospital in Aix. Dr. Bonnet told Marine this morning that he told Eric that he didn't have long to live; perhaps weeks, or months." Verlaque noted that he referred to the poet by his first name, as if they had been friends.

"He's at peace now," Hobbs said. "I didn't know he was ill."

"Late last night," Verlaque said. "I took a good look at your passport and thought you were the murderer."

"No."

"But you're a part of the story," Verlaque suggested. "Your wife, does she — ?" Verlaque said, shielding his eyes from the sun so that he could look at Bill Hobbs.

"Know I'm half French? No," he answered. "When we met, I never spoke of my childhood," he said. "It was partly because

412

of my mother's terrible death, which I told Shirley happened in the Pacific off of the coast of Seattle."

"But it was at Sordou," Verlaque said. "With Élodie, the love of Eric's life." Verlaque remembered Eric Monnier, on the boat ride over, mentioning a woman that Marine reminded him of. But he hadn't said her name. And had he known that Verlaque was an examining magistrate, he probably wouldn't have even mentioned her.

"Yes," Bill quietly said. "Élodie too."

"Was it Alain Denis's fault?" Verlaque asked.

"Mostly," Hobbs said, his voice quivering. "We were diving in those days."

"You all knew each other?"

"Yes, our families all had cabins on Frioul," Hobbs replied. "My mother grew up in Marseille. She met my father, who was an American soldier, during the liberation of Marseille in 1944; he took her back to the U.S., but we came back here every other summer."

Verlaque stayed silent, not wanting to stop Hobbs's story. He reached out and touched the book of poems.

"Alain would come over to the islands with buddies from the swim club," Hobbs went on. "We were diving, as I said, without equipment. . . . None of us had enough money for masks, and Alain was such a good swimmer he didn't need one."

"What were you diving for?" Verlaque asked.

"Amphoras."

"Greek?"

"Mostly," Hobbs answered. "The Greek ones got us the most money at any rate; and the Etruscans'. There was some sleazy Armenian guy up near the Cours Julien who would give us a bit of cash for them and then send them on their way around the world. A bit of cash. That's what we were doing it for; teenage thrills, and a bit of cash."

Verlaque looked down at his shoes.

Hobbs said, "Alain had discovered a bunch of amphoras here, just on this side of Sordou. We'd go out a few times a week, whenever we could get an older cousin or someone to bring a boat out. We had to be careful. But one time my mother and Élodie decided they wanted to come; they thought we were just swimming over here, you see."

"Your French is good after all these years," Verlaque said.

Hobbs laughed a bit. "It's tiring to speak it," he said in English. "You caught me understanding the French, didn't you?"

"More than once," Verlaque said. "But it bothered me that you knew the word for 'whip.' And yesterday one of our policemen found a record of the accident in an archive in Paris; Élodie's name didn't ring a bell with me, but your mother's name certainly did: Cécile-Marie Hobbs. It was then that I remembered seeing your passport: Cyril William Hobbs. I have an uncle named Cyril, but Cyril is also an English name, so it didn't seem odd to me at the time. Lots of people prefer using their second name."

Hobbs smiled. "And I'm no Cyril. Besides, after the drowning, my father and I wanted to erase France from our lives."

"I understand."

"It has nothing to do with this beautiful country," Hobbs continued, switching back into French. "It just hurt too much. *On était blessé.*"

"And Alain Denis would have called you Cyril in those days?"

"*Oui, bien sûr,*" Hobbs replied. "That's how I was sure he wouldn't recognize me this week. The fact that I was going by Bill would have thrown him off, and I'm not as slim as I once was." He patted his stomach and tried to smile.

Verlaque nodded. "But Eric?" he asked.

"Did M. Denis recognize him?"

"If he did, he didn't let on," Hobbs said. "We were quite sure that the film-star snob wouldn't acknowledge someone from his past, if he did recognize Eric, or even me. Not until Eric sent him a note, getting him to go down to the cove."

"What happened that day in 1957?"

"With Maman and Élodie along, we knew there would be no amphora searching," Hobbs said. "We came out to Sordou with a cousin of Eric's driving the boat, and we dove off the boat to show Maman and Élodie an underwater cave we liked. Neither of them was as strong a swimmer as us — we had plenty of practice after all — but we knew they could make it to the cave with our help. We swam under the water — getting to the cave took about a minute — and Maman and Élodie were enchanted. There was a small stone projection you could sit on, and there was about a foot of air above your head. But just after we arrived, Eric got bit by a jellyfish; I told the women that I'd head back up to the boat with Eric — we always had a bottle of vinegar on board for stings — and I'd be right back. Alain was to stay with them."

"But he didn't," Verlaque said.

"No, left them there alone," Hobbs replied, his voice once again cracking. "He was supposed to stay; if he had, they would have . . ." He swallowed, and then went on, "Just around the corner from the cave was our amphora spot; Alain couldn't resist going and getting one . . . either to sell, or to show off in front of the women. So he swam away. He later told us that the amphora had been stuck, so it took longer than usual to get it out. And when I got Eric back to the boat he started throwing up; his cousin was freaking out and wanted to take him back to Frioul, where a Marseille doctor had a vacation house. I begged him to wait, so I dove back under to return to the cave. But the water was murky; that was a bad sign . . ." He stopped again, looking down at his knees. "Someone had stirred up the sea bottom, and you couldn't see a thing. Usually we used the light from the sun on the water's surface to guide us. But that water was gray-black."

"Did you have to turn around?"

"Yes," Hobbs whispered. "A few seconds later Alain popped his head out of the water, with the bloody amphora in his hands. But the women never came back up."

"My God," Verlaque said, staring out to sea.

"We figured they panicked," Hobbs said.

"It was such an easy dive down to the cave — easier than they both had expected — that they decided to swim back up to the boat on their own. Maybe that's what they thought we had agreed upon."

"And they somehow swam the wrong way and agitated the sand?"

"Or Alain did, trying to get the amphora loose," Hobbs answered. "It's so easy to get turned around down there, if you can't see."

"Why now?" Verlaque asked. "That happened so long ago."

"There was a botched attempt, when we were in our thirties," Hobbs said, almost laughing. "Eric followed Alain to the Venice Biennale; but there were too many security guards around. Alain was a huge star then."

"You stayed in touch all this time?"

"Yes, easy to do when neither of us has moved in forty years," Hobbs said. "We were careful never to e-mail; I would phone Eric sometimes, or he me, pretending he got the wrong number if Shirley answered. Since that time in Venice, I had hoped that Eric had given up with his idea of killing Alain. But then in May he saw Alain on television. Eric said that Alain was vague about the island he would be vacationing on, but a few days later Eric read in *La Provence* that the hotel was opening again."

"And he called you and said that M. Denis would be vacationing in Sordou," Verlaque suggested.

"Yes," Hobbs replied. "We already had our flights for a trip to Provence. Shirley loves it and the older I get the more I want to come back here; I never could when my father was still alive. Coincidently, Shirley saw photographs of a similar type hotel in Capri in some decorating magazine, and so I said that I'd treat her for our anniversary. I've done well in the plumbing trade. Stores all over Washington State."

Verlaque smiled; the president of his cigar club was also independently wealthy thanks to "the plumbing trade," as Hobbs called it. "*Design* magazine, Bill."

"Touché," Bill said, trying to smile. He continued, "So the visit here was perfect; Shirley would be thrilled, and I could talk Eric out of murdering Alain."

"That's what you were discussing on the dock that evening?" Verlaque asked.

"Yes," Bill answered. "And Eric was being flippant; I half-believed he wasn't going to go through with his plan. I had no idea he had written Alain a note."

"Did you hear the shot?"

"I thought it was Prosper," Bill said. "I honestly thought that I had convinced Eric not to do it; but he couldn't forget about what happened in 1957. Eric said that he recognized me straightaway that first day on the boat, and he was envious of our happiness; Shirley was squealing about the waves. It's too bad he couldn't just forget, as I did. But having a family helps with that, don't you think?"

Verlaque looked at the sea and then at Hobbs. "I would imagine, yes," he said.

"I hadn't seen Alain pass by the dock, so when Eric said he needed a walk, it didn't worry me," Hobbs said. "But now I realize that Alain must have gone to the cove on the path behind the hotel."

Verlaque remembered Mme Poux's story of Alain Denis walking behind the hotel, in view of her laundry room. As a paranoid star, Denis purposely strolled around in the less visited corners of the island.

"It was only the next morning, when that sweet waitress found Alain's body, that I knew."

Verlaque took a deep breath, and began, "You realize that you —"

"Withheld valuable information," Hobbs cut in. "As they say on television. Eric was my friend. It takes effort to stay in touch — over an ocean — and over fifty years. I know it was wrong what Eric did," he said, "and for years I wanted to do the same thing to Alain." He held up his shaking hand and said, "Fortunately for this, I couldn't have fired a trigger. But I didn't do much to stop Eric, either."

Marine ran down the hotel's steps when she saw Antoine Verlaque and Bill Hobbs walking toward the gardens. Antoine carried something in his arms. She walked quickly, as if in a dream, surrounded by the reds and pinks and purples of the flowering plants so carefully chosen by the Le Bons. Palm fronds brushed up against her bare legs, almost scratching them, but she ignored it. The brilliant afternoon sun made the colors pale, as if filmed in the early 1960s. The closer she got, she saw that Antoine held a bundle of clothes, and a black book. Her heart sank. "Eric," she said when she got up to the men. Verlaque nodded and stepped aside so that Shirley Hobbs, who had been behind Marine, could hug her husband.

"What happened, Bill?" Mrs. Hobbs asked.

Bill Hobbs looked at Verlaque, who answered, "Eric Monnier shot Alain Denis and today committed suicide by drowning."

Shirley Hobbs held her hand to her

mouth. "How did you know, Bill?"

"Shirl," he slowly began. "Let's go up to the hotel. There's a lot I need to tell you."

"Did you know Eric?" Shirley asked. "From your Marseille days?"

Marine shot Verlaque a look.

"How did you know?" Bill Hobbs asked his wife, wide-eyed.

Shirley laid her hand on Bill's shoulder. "It was getting harder and harder for you to pretend you didn't understand French," she said. "But I've known for years; I found your mother's birth certificate once. It was when we bought our first house, in the sixties, and you still needed all that kind of information to get a bank loan . . . remember?"

Bill nodded. "I tried to hide it from you."

"You were so nervous and excited about the house," Shirley said. "You accidently left it out."

"And you didn't say anything?"

"No, what for?" Shirley said. "I knew that it must have something to do with your mother's tragic death — which I then realized must have been here, in France — and the memories were too painful. I respected you and your father too much to pry." Shirley's expression then turned sad, and she looked at Verlaque and asked, "Will

Bill get charged for withholding evidence?"

"Yes," he answered. As much as he wanted to protect Bill Hobbs, his work as a judge came first. "But the charge will be much more benign than had Bill assisted in the murder," he added.

Two hours later Bill and Shirley Hobbs were packed, and standing on the dock about to get into a police boat with Bruno Paulik. "When does your elder son arrive at the Marseille airport?" Verlaque asked. "Jason, right?"

"Tomorrow at noon," Shirley said. She looked at her husband, who had turned silent, and was standing at the edge of the dock, staring down at the water.

"I'll arrange to have an officer pick up your son," Verlaque said.

"That's very kind."

"I've also talked to Bill about a lawyer I once worked with in Paris, who may agree to work on Bill's defense," Verlaque said. "If that's okay by you; your husband told me that money wasn't a problem. Oddly enough, Niki Darcette knew the lawyer when she was young."

A young police officer gave Shirley Hobbs his elbow, helping her onto the boat. Bill Hobbs followed, holding his trembling hand up to Verlaque in a wave.

"Will you stay on the rest of the week?" Paulik asked his boss.

"Yes," Verlaque replied. "Mme Denis and Brice are leaving in a few minutes. . . . Hugo's taking them to the Marseille train station to catch the Paris TGV, along with the Viales. But we're staying, and so is Sylvie."

"Have fun, then," Paulik said over the sound of the boat's motor.

"Just look straight ahead at the horizon, Bruno," Verlaque said, rubbing his stomach.

The rest of the staff and clientele were waiting in the Jacky Bar, and Verlaque took a deep breath before going in. A police officer had accompanied the Hobbses back to their room so that they could pack; Verlaque had made sure that they passed through the main doors, avoiding the bar. He knew that the minute he walked into the bar he would be bombarded with questions. He opened the door and walked in, and to his surprise, the bar was quiet. He could see by the look on everyone's face that they already knew of Bill Hobbs's involvement.

"I saw them," Max Le Bon began, walking toward the judge. "I was in the office, and I saw the policeman accompany them to their room. What on earth is going on?"

Verlaque gathered the group together, around the bar, and told them the long story of the amphoras, and the connection between Eric Monnier, Bill Hobbs, and Alain Denis. When he had finished, Marie-Thérèse said quietly, "That's the saddest story I've ever heard," and she slowly sat down. Serge Canzano began wiping down the bar, and Émile Villey sighed and went into the kitchen.

Emmanuelle Denis was the first to approach Verlaque, and she said, "I want to thank you for everything you've done. I think that Brice and I will go back to Paris early."

"I understand," Verlaque replied.

"If you're ever in Paris . . . Neuilly, actually . . ."

"I don't get up there often," Verlaque replied, lying.

"Oh well," she said, sighing. "Brice," she called to her son.

Brice walked over to Verlaque and shook his hand. "Thanks," he said.

Verlaque reached into his jacket pocket and gave Brice Eric Monnier's copy of Frank O'Hara's *Lunch Poems*. "Try some poetry for a change," Verlaque said. "There's a beautiful poem about Billie Holiday in there."

"Sweet, thanks," Brice replied, taking the book. "I like her singing."

"So do I," Verlaque said. "Goodbye then, Brice. Goodbye, Mme Denis."

He turned around and was about to find Marine when Clément Viale tapped him on the shoulder. "Goodbye, old Dough Boy," he said.

"Leaving early?" Verlaque asked. He hoped the Viales wouldn't be on the TGV back to Paris with Emmanuelle and Brice.

" 'Fraid so," he replied. "Delphine misses the children, and frankly, so do I."

Verlaque smiled and shook his old friend's hand, hoping that the Viales would make a go of their marriage. "Good luck, Clément," he said.

Marie-Thérèse sat in Eric Monnier's usual spot, with Niki's arm around her. Émile waved from one of the *hublots;* a chef's work was never done, and he was busy preparing their dinner.

"Thank you for your help, Judge Verlaque," Max Le Bon said. "By the way, Mme Denis's emerald ring turned up; I don't know if you noticed that she was wearing it. Serge found it in a bowl of lemons that he keeps on the bar."

"Yes, I saw that she had it on. I'd almost forgotten about the ring until this morning," Verlaque said. "Bill Hobbs told me that he took it; Mme Poux had left the door of the Denises' room open when she ran back to the laundry room to get more towels. Bill said he could practically see it from the hallway, so he walked in, grabbed it, and immediately threw it in with the lemons."

"What on earth for?"

"To buy Eric some time," Verlaque answered. "To create a diversion. Bill hoped that we'd make more of a fuss about the ring than we did, and Eric could slip off the island."

"Oh, I almost forgot," Le Bon said, taking a folded piece of paper out of his pocket and handing it to the judge. "We took this message for you earlier," he said. "The officer said you'd understand."

Verlaque read the note and smiled. It read: "I just spoke with Mme Navarre; her husband has been filming on location in Thailand the past fifteen days. Officer Flamant."

"Can I get you a stiff drink?" Le Bon asked.

Verlaque paused before answering. "Perhaps later," he said. "What I'd really like now is a swim, since we still don't have water. A sea swim."

"So would I," Max Le Bon said. "I've only been in the sea once since we came to Sordou. Should we invite the others?"

"Good idea."

"Dear guests and staff," Max called out. "There will be an informal swim, followed by champagne on the terrace, in about" — Max looked at his watch — "thirty minutes."

"May I come?!" Marie-Thérèse called out, then quickly covered her mouth.

"May she?" Verlaque asked.

"Of course," Cat-Cat Le Bon said. "Who else wants to go for a swim?"

"I do," Niki replied.

"I'll stay here and keep Émile company," Serge Canzano said, drying off a wineglass. He found his boss's newly found enthusiasm a bit childish, embarrassing even. Besides, he hadn't swum in thirty years.

"Mme Poux!" Marie-Thérèse said. "You should come!"

Mme Poux, who had been sitting with Cat-Cat, unconsciously touched her carefully coiffed head. "Just to watch, my dear. And perhaps to sun a bit."

"Then it's decided," Max said. "We'll all meet at the ladder by the dock in thirty minutes."

Verlaque gave Marine more detail into

Hobbs's story while they changed into their swimsuits. Once changed, Marine sat on the edge of the bed, her hands on her knees. She hunched over and began to cry, and Verlaque sat beside her and held her. "We didn't have dinner with Eric Monnier," she finally said, after blowing her nose. "I wanted to, that night we had the wine from Calabria and the puttanesca, but he declined. He didn't want to get to close to anyone."

"Yes. But you took the time to play cards with Eric."

"I asked Eric to play cribbage so that I could observe him," she said. "But by the end of the game I had forgotten that he was a murder suspect. We had such a good time. I was comfortable with Eric. I even thought of giving him my mother's phone number, so that he could go to one of her book clubs; I think she belongs to three. But when my father told me that Eric had cancer, I knew that he was the murderer."

"I was convinced it was Bill Hobbs," Verlaque said. "I hope not to work on another murder for a long time."

"You liked Eric too."

Verlaque nodded.

"Perhaps the next murderer will be a horrible person," Marine said, trying to smile.

"Yes, let's hope," Verlaque answered. "Someone we both detest."

"You know, there were one or two times when Bill Hobbs understood the French," Marine said. "I just thought he was picking it up . . . that same night, when we had the puttanseca, remember?"

"Yes, he knew how to translate *supions* into squid," Verlaque said. "Up to that point I still had no idea he played a part in this. But there was something that early on in the week Sylvie said to Bruno, about *le général* and Shirley Hobbs not being able to recognize each other — if they had crossed paths in Vietnam — after all these years. I kept thinking what a good plan that would be; a man as self-obsessed as Denis wouldn't recognize someone from his past, and we had all these people on the island who were born around the same time, and who lived at one time or another in Marseille. We change, I daresay, from eighteen to sixty years. Because of that I thought that Mme Poux had killed Denis. She didn't have an alibi, either. And when we looked at Bill Hobbs's passport last night, we both thought he shot Denis."

"Wait," Marine said. "What about their alibi? People saw Eric and Bill together, down at the dock."

"Yes and no," Verlaque said, getting up and taking their beach towels. "Think about it; there were all kinds of people who saw the two men together, at the dock, pretending that they didn't understand each other. Bill and Eric were each other's alibi, which should have rung alarm bells for me, since up until then they hadn't spent much time together. But no one was really sure of the time; only that Eric and Bill were down there at *some time.* And when Hugo saw them from his cabin, he admitted that he could only see Bill Hobbs, not Eric."

Marine sat on the flat rocks, letting the seawater wash up over the rocks and onto her lap. She could see Antoine and Sylvie, not far from the sea; they had been swimming lengths, along Sordou's south coast, and were now treading water and chatting. It was Friday, their last full day on the island. *Le Sunrise* would be back for them tomorrow after breakfast, but minus a few guests. She closed her eyes, not wanting to think of the Hobbses, now in a Marseille hotel, having interviews with their lawyer, and certainly not of Eric Monnier. A coast guard boat had pulled up to Sordou's dock the previous evening, and the captain had got off the boat and asked to speak with

Judge Verlaque, holding his cap in his hand. Marine had been sitting on a bench with Sylvie and Hugo Sammut, and Hugo had said, "Looks like they found Eric's body. The coast guard never comes around here."

Marine waved to her friends and leaned back, knowing she should have put more sunblock on, but reveling in the warm water against her skin. It was so refreshing she could hardly feel the July sun beating down on her. In Aix during the two summer months she avoided the sun, walking on the shady side of the street. Here, the sun felt good.

"Hello there."

Marine looked up and saw Émile Villey standing beside her. *"Salut, Émile,"* she said. *"Ça va?"*

"Just out foraging for our last dinner," he said, kneeling down on the rock and tilting his basket toward her. "And the generator's been fixed, by the way."

Marine lifted out a bunch of dark-green leaves and held them in her hands. "It looks like a cross between spinach and Swiss chard."

*"Betterave maritime,"* Émile said.

"Maritime beetroot?"

"Yep. It grows all over here, by seaside rocky or sandy coasts. I first discovered it when I worked in Arcachon."

"It's how our ancestors ate," Marine said.

"Certainly Sordou's first inhabitants," Émile said. "I'm going to fry it in lemon and garlic and olive oil."

"What else is on the menu?"

"Top secret," Émile said. "There's some meat for him," he said, gesturing with his head toward Antoine Verlaque, who was now swimming toward the rocks with Sylvie.

"Antoine will appreciate it," she said. "For someone who spent a lot of his youth near the ocean in Normandy, he's a real meat and potatoes guy."

"I'll see you later then," Émile said, picking up his basket. "Still one or two ingredients to hunt down, then into the kitchen I go." He looked out at the sea and said, "I'm glad they found the body."

"Me too."

"I didn't want to think of M. Monnier out there."

"No," she answered.

"I saw you playing cards with him," Émile said, "from one of the *hublots*. It looked like you beat him."

Marine smiled. "I did," she said. "But he took it well."

Max Le Bon banged the edge of a glass with

a small spoon.

"Don't break the glass," Cat-Cat said.

"I'm being careful," Max whispered, vexed. "Good evening everyone," he called out. "Welcome to our last dinner on Sordou. Émile has prepared yet another stellar meal, and I hope you all enjoy it. Cat-Cat and I will be joining you for dinner, and we've taken the liberty of inviting the rest of our small staff to join us as well. We thought, that given the eventful week, they merited a gastronomic meal."

"Plus there are no more guests left," Sylvie whispered. They applauded, and Marie-Thérèse, Niki, Mme Poux, Hugo, Serge, and Émile stood up and bowed.

"Although they will be getting up periodically to help serve," Max said, smiling. "I'd also like to welcome M. Buffa and Général Le Favre. You both look very regal this evening, gentlemen."

Prosper Buffa beamed, fingering his bow tie. *Le général* straightened his back, as if that would allow the guests to better see his medals.

"Most of all, Cat-Cat and I would like to thank Judge Verlaque and Dr. Bonnet for their help this week," Le Bon went on. The staff applauded. "You managed to keep us all calm, be discreet in your investigation, and you both retained your smiles and good humor throughout. Thank you."

Cat-Cat stepped forward to speak. "Thank you all, from the bottom of our hearts. And on a business note, I'd like to congratulate Niki Darcette, whose hard marketing work has paid off; we're now fully booked until the end of September." She paused while the guests finished clapping. "Despite the fact that some of you seemed to think that Alain Denis's death may bring clients to Sordou," she said, avoiding looking at Verlaque and Bonnet. Marine kicked Antoine under the table. "It was Niki's riveting press releases and gorgeous photographs that did the trick, and now six of the world's best travel and architecture magazines will be publishing articles on Sordou, including Mme Hobbs's favorite, *Architectural Digest.* And, thanks to Mlle Darcette's persistent phone calls, Chef Émile will be interviewed and photographed next week for *Le Figaro.*"

Antoine Verlaque clapped, remembering that at the time of the murder Niki had been making phone calls. She had been trying to promote the hotel on its merits — its beauty, and Émile Villey's talent — not using the murder to win clients, as he had accused her of.

"I'd also like to congratulate Marie-

Thérèse," Cat-Cat continued, "who just this afternoon found out that she has been accepted into the prestigious École hôtelière de Lausanne."

Marie-Thérèse got up and did a quick curtsy, then shrugged and sat down, staring at the tablecloth.

"It was a great honor for Marie-Thérèse to have been selected out of the thousands of applicants the school gets every year," Cat-Cat said. "And although she won't be able to accept their invitation, we're all so very proud of her all the same."

"Time for dinner," Max said, taking his wife's arm. "Chef Émile's appetizer has been made using a local plant found here on Sordou, isn't that right, Émile?"

Émile stood up. "Yes," he answered. "Marie-Thérèse and I will go and get it. I've made butter biscuits that incorporate little pieces of Serrano dried cured ham, topped with slices of powdered black currant and Sordou's own delicate *pourpier*."

"*Pourpier?*" Sylvie called out.

"It's a seaside lettuce," Émile said.

"Emmeline picked that in Normandy," Verlaque whispered to Marine. "Purslane, she called it."

"*Bon appétit, tout le monde,*" Max said, raising a glass of champagne in the air.

■ ■ ■ ■

Later that evening, Marine and Verlaque sat out on their private terrace, drinking herbal tea. Sylvie was spending what she called "a last hurrah" with Hugo, in his cabin. "How do you feel about leaving tomorrow morning?" Verlaque asked.

"I leave Sordou with mixed feelings," Marine said.

"Me too."

"I love it here," she continued. "But I somehow think if we were to come again it wouldn't be as good."

"Well, at least there wouldn't be a murder," joked Verlaque.

"It's more about the people," Marine said, as if she hadn't heard his comment. "I'd miss Eric, and the Hobbses."

"Even Mme Denis and Brice added something special to our little gang," Verlaque suggested. "It's only the Viales I don't miss."

"I agree," Marine said. "Some people mark you more than others, don't they?"

"I love the silence here, and the breezes."

"And the smells," Marine said. "Part sea and part plant. I'm not looking forward to the summer's heat and lack of air in downtown Aix."

"Perhaps it's time we buy a seaside apartment," Verlaque suggested. "In Provence, or Italy. Remind me to call my banker on Monday afternoon."

Marine turned toward Verlaque. "You're not serious?"

"It's about something else," he said, his voice slightly quieter. "Mme Médéric, my bank manager, gets anxious if I don't check in every week."

"Oh, I see," Marine said, nodding. "You're going to pay Marie-Thérèse's tuition, aren't you?"

"Wouldn't you?"

"Yes," Marine answered. "I would." She reached over and squeezed his hand. "You know," she continued. "Our personalities were reflected in the way we — each one of us — entered the sea yesterday afternoon." They laughed, remembering the impromptu group swim: Marie-Thérèse had run the length of the pier and jumped in, plugging her nose. She resurfaced yelping for joy. Niki Darcette carefully dove in, after testing the water with her toes, her hands and feet perfectly parallel. Cat-Cat's dive was almost as faultless as Mlle Darcette's, and Max tried, with not much success, to do a cannonball. Mme Poux sat down, her slim legs dangling over the pier's edge. She wore a brightly colored silk kimono, a stark contrast to her usual black-and-white uniform. Marine jumped in, although with less child-like glee than Marie-Thérèse, and Sylvie did a backflip, followed by the aahs of the swimmers, who were now all treading water. "Come on, judge!" Marie-Thérèse yelled.

"Cannonball coming up," Verlaque called out. "And this one will soak Mme Poux."

Antoine Verlaque ran the length of the pier, trying to blot out the faces of Élodie, and Cécile-Marie Hobbs, and Eric, and Bill, and Alain Denis. As his body soared over the sea, he brought his legs to his chest, wrapping his arms around them and preparing his body for the shock of hitting the water. It hurt more than he had remembered. As he surfaced he heard everyone laughing. Mme Poux was now standing, and thoroughly soaked.

"I'm sorry," he called. "I wasn't expecting it to have been that powerful."

"Just come in, Mme Poux!" Marie-Thérèse cried. "It's beautiful!"

Mme Poux smiled and slipped off her kimono, revealing her modest one-piece suit and toned body that a thirty-year-old would have been proud of.

"Wowsa," Sylvie whispered, treading water.

"Yolaine, if you go in by the ladder," Cat-Cat called out, "you won't get your hair wet."

Yolaine Poux didn't respond but stood at the dock's edge, standing still and straight. And with one quick movement she put her head down and dove in.

# ABOUT THE AUTHOR

**M. L. Longworth** has lived in Aix-en-Provence since 1997. She has written about the region for the *Washington Post,* the *Times* (UK), the *Independent,* and *Bon Appétit* magazine. She is the author of a bilingual collection of essays, *Une Américaine en Provence,* published by Éditions de La Martinière in 2004. She divides her time between Aix, where she writes, and Paris, where she teaches writing at New York University.